THE GHOST BOOK
of
Charles Lindley, Viscount Halifax

THE GHOST BOOK
of
Charles Lindley, Viscount Halifax

Carroll & Graf Publishers, Inc.,
NEW YORK

Carroll & Graf Publishers, Inc.,
260 Fifth Avenue
New York, NY 10001

First Carroll & Graf edition 1994

First published in the UK in two volumes, as *Lord Halifax's Ghost Book* and *Further Stories from Lord Halifax's Ghost Book*, by Geoffrey Bles, 1936 and 1937

A copy of the Cataloguing in Publication Data for this title is available from the Library of Congress

ISBN 0-7867-0151-X

Printed and bound in the UK

10 9 8 7 6 5 4 3 2 1

CONTENTS

CONTENTS

FOREWORD
by
Simon Marsden

Unhinged the iron gates half open hung,
Jarr'd by the gusty gales of many winters,
That from its crumbled pedestal had flung
One marble globe in splinters.

'The Haunted House', Thomas Hood (1799–1845)

'It was in the gathering dusk that the mysterious woman, dressed in a beautiful green silk dress, descended from the carriage near the entrance to the Hall. Passing through the gates she slowly walked up the long driveway, through the beautiful gardens, towards the old house. She began to hear the sounds of excited voices and laughter from within. Peering through a lighted window she saw, seated at a candlelit dinner table, the man she loved surrounded by his wife and children. She had no place there. Unable to bear either his happiness or her own grief, she fled tearfully into the great park where she stabbed herself to death beside an ancient oak tree. It is her sad ghost that still haunts the house and grounds.'

As children, we often sat nervously listening in the drawing room of the sixteenth-century house, our eyes occasionally daring to glance up at the portrait of the phantom Spanish aristocrat that hung above the fireplace, as my father told us this story of our 'family ghost'. He had an extensive collection of books in the genre and amongst them, as in most of the libraries of large country houses at that time, were the two volumes of *Lord Halifax's Ghost Book* that were first published in the 1930s, shortly after Lord Halifax's death. These books contained extracts from his own journal, known to his family as 'The Ghost Book', and from which he would read aloud to them on special occasions such as Halloween or Christmas. It includes many eye-witness accounts of supernatural phenomena, related to him by friends and acquaintances who were privileged to stay in many of the great houses of the age.

Britain and Ireland are without doubt the spiritual home of ghosts, with so many historic houses and castles that, in many cases, have belonged to the same families for centuries, and within their dark panelled corridors, alongside the suits of armour and ancient tapestries, hang eerie portraits of ancestors of dubious repute, a host of phantoms from an illustrious past. Many of these ancient piles are included here in *The Ghost Book* and there are several that I have visited and photographed for my own books on hauntings, including the infamous Glamis Castle in Scotland with its mysterious secret room that was reputed to contain a hideous monster, and the phantom of the 'Hooded Monk' at Bolton Priory in Yorkshire that was once described as 'something very black and evil'. This apparition was seen by the owner's son, the Marquis of Hartington, in 1912, and (according to Lord Halifax) his signed statement was endorsed by George V, the then King of England.

During dinner party conversations the mere mention of the word 'ghosts' inevitably alters the atmosphere of the evening. Everyone it would seem has an opinion on the subject which covers so many controversial topics such as life, death and religion, often encroaching on the borders of rationality. More often than not those present have experienced some form of paranormal phenomena, or if not themselves, they know of a relative or friend who has. This overwhelming weight of evidence, together with my own personal experiences of the supernatural, has left me in no doubt that a hidden, very different 'spirit world' runs parallel to our own so-called 'reality', and that this other secret existence can be revealed to any one of us if the conditions are right and if we allow ourselves to be receptive to it by conquering our innermost fears of the unknown. The Celts, for example, believed that human beings could cross over into this supernatural world at certain ancient and sacred sites which were energized with nature's primeval powers. This I believe would explain why so many of our ancient buildings become the focus of paranormal phenomena, as they are invariably built on or near such places, and contain these ancient and perpetual forces within their foundations. It would also help to explain the so-called 'tape-recording' theory of ghosts, where inanimate objects such as wood and stone, which are frequently found in old buildings, are thought to give off their own individual energy fields, on to which extreme human emotions can be imprinted and then played back when re-activated.

Lord Halifax's Ghost Book stands today as a unique record of the personal experiences of people who visited and lived in such places, and the manner in which they are retold gives a very real impression of the atmosphere and life in these haunted gothic mansions. Imagine yourself climbing the ancient stairway to your bedroom at midnight as the moonlight begins to cast its long shadow across the Hall. Locking the door you retire to the safety of your four-poster bed and switch off the bedside light. It is only then that you realize you are not alone, for in the dark room, within the heavy oak cupboard, or behind the faded curtains, lurks a creature from the distant past, the family's ghost, silently watching you . . .

Simon Marsden is a professional photographer who specializes in the fantastic and the supernatural. The powerful and haunting image on the cover of this book is his work – an original black and white picture, hand coloured. He has published several books on the subject, and his Journal of a Ghosthunter *is to be published in autumn* 1994.

VOLUME I

The Harper
of
Inveraray

¶ *Mr. H. W. Hill*, who contributed these experiences, was an old friend of *Lord Halifax* and was for many years secretary of the English Church Union, of which *Lord Halifax* was President. He paid several visits to *Inveraray Castle*, the home of the Dukes of Argyll.

I

LORD ARCHIBALD CAMPBELL DIED AT EASTER, 1913. I saw the announcement that he was very ill and had gone from Coombe to Inveraray. His son, Mr. Niall Campbell, was in France for Easter, but came home when he heard of his father's serious condition. Having been told by a friend that Lord Archibald, before going to Inveraray, was heard to say that he felt he would not come back and to express certain wishes which were to be carried out after his death. I wrote to Mr. Niall Campbell, who very kindly sent me a description of all the arrangements he had made for the funeral and asked me to keep myself free to dine with him at the Bachelors' Club one evening on his return, so that he might tell me all his news.

I dined with Mr. Campbell, who had now become Duke of Argyll, at his club, on May 28th, and mentioned what I had been told about his father. He replied that he was glad to have my information, since it explained something which had been puzzling him. I then went on to mention some of the stories which I had read in West of Scotland newspapers. There was a tale about ravens, which came down from the glens and were seen hovering about Inveraray while his father was passing. It was said that this always happened when the Chief or anybody closely related to him was about to die.

3

Mr. Campbell said he believed that the story was true, but that they did not take much notice of the ravens. However, he then told me that the 'Galley' had appeared on Loch Fyne. When I asked him to explain what this was, he told me that the 'Galley' was a little ship like the one in their Arms, and that when the Chief or one near to him was dying it appeared on Loch Fyne with three people on board, one of whom is supposed to be a saint connected with St. Columba. When his father was dying the 'Galley' was seen to pass silently up the Loch and to come to land at a particular point. It then passed overland and finally disappeared at the site of a holy place associated with St. Columba and given to the Church by the forbears of the Campbells. A great many people saw it on the occasion of his father's passing, including a 'foreigner', that is to say, one who was not a Campbell or even a High-lander, but a Saxon. When the 'Galley' was seen to pass over the land, this man called out, 'Look at that funny airship!'

II

In August 1914 I was staying at Inveraray, arriving there after luncheon on the 18th. That afternoon, when tea was served in the library, there were present the Duke, his sister (Lady Elspeth), the Bishop of Argyll and the Isles, the Cham-berlain of Argyll and his wife, Mr. Samuel Gurney and my-self. I remember that we were all sitting having tea round a big table, when presently I heard a tremendous noise at my side, like the banging of books. It was as though a whole shelf full of books had been taken out and thrown violently on to the floor of the open gallery, which runs round the library.

I looked up, but said nothing. In fact, no one uttered a word, but I noticed that the Duke and his sister exchanged glances and then looked at me. I had the impression that no one else in the room had heard anything.

After tea, the Duke spoke to his sister and then took me into his private room. He said to me: 'You heard a noise while we were at tea. My sister and I saw that you heard it and that no one else did.'

He went on to tell me that that side of the Castle was haunted, and that that particular noise had been heard there for many years. On one Sunday evening, when he was working in the library, it went on for an hour. 'My sister', he said, 'will tell you all about it.'

Next day, when Lady Elspeth was out walking with me, she told me the story. She was good enough to say that she and her brother regarded me as quite one of the 'elect', since I was the only person besides themselves who had heard the noise. She had been expecting to hear it, because when she went into the library before tea she saw 'the old man'. This was the ghost of the Harper, who was hanged at Inveraray by Montrose's men when they came up the glen in pursuit of the great Marquis of Argyll. The Harper always appears in the Campbell tartan and is a harmless little old thing. She generally both sees and hears him; but the Duke only hears the noise.

The story struck me as strange because the present Castle is comparatively new, having been built in 1750 and not on the site of the previous building. Probably the poor old man appears on the spot where the tree grew on which he was hanged.

Lady Elspeth went on to say that when we had gone in to tea she had distinctly seen the 'little man' standing in the gallery. As for the others present, she was quite contemptuous about Highland bishops and 'Norfolk dumplings'.[1] It was more surprising that the Chamberlain and his wife had noticed nothing, while I, a mere Saxon, had heard the noises. I suggested that the visit of the Bishop to the Castle was a good opportunity for putting the 'little man' to rest, but she would not hear of this. He was, she said, a friend and in some sense a guardian; he was quite happy and never did anyone any harm.

Since that time I have often heard the Harper. In 1918, when I had lately recovered from a long and almost fatal illness, I was at Inveraray. I was put in the 'Archie' Room, which is above the Green Library and like it has a turret attached. During the whole of the fortnight of my stay I never ceased to be conscious of a presence in the bedroom and in the turret, which I used as a sitting-room.

I did not mention my sensations to anybody except the

[1] Mr. Samuel Gurney was a Norfolk man.

Duke's aunt, the late Mrs. Callander of Ardkinglas and Cramond, who asked me which was my bedroom. When I told her she said, 'I know and have *seen*!' She then put her finger on her lips.

When I was leaving Inveraray, Lady Elspeth walked down to the Lodge with me. I asked her why she had put me in that room and she replied: 'For your own good. My aunt, Lady Mary Glyn, who was so ill here lately, would have died if she had not been placed in that room.'

Other people have also seen the Harper. Lady George Campbell saw him in the Blue Room, which is in the same part of the Castle as the 'Archie' Room, and one of her daughters saw him on the stairs. During the night, the music of the harp is often heard. Last autumn Mrs. Ian Campbell was staying at the Castle and took her harp with her. She occupied the 'Archie' Room and kept the harp in the turret. In the night she heard someone playing it, and it was, of course, the 'little man'. The lady had had the same experience on a former visit.

III

I was again staying at Inveraray in October 1922, towards the end of the month. The Duke was unwell and had retired to bed early, having decided that he would not be able to attend the funeral next day of the Marquess of Breadalbane.

That evening Lady Elspeth and Mr. Ian Campbell, a lad of

7

nineteen, who was Lord Walter Campbell's grandson and the Duke's second heir, were sitting together in the Green Library, to which a round turret room is attached. Presently they heard great noises, as though books were being thrown about in the turret; and after a few minutes the doors from the turret into the library opened. Nothing could be seen, but something had entered and was slowly and deliberately scuffling about the room. Lady Elspeth and Mr. Ian Campbell ran upstairs to tell the Duke, who remarked that the visitor must be 'the old man'. He must, the Duke said, have appeared on account of the funeral of Lord Breadalbane, such apparitions being by no means unusual on the death of great clansmen.

A few days later the Duke wrote to me to tell me of these occurrences; and on the same day I had a letter from Lady Elspeth, in which she reported that 'the Little Harper had been very active' about the time of the funeral. It would seem that this was his way of showing his annoyance at the absence of the great Chief from the obsequies of his vassal.

The Man
in the
Iron Cage

¶This story was a great favourite with *Lord Halifax*. It is preceded by the following note: 'I certify this to be a correct copy of the account written by *Mr. Pennyman*, of the ghost that haunted the hotel at *Lille*. O. BARRINGTON.'

YOU EXPRESSED A WISH TO KNOW WHAT CREDIT MIGHT BE given to a story, a garbled version of which, after a lapse of between thirty and forty years, appeared recently as a 'true ghost story'. I will accordingly state the facts as they were recalled to me about a year ago by an old friend of mine, a daughter of the late Sir W. A. Court. She sent me the album in which the story had been written, requesting me to read it and let her know if there was any truth in it. She had been intimate with my mother and the whole family, and since she had never heard the matter mentioned she could not believe that it was true. I read the story with the greatest surprise. Clearly it could not have been written by any member of the family alive at the time, or indeed by anyone who was at all intimate with us. It was full of mistakes as to names, etc., yet in some parts was so near the truth that I was frankly puzzled. So many years had elapsed and so much had happened to drive the incident from my mind, that I had some trouble in recalling exactly what had occurred. However, I succeeded in doing so and am now able to answer your enquiries.

My father and mother, with myself, my sisters and one of my brothers (the other, Harry, was too young for the University and was nearly the head boy of Westminster), went abroad in the late autumn of 1865 or 1866. We children were supposed to be learning French, and after we had visited two or three towns in France our parents decided to make a rather longer stay at Lille. Besides finding the teaching particularly good there, we had letters of introduction to some of the leading families in the neighbourhood.

The first lodging we had was very uncomfortable and my father soon began to look about for a house. In due course he discovered a very large and well built residence, to which we took a great fancy. We were told that we could rent it at what was a remarkably low figure, even for that part of the world. Accordingly we took the house and moved into it without delay.

About three weeks later I went with my mother to the bankers with a letter of credit, which we cashed. As the money was paid in large six franc pieces we could not take it with us and the banker offered to send his clerk. He asked our address and when we told him that our house was in the Place du Lion d'Or, he looked surprised. There was, he said, nothing there that would suit our family except indeed a house that had been long unlet on account of a *revenant* that walked about it. (This he said quite seriously and in a natural tone of voice.)

My mother and I laughed, but asked the clerk not to mention the *revenant* to the servants; and as we were walking home my mother remarked in fun: 'I suppose, Bessie, that it was the ghost which woke us up by walking about over our heads.' I was sleeping in the same room with her and on three or four nights we had been awakened by a slow, heavy step overhead, which we thought must be one of the menservants walking

12

about. Our staff consisted of three Englishmen—a footman who had been with us for years, a coachman and a groom; three Englishwomen—my mother's maid and housekeeper, my own maid, and a nurserymaid. All these English servants returned to England with us and never had any idea of leaving us. The other women in the house were French, and so were the butler, the cook, the footman and Louis (a boy who came home with us).

A few days after our visit to the bankers, having been again awakened in the night by steps overhead, my mother asked Cresswell, her maid, who it was who was sleeping in the room over us, She replied: 'No one, my lady. It is a large empty garret.'

A week or ten days later, Cresswell came in one morning after breakfast and told my mother that most of the French servants were talking of leaving because there was a *revenant* in the house.

'Indeed, my lady,' she said, 'there is a very strange story about a young man who was heir to this and another house, with an estate in the country, and is said to have been confined by an uncle in an iron cage in this house. As he disappeared and was never afterwards seen, they supposed that he was killed here. The uncle left the house in a hurry and afterwards sold it to the father of the man from whom you took it. No one has ever remained in it for so long as we have done, and it has been a long time without a tenant.'

'And do you believe this, Cresswell?' asked my mother.

'Well,' she replied, 'the iron cage is in the garret over your head, my lady, and I wish you would all come up and see it.'

At this moment a friend of ours, an old officer with the Cross of St. Louis, arrived to call on us. We told him the story with some amusement and asked him to accompany us upstairs to see the cage. We found ourselves in a long, large garret, with bare brick walls. It was quite empty, except that in the further corner there was an iron cage attached to the wall. It recalled to us the kind of cage in which wild beasts are kept, only it was higher. It was about four feet square and eight feet high and there was an iron ring in the wall at the back, to which was attached an old rusty chain with a collar.

We really began to feel rather creepy at the idea that any human being could have been kept in such an unpleasant place, and our French friend was as horrified as we were. All the same, we were quite certain that the footsteps we had heard in the night were part of a plan to keep the house untenanted, and we were rather uncomfortable at the thought that there was a private way in, of which we knew nothing. We therefore decided to look about us for something else, but to stay in our present quarters until we were successful in finding it.

About ten days after our visit to the garret, Cresswell came to dress my mother in the morning, looking so pale and ill that we asked her what was the matter.

'Indeed, my lady,' she said, 'we have been frightened to death. Neither Mrs. Marsh (my maid) nor I can sleep again in the room we are now in.'

'Well,' said my mother, 'you may come and sleep in the little spare room next to ours. But what has frightened you?'

'Someone, my lady,' she said, 'went through our room last night. We both saw the figure, but hid under the bedclothes and lay in a dreadful fright till the morning.'

I burst out laughing, but Cresswell began to cry, and when I saw that she was really upset I tried to comfort her. I told her we had heard of a very good house and would soon move into it. Meanwhile, they could sleep in the room next to ours.

The room in which they had been so frightened had a door recessed from the first landing on a very wide staircase, leading to the passage on to which the best rooms opened. The door of my mother's room faced the staircase. In Cresswell's old room there was a second door which led to the backstairs, making it a kind of passage.

A few nights after the change of rooms my mother asked Charles and me to fetch from her bedroom her long embroidery frame, so that she might get her work ready for the morning. Although it was after supper and quite dark, we did not take a candle, as there was a lamp at the bottom of the staircase and we thought we could find the frame by leaving open the door of my mother's room. When we reached the foot of the stairs we saw a tall thin figure in a powdering gown and wearing hair down the back going up the stairs in front of us. We both thought it was Hannah and called out, 'It won't do, Hannah. You can't frighten us.' At these words the figure turned into the recess and when, in passing it, we saw nobody there, we concluded that she had gone through Cresswell's old room and down the back staircase.

When we returned with the frame we told my mother of Hannah's trick. She said, 'That is very odd. Before you came in from your walk, Hannah went to bed with a headache.'

We went at once to Hannah's room, where we found Alice at work, and she told us that Hannah had been sound asleep for more than an hour. A little later, on our way to bed, we saw Cresswell. When we told her of our mistake she turned quite white and exclaimed: 'That is exactly the figure we saw!'

About this time my brother Harry came to spend ten days with us. He was sleeping up another staircase at the far end of the house and one morning, when he came down to breakfast he asked my mother quite angrily if she had thought he was drunk the night before and could not put out his candle, since she had sent some of those 'French rascals' to watch him. He added: 'I jumped up and opened my door and by the moon through the skylight I saw a fellow in his loose gown at the bottom of the stairs. If I had had anything on I would have been after him and taught him to come spying on me.'

16

My mother assured him that she had not sent anyone.

That very day we had arranged to take a delightful house with a charming garden belonging to a young nobleman who was going to Italy for a few years. An evening or two before we moved in, a Mr. and Mrs. Atkyns and their son, who lived three or four miles from Lille, came on horseback to call on us. We told them how frightened our servants had been and how disagreeable it was to be in a house which a person might enter unknown to us. We told them that no one now would sleep in the room in which Cresswell and my maid had seen the *revenant*. Mrs. Atkyns laughed and said that with my mother's permission she would much like to sleep there and that with her terrier to keep her company she would not be in the least afraid. On my mother replying that she had no objection, Mr. Atkyns rode home with the boy to fetch Mrs. Atkyns' things before the gates were shut.

In the morning Mrs. Atkyns looked ill and did not appear to have slept much. When we asked her if she had been frightened she declared that she had been roused from a sound sleep by someone moving about her room. The dog did not stir although he generally flew at an intruder, but by the lamp in the chimney she distinctly saw a figure. She said that she had tried to set the dog at it, but our belief was that she was much too frightened, and we were greatly entertained when Mr. Atkyns arrived to take her home and, to her indignation, said in his droll way, 'Perhaps you dreamt it all.'

After they had gone my mother said, as she had often done, 'I cannot for an instant fancy it is a ghost, but I most sincerely hope I shall get out of the house without seeing what seems to frighten people so much; I know that to see any person in my room at night would alarm me dreadfully.'

Three days before our move into the new house I had been for a long ride and went to bed tired. It was hot and the curtains of our bed were undrawn on my side and at the foot. I was sleeping soundly when I was awakened, though by what I could not say (we were so accustomed to the footsteps overhead that by this time they never awakened either my mother or myself). We kept a light always burning in the room, and by it I saw a tall, thin figure in a long gown. One arm rested upon the chest of drawers that stood between the window and the door. The face was turned towards me; it was long and thin and pale, the face of a young man with a melancholy look on it which I shall never forget. I was certainly very frightened, but my worst fear was that my mother would wake. Fortunately she seemed to be in a sound sleep. At that moment the clock on the stairs struck four and I lay for nearly an hour before daring to look again towards the chest of drawers. When at last I did so I could see nothing, though I never heard the door opened or shut, or any other noise.

I did not close my eyes for the rest of the night, and when Cresswell came as usual I called out, 'I need not get up to let you in, for you must have forgotten to put the key upon the

18

chest of drawers last night.' She said she had not forgotten and, to my surprise, when I got up, I found the key in the usual place. When I told my mother she was most grateful that I had not wakened her and insisted that we should not run the risk of spending another night in the house. So directly we had had breakfast we set about moving all our things, so that we were able to sleep in our new quarters.

Before we left, Cresswell and I examined every part of our room, but without discovering any secret way of entering.

In the disturbances that followed in France and various troubles of our own, we almost forgot about our *revenant*. On one winter evening, however, my mother made me tell the story to Mrs. Hoare.

The 'garbled version' referred to in the first paragraph of this story was evidently a narrative which appeared in the *Cornhill Magazine* from the pen of the Rev. S. Baring-Gould, the well-known author. He subsequently wrote to Lord Halifax enclosing the following letter which he had received:

DEAR SIR,

The November number of the *Cornhill Magazine* has only lately come into my hands. I find your story of 'the man in the Iron Cage' particularly interesting because of an experience I had at the Hôtel du Lion d'Or at Lille some thirty years ago. As I think this may interest you I venture to write you an account of it.

In May 1887, I was travelling with two friends from Bou-
logne to Brussels. One of my friends, an aged lady unaccus-
tomed to long railway journeys, became so tired that her sister
decided it would be best to stop short at Lille and spend the
night there. We arrived towards evening. Knowing nothing of
the place and intending to go on next morning, we asked for
the hotel nearest the station, which proved to be an old-
fashioned, unpretentious hostelry, the Hôtel du Lion d'Or.

We were soon settled in a comfortable suite of rooms on the
first floor. The larger bedroom, occupied by my friends, had
two doors, one opening on the landing to the right of the staircase, the other into a small narrow ante-room or dressing-
room, of which the opposite door communicated with my
room. At first we thought this was the only entrance to my
bedroom, but on examination we found a second door at the
further end of my room. This, the landlord said, was usually
kept locked and he did not seem disposed to open it. My
friend, however, insisted on the door being unlocked and the
key left in our possession. It opened into a small recess off the
landing and, as far as I can remember, about opposite to the
head of the stairs. This recess appeared to be used as a housemaid's closet, for it was full of pails and brooms, which we
thought explained our host's objection to unlocking the door.

My friends retired very early to rest, encouraged by the
chambermaid's assurance that they would have a quiet night
as they were the only occupants of that floor. Indeed we seemed

to be the only guests in the hotel—a fact which did not surprise us, as it was early in the season.

Since I did not feel at all tired, after wishing my friends good night I sat down in my room to write some letters home. So engrossed was I in this occupation that the time slipped away quickly and it must have been between eleven and twelve o'clock when I became aware that, although the house had long been perfectly quiet, someone was apparently walking up and down in a rather stealthy fashion just outside the door which opened into the recess. The 'slow, dragging steps' mentioned in your story exactly describes the sound I heard.

I paid little heed to it, thinking the steps were those of some belated servant. Suddenly there was a knock at the outer door of my room and the younger of my friends, whom I had thought asleep hours before, looked in, anxiously asking if anything was the matter, as she had been awakened by hearing me, as she supposed, walking up and down my room. I assured her that I had not stirred from my chair and that I too had been surprised at hearing the same noise, which seemed to come from outside my door on the landing. We opened this door and with a light examined the recess and then the landing, but all was perfectly still and no one was to be seen.

Concluding that, although the footsteps seemed to have been so near, the sound must really have proceeded from an upper storey, we re-locked the door. My friend returned to her room and I went to bed, still hearing from time to time, until I fell asleep, that stealthy dragging step.

We left Lille by an early train next day and I thought little more of this occurrence. It did not, however, completely pass from my mind, as I mentioned it in recounting my travels on my return home about two months later. Very likely I should not have given it another thought had it not happened that a friend of my mother's, who knew her to be interested in ghost stories, gave her a manuscript account, almost exactly similar to yours, of a haunted house in the Place du Lion d'Or at Lille. It then struck me that probably this was the very house in which I had spent the night and that the footsteps I had heard were not those of any living denizen of the hotel.

I have given you this account, thinking it may help you to identify the house to which your sad story is attached.

Believe me to remain,

Yours faithfully,

A. C.

The Secret
of
Glamis

¶ Much has been written about *Glamis Castle*, the home of the *Earl of Strathmore*. The following account was given to *Lord Halifax* by *Mrs. Maclagan*, wife of the *Archbishop of York*. *Miss Virginia Gabriel*, to whom she refers, was a composer of songs and music.

IN 1870 WE MET MISS VIRGINIA GABRIEL, FRESH FROM A long visit to Glamis and full of the mysteries which had assumed such prominence since the death of our poor brother-in-law in 1865. The Chapel had been cleaned and re-dedicated with great solemnity, and the gossip was that the ghosts were endeavouring to terrify Claude (Lord Strathmore) and his family from making the Castle their home.

I will try to write down all that Virginia told us, much of which was afterwards confirmed by Lady Strathmore. It appears that after my brother-in-law's funeral the lawyer and the agent initiated Claude into the family secret. He went from them to his wife and said: 'My dearest, you know how often we have joked over the secret room and the family mystery. I have been into the room; I have heard the secret; and if you wish to please me you will *never* mention the subject to me again.'

Lady Strathmore was too good a wife not to obey, but she talked freely to other people, and her mother, old Mrs. Oswald Smith, was one of the chief propagators of stories which, of course, lost nothing in the telling.

Claude made a good many alterations and improvements at the Castle, one being a staircase from the lower hall or crypt, as it was called, to the Chapel, which had previously been accessible only through the great drawing-room. One day, when the family were in London, a man working in, I think, the Chapel, came upon a door opening up a long passage. He went some way down it; then became alarmed and went back and told the Clerk of the Works. Immediately all the work was stopped and the head man telegraphed to Claude in London and to Mr. Dundas, the lawyer, in Edinburgh. Both arrived by the earliest possible train and subjected the workman to a severe examination as to what he had or had not seen, the end of it being that he and his family were subsidized and induced to emigrate.

It is unquestionable that for many years, after the revelation of the secret, Claude was quite a changed man, silent and moody, with an anxious scared look on his face. So evident was the effect on him that his son, Glamis, when he came of age in 1876, absolutely refused to be enlightened.

Virginia further informed me that in several of the bedroom cupboards there were stones with rings in them. Claude converted all these cupboards into coal-stores, with strongly boarded fronts, and ordered them to be kept always full, so that no inquisitive visitor might attempt an exploration. She told us a wonderful tale of the first house-warming—a dance in the new dining-room in November 1869. They had all been very merry and dancing went on until the small hours. The three sets of rooms on the Clock Landing were occupied by the Streatfields (Lady Strathmore's sister), Mr. and Lady F. Trevanion (Lord Strathmore's sister), and Mr. and Mrs.

Monro from Lindertis. The latter were in the Red Room, their little boy sleeping in the dressing-room, the outer door of which was rather stiff and difficult to open. In the middle of the night, Mrs. Monro awoke with a sensation as though someone was bending over her; indeed, I have heard that she felt a beard brush her face. The night-light having gone out, she called her husband to get up and find the matches. In the pale glimmer of the winter moon she saw a figure pass into the dressing-room. Creeping to the end of the bed she felt for and found the matchbox and struck a light, calling out loudly 'Cam, Cam, I've found the matches.'

To her surprise she saw that he had not moved from her side. Very sleepily he grumbled, 'What are you bothering about?'

At that moment they heard a shriek of terror from the child in the dressing-room. Rushing in, they found him in great alarm, declaring that he had seen a giant. They took him into their own room, and while they were quieting him off to sleep they heard a fearful crash as though a heavy piece of furniture had fallen. At that moment the big clock struck four.

Nothing more happened, and the next morning Mr. Monro extracted a reluctant promise from his wife to say nothing about her fright, as the subject was known to be distasteful to their host. However, when breakfast was half over, Fanny Trevanion came down, yawning and rubbing her eyes and complaining of a disturbed night. She always slept with a night-light and had her little dog with her on her bed. The dog, she said, had awakened her by howling. The night-light had gone out, and while she and her husband were hunting for matches they heard a tremendous crash, followed by the clock striking four. They were so frightened they could not sleep again.

Of course this was too much for Mrs. Monro, who burst out with her story. No explanation was offered and the three couples agreed on the following night to watch in their respective rooms. Nothing was seen, but they all heard the same loud crash and rushed out on to the landing. As they stood there with scared faces the clock again struck four. That was all; and the noise was not heard again.

We did not go to Glamis that year, but with our heads full of all these wonderful tales paid a visit to Tullyallan Castle, a large and comfortable modern house. It was inhabited by a most cheerful old couple, Lord and Lady William Osborne, and there was nothing about it to suggest a ghost. On the night of the 28th of September I dreamt I was sleeping in the Blue Room at Glamis, which Addy and I occupied during our memorable and delightful visit in 1862. The dressing-room has a well-known trap-door and a secret staircase leading to a corner of the drawing-room. I dreamt that I was in the park watching some horses when I heard the gong sound for dinner and rushed upstairs in a great hurry, begging the others not to wait for me. In the passage I met the housemaid coming out of the Blue dressing-room with her arms full of rusty bits of iron which she held out to me.

'Where did you find those?' I asked.

She replied that in cleaning the grate she had seen a stone with a ring in it which she had raised and in the hollow space below had found these pieces of iron.

I said, 'I will take them down with me. His lordship likes to see everything that is found in the Castle.'

As I opened the door of the Blue Room the thought crossed my mind: 'They say the ghost always appears if anything is found. I wonder if he will come to me.' I went in and there, seated in the armchair by the fire, I saw a huge figure of a man with a very long beard and an enormous stomach, which rose and fell with his breathing. I shook all over with terror, but walked to the fireplace and sat down on the coalbox staring at the ghost. Although he was breathing heavily I saw clearly that it was the face of a dead man.

The silence was unendurable, and at last I held up the pieces of rusty iron, saying, 'Look what I have found'—an untruth, for the housemaid was the finder.

Then the ghost, heaving a deep sigh, said, 'Yes, you have lifted a great weight off me. Those irons have been weighing me down ever since. . . .'

'Ever since when?' I asked eagerly, forgetting my alarm in my curiosity.

'Ever since 1486', replied the ghost.

At that moment, to my great relief, I heard a knock at my door.

'That is Caroline' (my maid), I thought, 'coming to dress me. I wonder if she will see this dreadful creature.'

'Come in', I called and woke up.

It was Caroline opening my shutters, and the sun was streaming cheerfully into the room. I sat up in bed and found that my nightgown was quite wet with perspiration. I came downstairs very full of my dream, and still more of the fact, as I believed, that although the room was in all other respects exactly like the one I thought I remembered so well, the fireplace was in a different corner. So persuaded was I of this that when next year I saw the room at Glamis and found that my dream memory was right and my waking memory wrong, I could scarcely believe my eyes. I even brought upon myself some ridicule by asking Claude if the fireplace had been changed, which would be neither easy nor likely in a house of that age and with walls of that thickness.

This part of my dream greatly interested Dr. Acland and other Oxford dons as a striking confirmation of the theory that the brain receives impressions which are always accurate when it is undisturbed by outside influences. I wrote my dream down, but told it to very few people.

A year or two afterwards Mrs. Wingfield, a daughter of Lord Castletown's, met my brother Eric at a water party and began asking him about my dream. She had had an odd experience of her own which unfortunately I can only relate second-hand, as I have never had the opportunity of meeting her.

So far as I could make out she was staying at Glamis for the first time during the same week, if not on the very same day, that we went to Tullyallan. She was occupying the Blue Room, but had heard none of the stories about Earl Beardie and his crew of ghosts. She went to bed with the usual night-light, which was so bright that she read by it before going to sleep. During the night she awoke with the feeling that some-one was in the room, and sitting up in bed she saw, seated in front of the fire, a huge old man with a long, flowing beard. He turned his head and gazed fixedly at her, and then she saw that although his beard rose and fell as he breathed the face was that of a dead man. She was not particularly alarmed, but unfortunately made no attempt to enter into conversation with her visitor. After a few minutes he faded away and she went to sleep again.

Next morning, when Mr. Oswald Smith began to tell her some of the tales of the Castle, she said, 'Let me tell you first what I saw last night.'

Whether she saw or dreamt it the coincidence was curious. Nothing came either of her dream or of mine, but some years afterwards, when we were driving from Glamis to Cortachy, my mother asked me if I had ever told my dream to Lady Strathmore. I replied that I had not thought it worth telling, but she insisted on my relating to Lady Strathmore just what I have written here. When I came to the date, Lady Strathmore gave a start, and turning to Fanny Trevanion, said, 'Oh, that is too odd.'

I said, 'Surely that isn't the right date? I thought it was fifteen hundred and something.'

'No,' she answered, 'it was in 1486, nearly four hundred years ago.'

Of course I may have heard the date at some time, but have no recollection of it.

After 1870 we went to Glamis every year, nearly always spending my mother's birthday there. St. Michael was the patron saint of the Chapel, people pretending that when it was re-dedicated he had been chosen for the purpose of keeping away evil spirits. I generally had a most ghostly little room, King Malcolm's Chamber, but never slept there, for my mother was so afraid of waking in the night and felt so nervous when she was alone that at Glamis I always slept with her.

We never saw or heard anything, and eager believers in the ghosts affirmed that this was because we had Lyon blood and the ghosts never appeared to any of the family. My mother's grandmother, Lady Anne Simpson, who was a Lyon, tried hard to see something and I often found her in her room with her face pressed against the window pane, straining her eyes for a glimpse of the White Lady, a most harmless apparition, who is supposed to flit about the avenue. One year on our arrival we found the whole house in great excitement as the White Lady had been seen by Lady Strathmore, her nieces and Lady Glasgow, from different windows at the same moment. Their descriptions were exceedingly vague and incoherent.

One more tale, related to me by old Dr. Nicholson, the Dean of Brechin, I must put down. He said that once, when he was staying at Glamis, he had gone to bed in the room halfway up the winding stair. The door was locked, but he saw a tall figure enter, draped in a long, dark coat, fastened at the throat with a clasp. Neither spoke and the figure disappeared in the wall.

The Bishop of Brechin, Dr. Forbes, who was also staying in the Castle, was very incredulous about this apparition and teased his friend by saying, 'Now, Mr. Dean, we all know you are the most persevering beggar in Scotland. I am sure you brought out your collecting book and laid the ghost by asking him for a subscription.'

Next night, to the delight of Dr. Nicholson, the Provost of Perth, who had joined the party, said he had had a similar mysterious visit the last time he slept in that room. The Dean at once hurried him off to the Bishop and made him repeat his tale to that sceptical prelate.

Bishop Forbes and Uncle Robert Liddell[1] both offered to hold a service of exorcism in the Castle, but this was never

[1] The Hon. and Rev. Robert Liddell, for many years Vicar of St. Paul's, Knightsbridge.

done. I think Claude would have been afraid to have it. Unquestionably, there is something strange about the place. The Chaplain told me that he felt this more and more the longer he lived there, while the Factor, Mr. Ralston, a dry, shrewd, hardheaded Scotsman, after he had been initiated into the secret could never be induced to sleep in the Castle. One winter evening, when he had come up for the theatricals, a sudden snowstorm came on and the road back to his home appeared impassable. However, he resolutely refused to spend the night on a sofa and insisted on rousing the gardeners and stablemen to dig out a path to his house nearly a mile off outside the Park. Lady Strathmore herself told me that she once disclosed to Mr. Ralston her great curiosity about the mystery. He looked earnestly at her and said very gravely: 'Lady Strathmore, it is fortunate that you do not know it and can never know it, for if you did you would not be a happy woman.' Such a speech from such a man was certainly uncanny.

Many years afterwards, in September 1912, I visited Glamis with my daughter, Dora, for the first time after Claude's death. His son, the present owner, has no objection to talking about the ghost. He and his wife were much interested in my dream and got me to give them a copy of my account of it. Lady Strathmore told me that on her first visit to Glamis after her marriage she and her husband occupied the Blue Room. During the night she dreamt that she saw a big man gazing at her from the other side of the bed; only he was thin, not fat like

34

my ghost. She woke in a great fright and roused her husband, but of course there was nothing there. Two of her children, Rose, the second girl, and David, the youngest boy, often see shadowy figures flitting about the Castle. They are not alarmed by them, but Rose says she would not like to sleep in the Blue Room. Figures have been frequently seen by them and by a housemaid in the Oak Room, which my mother always had, but it has now been turned into an extra sitting-room. King Malcolm's Chamber, the little room where I used to dress, has also been dismantled and thrown into the passage. This is a great improvement, as it provides a better access to the great drawing-room and the Chapel.

The Grey Man
of
Wrotham

¶This story is prefaced by the following letter to *Lord Halifax*, dated April 29th, 1883. The signature of his correspondent has been cut away.

'Knowing your fondness for an authenticated ghost story, I send you the enclosed. It was told to the *Bishop* at *Hyères* by a *Mrs. Brooke*, wife of *Major Alured de Vere Brooke*, Royal Engineers. When we received it we thought that could any corroboration be obtained it would be as well, and so the evidence of the nurse (*C. E. Page*) was got and we have it. Should you wish for it, it is at your service.'

IN THE AUTUMN OF THE YEAR 1879, WHEN MY HUSBAND was Captain and Adjutant of the Royal Engineers at Chatham, we were invited to spend a couple of nights with some friends at Wrotham, an old place of historic interest about eight miles from Maidstone. We drove over in our own carriage, and the weather being cold and wintry were glad of the warm bear rugs and robes which we had bought in Canada a few years previously.

We arrived at Wrotham House only just in time to dress for dinner and were immediately shown to our rooms. These were at the extreme end of a long passage up a short flight of stairs in a distant wing of the old house. The bedroom, which was large, was not connected with the dressing-room, which was a few paces down the passage. The fire appeared to have been lighted only a few seconds before and the room struck so cold that I begged my husband to fetch up the robes we had left in the carriage, as I thought we should need them at night. This he did.

After dinner we went to a Penny Reading at which we had been invited to sing and act, and on returning, as a number of people had come in to supper, dancing was proposed, with the result that it was nearly two o'clock before we retired to bed.

Neither on that night nor on the next one, when we again danced until a late hour, did we get any rest. In spite of the fire

39

and of our furs we were horribly cold and my husband even went so far as to declare that he would never sleep in the room again. We attributed this intense cold to damp mattresses and to the fact that probably the room had not been used for some time. Neither of us thought that it was due to any supernatural cause.

In the following spring Captain Brooke and I, with our little girl, aged five, were invited to Wrotham for a week. My husband was unable to leave his duties, but urged me to accept the invitation for myself and for the child who had been ill and would, we thought, benefit by the change.

Accordingly we went there, taking the nurse with us, but remembering my previous experience I wrote beforehand to ask that our rooms might be thoroughly warm and the mat-tresses aired. We arrived at Wrotham on a Saturday, intending to stay till the following Saturday. Finding that the rooms allotted to us were the same as those which I had occupied with Captain Brooke, I arranged that the nurse should sleep in the dressing-room and the child with me.

That evening I sat up very late talking to Lady M. and her daughter. I remember that as we passed through the hall on our way to bed, a large old-fashioned clock on the stairs struck one o'clock and I remarked that it was Sunday morning.

The instant I reached my room I was struck by the vault-like coldness of it and anxiously approached my child to see if she felt it. She appeared to be perfectly warm and was sleeping soundly, but for more than an hour after I had lain down beside her I shivered and shook with cold.

At eight o'clock on Sunday morning the nurse came in with a white face, red eyes and frightened looks. When I exclaimed at her appearance she told me she had had a very bad night. Up till one o'clock someone had been playing practical jokes in the passage, 'opening her door, laughing outside and then going away and coming back.'

'Why did you not lock your door?' I asked.

'I did, twice,' was her reply, 'but soon afterwards it was opened again.'

I quite thought she had been dreaming and rallied her about what she had eaten for supper. She went to her breakfast, from which she returned, looking excited.

'Oh, ma'am,' she said, 'is it not too bad? These rooms are haunted and the doors can never be kept shut before one o'clock.'

It appeared that the servants had excited her suspicions by questions as to what sort of a night she had had and had then told her she need not be afraid another night as she had only to leave her door open and nothing would happen. I told her that it was very unpleasant, if no more than that, and that I would make enquiries. On the way back from morning church I questioned Lady M. about the house, asking which was the most ancient part and so on, and whether there was a haunted room. A look of intelligence flashed from my hostess to her daughter and back again. The latter then said, 'Yes, there is a haunted room, but we will not tell you which it is, as you might imagine things.'

'I think I know already,' I replied, 'and my nurse was frightened by the ghost last night.'

They would vouchsafe no further information on the subject, but offered to let their under-housemaid sleep with the nurse if she were feeling anxious. This I agreed to, and when we were going to bed I told the girl to leave the door of the room open and to go to sleep without thinking of any foolishness, as of course ghosts did not exist.

I undressed and sat down by the fire to analyse my own feelings. I must insist that I was not in the least nervous or uneasy, only rather curious as to what might happen. I made up the fire, locked the door, and took the further precaution of putting a chair under the handle. At first I thought of sitting up to watch, but, being tired, I at last went to bed and to sleep.

I awoke after what had seemed a short time and heard the clock strike twelve. Although I tried to sleep again I found myself getting colder and colder every moment and sleep was impossible. I could only lie and wait.

Soon I heard steps coming along the passage and up the stairs, and as they slowly approached my door I felt more and more alarmed. I scolded myself. I even prayed fervently.

Then I heard a slight fumbling, as it were, with the handle of the door, which was thrown open quite noiselessly. A pale light, distinct from the firelight, streamed in, and then the figure of a man, clothed in a grey suit trimmed with silver and wearing a cocked hat, walked in and stood by the side of the bed furthest from me, with his face turned away from the window. I lay in mortal terror watching him, but he turned, still with his back to me, went out of the door uttering a horrid little laugh, and walked some paces down the passage, returning again and again.

After that I think I fainted, for it was nearly two o'clock when I became fully conscious again. I did not get up and, still believing that I had had a fearful dream, tried to go to sleep. When the maid opened my door in the morning and pushed aside the chair, my belief in the supernatural was not so strong.

On the Monday evening I asked the nurse, who, by the by, had not been disturbed the previous night, to come and sleep on the sofa in my room. I did not tell her what I had seen or thought I had seen and had still enough courage to be anxious to discover whether the events of the night would be repeated. Again, on this third night, I awoke to hear the clock strike twelve. I called in a whisper to the nurse and found that she was also awake, and presently we both of us began to have the cold sensation. Presently the nurse said, 'I hear steps, ma'am. Do you?'

'Yes,' I replied. 'I will get up and meet it, whatever it is.'

In fact, I did try to get up more than once, but in vain. It was as though I was bound to the bed, and this time all my courage left me. Once again the door opened noiselessly and the grey figure made his entry and uttered his diabolical little laugh. The nurse saw and heard all this as plainly as I had done and also declared that she could not have moved or spoken while it lasted.

Next day I told the ladies in the house what had happened, adding that since my nerves could not stand a further trial we must return home. In vain they assured me that my visitor would not trouble me again, that he 'only appeared three times and always to strangers, and never did any harm', and much more to that effect. I refused to repeat the experiment, and by leaving my hostess's roof there and then I forfeited her friendship.

I believe the family has suffered from these visitations for seventy-five years and that the ghost is supposed to be that of a man who murdered his brother in the room in which I slept and threw his body out of the window. I am told that there is in existence a portrait of one of these brothers, dressed as I have described him.

HYÈRES, 1883.   M. A. DE V. B.

Copy of a Letter from the Nurse who slept with Mrs. Brooke and her child on the occasion when the ghost was seen.

MY DEAR MADAM,

Thank you so much for your very kind letter. I was so glad to hear that my Miss M. is better and that you think she will soon be her dear bright self again. I have often thought of you and wished I was with you to help nurse her, dear child. I sometimes say she is too good and sweet to live, but pray God to spare her to us.

Madam, you ask me to tell you as simply as possible what happened that night at Lady M.'s. I never like to think of it, but this is what I remember. You asked me to sleep in the room with you and Miss M., and at twelve o'clock we both woke and heard the hour strike and both said how cold it was, and then we heard the steps in the passage and you said, 'I will get up and see what it is,' but you did not, and then the door which you had shut and locked was opened and a man dressed in grey came in and stood looking out of the window and there was a bright light and I was so cold and my night-dress was quite wet; and then he went away and came back twice again and there was a wicked laugh at the door and the steps going away and I think you said, 'Thank God it's all over,' and we both cried, and you lit the candle and there was the door wide open and you said, 'We will pack up and go home to-morrow, I can't stop here without the Captain.' I think that was all.

Your affectionate dutiful servant,

—— ——

The Haunting
of
Hinton Ampner

⁋ This story is introduced by a note:

'The existence of the following narrative is alluded to in the recently published *Life of the Rev. Richard Barham*, but the version therein given is incomplete and consequently erroneous in some particulars.

'It, therefore, appears to the possessors of the two manuscript copies made by *Mrs. Ricketts* that it is now desirable to publish the original MS., and that they are fully justified in doing so, with the addition of extracts from letters of relatives and friends which bear strongly on the subject.'

The MS. appears to have been given to *Lord Halifax* by his friend, the *Bishop of Winchester* (*Dr. Harold Browne*).

The story itself is contained in a long statement by *Mary Ricketts*. This is preceded by some correspondence between her and her husband, *Mr. William Henry Ricketts* (who was away in *Jamaica* at the time), her brother *John Jervis* (the distinguished sailor, who afterwards became *Lord St. Vincent*), *Mr. Sainsbury*, agent to *Lady Hillsborough*, who was the owner of *Hinton House*, and others. For the most part these letters are merely a repetition of *Mrs. Ricketts'* narrative.

A full statement of all the circumstances by Mrs. Ricketts.

HINTON PARSONAGE, *July*, 1772.

To my dear children I address the following relation. Anxious that the truths which I so faithfully have delivered, shall be as faithfully transmitted to posterity, and to my own in particular, I determined to commit them to writing, which I recommend to their care and attentive consideration, entreating them to bear in mind the peculiar mercy of Providence in preserving them from all affright and terror during the series of wonderful disturbances that surround them. . . .

To the almighty and unerring judgment of Heaven and earth I dare appeal for the truth, to the best of my memory and comprehension, of what I here relate.

MARY RICKETTS.

The mansion house and estate of Hinton Ampner, near Alresford, Hampshire, devolved in 1755 to the Rt. Honourable Henry Bilson Legge, in right of his lady, daughter and sole heiress of Lord Stawell, who married the eldest daughter and co-heiress of Sir Hugh Stewkeley, Bart., by whose ancestors the estate of Hinton had been possessed many generations, and by this marriage passed to Mr. Stawell on the death of the said Sir Hugh. Mr. (who on the death of his elder brother became Lord) Stawell, made Hinton his constant residence.

49

Honoria, the youngest sister of his lady, lived with them during the life of her sister and so continued till her death in 1754.

On the evening of April 2nd, 1755, Lord Stawell, sitting alone in the little parlour at Hinton, was seized with a fit of apoplexy. He articulated only one sentence that could be understood, and continued speechless and insensible till the next morning, when he expired. His household at that time consisted of the following: Isaac Mackrel, house steward and bailiff, Sarah Parfait, housekeeper, who had lived in the family near forty years, Thomas Parfait, coachman, husband to Sarah, Elizabeth Banks, housemaid, an old family servant, Jane Davis, dairymaid, Mary Barras, cook, Joseph Sibley, butler, Joseph, groom, Richard Turner, gardener, and so continued by Mr. Ricketts. Lord Stawell had one son, who died at Westminster School, aged sixteen.

Thomas Parfait, his wife and Elizabeth Banks continued to have the care of the house during the lifetime of Mr. Legge, who usually came there for one month every year in the shooting season. On his death in August, 1764, Lady Stawell, so created in her own right and since married to the Earl of Hillsborough, determined to let Hinton mansion and Mr. Ricketts took it in December following. Thomas Parfait was at that time lying dead in the house and his widow and Elizabeth Banks quitted it on our taking possession in January, 1765.

We removed thither from town and had the same domestics that lived with us there. Nor till some time afterwards had we any house servant belonging to the neighbourhood. We had not long been settled at Hinton when I began frequently to hear noises in the night, as of people shutting, or rather slamming, doors. Mr. Ricketts often went round the house, supposing that someone had broken in, or that there was some irregularity among the servants. In these searches he never could trace any person. He found the servants in their proper apartments and no appearance of disorder.

The noises continued to be heard and I could conceive no other cause than that some of the villagers had false keys to let themselves in and out at pleasure. The only remedy was to change the lock, which was accordingly done, yet without the effect we had reasonably expected.

About six months after we came thither, Elizabeth Brelsford, nurse to our eldest son, Henry, then about eight months old, was sitting by him as he slept in the room over the pantry, used as the nursery. Since it was a hot summer's evening, she had opened the door facing the entrance into the Yellow Bedchamber, which, with the adjoining dressing-room, was the apartment usually occupied by the lady of the house. She was sitting directly opposite to this door and plainly saw, as she afterwards related, a gentleman in a drab-coloured suit of clothes go into the Yellow Room. She was in no way surprised at the time, but on the housemaid, Molly Newman, coming up with her supper, she asked what strange gentleman had arrived. Upon the other answering there was no one, she related what has been already described and desired her fellow servants to accompany her and search the room. This they did immediately, without finding any trace of what she had seen.

She was much concerned and disturbed, yet sure she could noways be deceived, the light being sufficient to distinguish any object clearly. When, some time afterwards, her story was mentioned to me, I treated it as the effect of fear or superstition, to which the lower class of people are so prone, and it was entirely obliterated from my mind till the late astonishing dis-turbances brought to my recollection this and other previous events.

In the autumn of the same year, George Turner, son of the gardener, who was then groom, crossing the great hall to go to bed, saw at the other end a man in a drab-coloured coat. He concluded that he was the butler who, being lately come and his livery not made, wore such coloured clothes, but as he passed upstairs to the room where all the menservants lay, he was astonished to find the butler and all the others in bed. Thus the person he had seen in the hall, like the person before described by the nurse, remained unaccounted for. George Turner, now living, avers these particulars in the same manner as he first related them.

In the month of July, 1767, about seven in the evening, there were sitting in the kitchen Thomas Wheeler, postilion, Ann Hall, my own woman, Sarah, a waiting-woman to Mrs.

Mary Pointz, and Dame Lacy. The other servants were out excepting the cook, who was washing up her things in the scullery. The persons in the kitchen heard a woman come downstairs and along the passage leading towards them. Her clothes rustled as though they were of the stiffest silk. The door was open, and, on their looking towards it, they saw the figure of a woman pass swiftly by, and, as they thought, out of the house door. Their view of her was imperfect, but they plainly distinguished a tall figure in dark-coloured clothes. Dame Brown, the cook, who came in at this moment, saw the figure pass close by her and then disappear. She described the person and drapery as before-mentioned, and while they were all discussing the appearance a man arrived through the yard and up to the house by the way the woman had gone out. On being asked he declared that he had seen no one.

Meanwhile, the noises continued to be heard occasionally, Miss Parker's woman, Susan Maidstone, was terrified by the most dismal groans and rustling round her bed, and at different times most of the servants were alarmed by unaccountable noises.

In the latter end of the year 1769, Mr. Ricketts went to Jamaica, while I continued at Hinton with my three infant children and eight servants. These latter, with the exception of the butler, who was a Swiss, were ignorant country people.

Some time after Mr. Ricketts left me, I, then sleeping in the bedroom over the kitchen, frequently heard the noise of someone walking in the room within. The rustling as of silk clothes against the door opening into my room was sometimes so loud and so continuous as to break my rest. Although we often made instant search, we never could discover any appearance of human or brute being. Repeatedly disturbed in this manner, I made it my constant practice to search the room and closets within, and to secure the only door that led from that room on the inside in such a manner as to be certain no one could gain entrance without passing through my own apartment, which was always made fast by a bolt on the door. Yet in spite of these precautions, the disturbances continued with little interruption.

About this time, an old man, living in the poorhouse at West Meon, came and desired to speak to me. When admitted he told me he could not rest in his mind without acquainting me with a story his wife had often related to him. In her younger days a carpenter whom she had known well had told her that he was once sent for by Sir Hugh Stewkeley and directed by him to take up some boards in the dining-room, known in our time as the lobby. The carpenter believed that Sir Hugh had hidden something which he conceived to be treasure underneath. Later he was ordered to put down the boards in the same manner as they had been before. I repeated this story to Mr. Sainsbury, attorney to Lady Hillsborough, suggesting to him that he might have the floor taken up and examined.

In February, 1770, two of my servants left and were replaced. A little later my butler also went away and I hired another man to succeed him. During the seven years that I was at Hinton I had many changes of servants, so that at the time of my leaving not one of those who had accompanied me there was still in my service. I mention this fact to show the improbability of a conspiracy among them.

In the summer of 1770, when I was lying one night in the Yellow Bedchamber, I plainly heard the footsteps of a man walking towards the foot of my bed. I thought the danger too near for it to be of any use to ring my bell for assistance, but sprang out of bed in an instant and fled into the nursery opposite. I returned with the nursemaid and a light, to make a search in my bedchamber, but found nothing. There was a light burning in the dressing-room within as usual, and there was no way out other than through the door that opened to the nursery. At the time when I heard the footsteps I was perfectly awake and collected.

For some months afterwards I did not hear any noise that particularly struck my attention until, in November of the same year, when I was sleeping in the Chintz Bedroom over the hall, I once or twice heard sounds of music and on one night in particular three distinct and violent knocks as though someone were beating with a club or other heavy weapon against a door downstairs. I thought that housebreakers must be forcing their way in and immediately rang my bell. No one answered it, but as the noise ceased I thought no further of it at the time. After this, and in the beginning of the year 1771, I was frequently conscious of a hollow murmuring which seemed to fill the whole house. It was like no other sound that I have heard and could not have been caused by the wind, as it occurred even on the calmest nights.

On the morning of the 27th of February, when Elizabeth Godin, my woman, came into my room, I enquired of her about the weather. Noticing that she replied in a very faint voice, I asked her if she were ill. She said she was well, but had never been so terrified as during the preceding night. She had heard the most dismal groans round her bed, and when she got up to search the room and look up the chimney she could discover nothing, though there was bright moonlight. I did not pay much attention to her account, but it occurred to me that she would be afraid to sleep in the room again if anyone should tell her that it was the one formerly occupied by Mrs. Parfait, the old housekeeper, who had died a few days before at Kilmston and had been buried in Hinton Churchyard that very evening.

Five weeks later, on the 2nd April, I awoke between one and two o'clock, as I found by my watch, which was on a table close by my bedside. I lay thoroughly awake for some time and then heard footsteps going to and fro in the adjoining lobby. I got out of bed and listened at the door for the space of twenty minutes, during which I distinctly heard the walking and in addition a loud noise as though someone were pushing strongly against a door. Being sure that I was not deceived I determined to ring my bell, which I had not done before because I did not wish to disturb the nursery-maid, who was very ill of a fever. My woman, Elizabeth Godin, was sleeping in the room with my sons and came immediately on hearing my bell. Convinced that there were persons in the lobby, I asked her, before I opened my door, if she saw anyone. On her replying that she did not I went out to her, examined the window, which was shut, and looked under the couch, which was the only piece of furniture which might conceal anyone. I further found that the chimney board was fastened and when I removed it there was nothing behind it. The door into the lobby was shut, as it was every night. After completing this examination I was standing in the middle of the room, wondering what could have caused the noise, when suddenly the door that opened into the little recess leading to the Yellow Room sounded as if it were being swung to and fro by someone standing behind it. This was more than I could bear and I ran into the nursery and rang the bell to the men's apartments. The coachman, Robert Camis, came to the door at the top of the landing, which was secured every night so that no one could get to that floor except through the windows. Upon opening it to him I told him that I had reason to suppose that someone was behind the door leading to the Yellow Room. He took a light and armed himself with a billet of wood, while Elizabeth Godin and I stayed behind. When he opened the door he found no one. The Yellow Room was locked, the key was hanging up and a great bolt was drawn across the outside door. After Robert had again secured the door and returned to his apartments, I went and lay down in my sons' room. About half an hour afterwards I heard three distinct knocks. They seemed to come from below, but I could not then or later discover the exact spot. Next night I returned to my own room, where I heard noises now and then and frequently the hollow murmur which I have described.

On the 7th of May this murmur was uncommonly loud. I could not sleep, apprehending it to be the prelude to some greater noise. At last I got up and went to the nursery, where I stayed till half past three, and then, it being daybreak, I returned to my own apartment to try to get some sleep. I lay there till ten minutes before four, when the great hall door directly under me was slammed to with the utmost violence so that my room shook perceptibly. I jumped out of bed and ran to the window overlooking the porch. There was plenty of light, but I could see nothing to account for what I had heard. The front door, when I examined it, was fast locked and bolted as usual.

From this time I determined to have my woman in a little bed in my room. The noises grew more frequent and she always heard them just as I did. I was still very unwilling to report these occurrences; although I had taken every means of investigating them I could not discover the least appearance of a trick. On the contrary I was convinced that the noises were beyond the power of any mortal agent. Still, knowing how exploded such opinions were, I kept them in my own bosom. After midsummer the noises became more intolerable every night. They began before I went to bed and continued with intervals till it was broad daylight. Frequently I could distinguish articulate sounds. Usually a shrill female voice would begin talking and presently two other voices, deeper and man-like, joined in. But though the conversation sounded as if it were quite close to me, I never could distinguish any words. One night in particular my bed curtains rustled as though someone were rushing by them. I asked Elizabeth Godin if she had heard anything and she reported exactly the same sensation. Several times I heard sounds of music within the room, not regular or distinct notes, but a kind of vibration, and every night the walking, talking, knocking, opening and slamming of doors were repeated.

My brother,[1] who had returned not long before from the Mediterranean, came to stay with me, yet so improbable was my story that I could not bring myself to disclose it even to him. One morning, however, I carelessly said, 'I was afraid the servants would disturb you last night and rang my bell to order them to bed.' He replied that he had not heard them.

[1]Afterwards Lord St. Vincent.

Next morning, about three o'clock, after he had left me to return to Portsmouth, Elizabeth Godin and I were both awake in bed. She had been sitting up looking round her, expecting as she always did, to see something terrible. Suddenly, to my astonishment, I heard a most loud, deep, and tremendous noise, which seemed to rush and fall with great velocity and force on the lobby floor adjoining my room. I started up and called to Godin: 'Good God! Did you hear that noise?'

She made no reply; but on my repeating the question she answered in a faltering voice that she was so frightened she scarcely dared to speak. At that instant we heard a shrill and dreadful shriek, apparently proceeding from under the spot from which the rushing noise had come. It was repeated three or four times, growing fainter as it seemed to descend, until it sank into the earth. Hannah Streeter, who was sleeping in the room with my children, heard the same noises, which so appalled her that she lay for two hours almost deprived of sense and motion.

Having heard little of the earlier noises, she had rashly expressed a wish to hear more and from that moment until she quitted the house there was scarcely a night when she did not hear the sound of someone walking towards her door and pushing against it as though attempting to force it open.

So dreadful was this last experience that I determined to unburden myself of the whole story to my brother on his return to Hinton. The frequency of the noises, the disturbance to my rest, and the necessity of often getting up at unreasonable hours gave me a fever and a deep cough, but though my health was much impaired my resolution remained firm. While I was waiting for my brother's arrival, which was delayed through his being detained at Portsmouth a week longer than he had foreseen, it occurred to me to endeavour, by changing my apartment, to obtain a little rest. Accordingly, I moved to the room formerly occupied by Elizabeth Godin. I did not mention my intention of doing so until ten at night, when the room was got ready for me. I went to bed and had scarcely lain down when the same noises that I have described began again. I mention the circumstance that I had changed my room without previous notice to prove how impossible it would have been for the plan to be suddenly conveyed by any human agent to another part of the house.

In the following week my brother arrived. Anxious though I was to tell him my story, I forbore until the next morning, wishing him to enjoy a night's rest. I had told him, however, that he must be prepared to hear on the morrow the most astonishing tale which would demand all his trust in my veracity.

In the morning I began my story, to which he listened with wonder and surprise. Just as I was finishing, Captain Luttrell, our neighbour at Kilmston, chanced to call and induced my brother to impart the whole story to him. He then in a very friendly manner offered to join in our investigations. We agreed that he should come late in the evening and divide the night watch with my brother, keeping their intention profoundly secret. During the daytime my brother, accompanied by his servant John Bolton, made a thorough search of the whole house and particularly of the rooms on the first floor and the attics. They examined every possible hiding-place and saw that every door was fastened, except those leading to the rooms occupied by the family.

That night he went to bed in the room over the servants' hall. Captain Luttrell and Bolton sat up, with arms, in the Chintz Room adjoining. I was sleeping in Elizabeth Godin's room and the children were in the nursery, so that every chamber on that floor was occupied. I bolted and locked the door leading from the back stairs, so that there was no extrance except through the room in which Captain Luttrell was keeping watch.

As soon as I had lain down I heard a rustling as though someone were close to the door. I told Elizabeth Godin to listen and if the noise continued to go and tell Captain Luttrell. She did so and instantly he threw open his door and spoke to us.

I must now give his account as he related it to my brother and myself next morning:

He declared that he had heard the footsteps of a person walking across the lobby. He had instantly thrown the door open and called out, 'Who goes there?' Something flitted past him and my brother cried, 'Look against the door.' My brother was awake and had heard Captain Luttrell's challenge, as well as the noise. He rose and joined the other. To their astonishment they continued to hear various noises, but, although they examined everything everywhere, they could see nothing and found the staircase door fast secured as I had left it. My brother and Bolton then went upstairs, where they found the servants in their rooms and all doors closed. All three men sat up together until daybreak, when my brother returned to his own room. About that time, as I imagined, I heard the Chintz Room door opened and slammed to with the utmost violence, and a moment later the hall door opened and shut in the same manner. I thought that my brother must have done this and mentioned to Godin my surprise that he who was so attentive not to alarm or disturb the children should behave so noisily. An hour later the front door again opened and slammed in the same way, so as to shake the house. No one was yet up, but about half an hour afterwards I heard the servants rise and go downstairs. At breakfast I remarked upon the noise my brother had made with the door. Mr. Luttrell replied: 'I assure you, Jervis made not the least noise; it was your door and the next which I heard opened and slammed in the way you described.'

My brother had not heard any of the doors opened or shut, but told me that when he had gone to bed and Captain Luttrell and I were sitting below, he had heard dreadful groans and various noises, for which he was unable to account. His servant was at that time below with the staff.

Captain Luttrell insisted that the disturbances of the night were such as to make the house an unfit residence for any human being. My brother, although more guarded in his language, agreed, and we decided to send an express to Mr. Sainsbury, Lady Hillsborough's steward, asking him to come over immediately on an urgent matter, with the nature of which he would be made acquainted on arrival. Unluckily Mr. Sainsbury was confined with the gout, and sent over his clerk, a youth of fifteen to whom we thought it useless and improper to divulge the circumstances.

My brother sat up every night during the week he spent at Hinton. In the middle of one of them I was alarmed by the sound of a gun or pistol, discharged quite close to me, and immediately followed by groans as of a person in agony or on the point of death. These noises seemed to come from some/where between my chamber and the next one, which was the nursery. I sent Godin to Nurse Horner to ask her if she had been disturbed, but she had heard nothing. Nor, I discovered next morning, had my brother. There were, however, several occasions when loud noises were heard by one or two people, whereas others, equally near to the spot whence the sounds appeared to come, were unaware of anything.

Since the night watch deprived my brother of his sleep, he usually lay down after dinner. Once, when he had retired in this way to rest, I sent the children and their attendants out for a walk. The dairymaid had gone to milk, the cook was in the scullery, and my own woman, with my brother's man, was sitting in the servant's hall. I was reading in the parlour when I heard my brother's bell ring very sharply. I ran up to his room and he asked me if I had heard any noise, 'Because', he said, 'as I was lying awake an immense weight seemed to fall from the ceiling to the floor just by that mahogany press, and it is impossible that I should be deceived.' By this time his man had arrived and protested that he had heard nothing, although he had been in the room below.

My brother now earnestly begged me to leave the house, offering, if I was unable to move before he had to return to Portsmouth, to send his Lieutenant of Marine, Mr. Nichols, who was an old friend of the family, to stay with me until I was ready to go.

One circumstance was so striking that I must not omit to re-late it. We were discussing the disturbances one evening when I mentioned the extraordinary effect they had had upon a favourite cat which was usually in the parlour with me. I had observed that she would sit for a while on a table or a chair with her accustomed unconcern, and then suddenly would crouch as though struck with the greatest terror, hide herself under my chair and put her head close to my feet. After a while she would come out quite unconcerned. Not long after I had told my brother about the cat my story was verified in a striking manner. Nothing happened that might alarm the animal, but she behaved exactly as I have described. My servants told me that a spaniel in the house had been similarly affected, but that is only hearsay.

MARY RICKETTS.

★

Mrs. Ricketts added, apparently at a later date, some notes to her story. She moved from Hinton Ampner to the old palace at Wolvesey, which was lent to her by the Bishop of Winchester. While the house was being got ready she stayed with a certain Dame Camis, who lived close to Hinton Manor. Several people by now had heard the story, to which they gave a mixed reception. She was greatly offended with Chancellor Hoadley, who refused to believe her. The Lord Radnor of the day expressed a great interest in it, and the Bishop of Winchester himself was most regretful that no attempt had been made at an exorcism. When Mrs. Ricketts left Hinton she gave the keys to Dame Camis, who came over every fair day to open the windows. The house was never again occupied and since its reputation was such that tenants were unobtainable, it was at last decided to pull it down. During the work of demolition the workmen found under the floor of one of the rooms a small skull said to be that of a monkey. It was in a box, and close by were a number of papers which had apparently been hidden under the floor of the hall during the Civil War.

The Death
of
Lord Tyrone

¶ The following story was sent to Lord Halifax by a member of the *Duke of Beaufort's* family, who had had it from a *Mrs. Wallace*. She was a grand-daughter of *Lady Charles Somerset,* who wrote out this version of the story about the year 1827. The *Lady Beresford* referred to was the widow of *Sir Tristram Marcus Beresford,* 3rd Baronet, who died in 1731. She was the daughter of *James, 3rd Earl of Tyrone.* Her brother was the 4th Earl.

LORD TYRONE AND LADY BERESFORD WERE BORN IN Ireland. Being orphaned in their infancy they were left to the care of a guardian who brought them up in the principles of Deism. He died when they were both about fourteen, and although his successor made every possible endeavour to eradicate the erroneous principles they had imbibed, it was all in vain. No argument could move them from the faith they had acquired in their childhood. Although now separated from each other, their affection was unchanged and after some years they made a mutual and solemn promise that whichever of them should be the first to die would, if permitted, appear to the other and declare what was the true religion.

Soon afterwards Lady Beresford married Sir Marcus. She still saw a good deal of her brother, with whom she frequently exchanged visits.

Shortly after one of these visits Sir Marcus observed one morning, when his wife came down to breakfast, that she was very pale and that her face carried evident marks of terror and confusion. He asked anxiously after her health and she assured him that she was perfectly well. He begged to be told if anything had occurred to distress her and she replied, 'No, no. I am as well as usual.'

'Have you hurt your wrist?' he asked, noticing that a black ribbon was bound round it. 'Have you sprained it?'

She replied that nothing had happened, but added: 'Let me beg you, Sir Marcus, never to enquire the cause of my wearing this ribbon. You will never again see me without it. If it concerned you as a husband to know why I wear it I would tell you. I never in my life denied you a request, but about this I must entreat you to forgive my silence and never to urge me again on the subject.'

'Very well, my lady,' replied Sir Marcus, smiling. 'Since you so earnestly desire it, I will ask no more.'

There the conversation rested, but breakfast was scarcely over when Lady Beresford eagerly asked if the post had come in. She was told that it had not. A few minutes later she again rang the bell for her servant and repeated the question. Once more she was told that the post had not arrived.

'Do you expect any letters,' asked Sir Marcus, 'that you are so anxious about the arrival of the post?'

'I do,' she answered. 'I expect to hear that Lord Tyrone is dead; that he died last Tuesday at four o'clock.'

'I never in my life', said Sir Marcus, 'believed you to be superstitious, but you must have had some idle dream which has alarmed and terrified you.'

At that instant the servant opened the door and delivered a letter sealed with black.

'It is as I expected,' exclaimed Lady Beresford; 'he is dead.'

Sir Marcus opened the letter. It was from the steward of Lord Tyrone and contained the melancholy intelligence that his master had died on the previous Tuesday at the very hour specified by Lady Beresford. Sir Marcus begged her to compose herself and to try as much as lay in her power not to make herself unhappy. She assured him, however, that she felt much easier in her mind than she had done for some time. She added, 'I can tell you something which I know will prove welcome to you. I can assure you beyond the possibility of a doubt that I am now with child of a son.'

Sir Marcus received this information with the pleasure that might be expected, expressing in the strongest terms the happiness he would derive from an event which he had so ardently desired.

After a period of some months Lady Beresford, who had previously had two daughters, was delivered of a son, whom his father survived by little more than four years.

On Sir Marcus's death Lady Beresford went very little from the house. The only family she visited was that of a clergyman, who lived in the same village. She devoted the rest of her time entirely to solitude, as though determined to avoid all human society.

The clergyman's family consisted of himself, his wife and one son, who at Sir Marcus's death was quite a youth. Nevertheless, after a few years of widowhood, Lady Beresford astonished the neighbourhood by marrying this young man, in spite of the disparity in years and rank. The outcome of the marriage justified the gloomy expectations of her neighbours.

She was treated by her young husband with contempt and cruelty, his conduct being that of an abandoned libertine, destitute of every virtue and human feeling. After bearing him two daughters, Lady Beresford was so estranged by his profligate conduct that she insisted upon a separation. They parted for several years when, on his expressing his deep contrition for his former misconduct, she consented to pardon him and once more to reside with him. After some time she bore him a son.

On the day on which she had lain-in a month, being the anniversary of her birthday, she sent for Lady Betty Cobb and a few other friends, asking them to spend the day with her. About noon, the clergyman by whom she had been baptised and with whom she had all her life maintained an intimacy, came into her room to enquire after her health. She told him she felt perfectly well and requested him to spend the day with her, 'For', she said, 'I am forty-eight to-day.'

'No, my lady,' replied the clergyman, 'you are mistaken. Your mother and I had many disputes about your age and I at length discovered that I was right. Happening to go last week into the parish where you were born, I searched the register and find that you are only forty-seven to-day.'

'You have signed my death warrant,' said Lady Beresford. 'I have not much longer to live and must entreat you to leave me at once as I have something of importance to settle before I die.'

When the clergyman had left, Lady Beresford sent word to put off her friends, but asked Lady Betty Cobb, and her own son by Sir Marcus, then about twelve years old, to come to her room. Immediately upon their arrival, having ordered her attendants to leave, she said:

'I have something of the utmost confidence to impart to both of you before I die, a period which is not far distant. You, Lady Betty, are no stranger to the close affection which existed between Lord Tyrone and myself. We were educated under the same roof and in the same principles, those of Deism. When our later guardian tried to persuade us of the error of our belief, his arguments, though insufficient to convince us, left us wavering between two opinions. In this perplexing state we promised each other that whichever of us should die first would, if permitted by the Almighty, appear to the other to declare what religion was most acceptable to Him.

'One night, when Sir Marcus and I were in bed, I awoke to discover Lord Tyrone sitting by my side. I screamed and tried to wake Sir Marcus. "For Heaven's sake," I said, "by what means and for what purpose have you come here at this time of night?" "Have you forgotten our promise?" he replied. "I died last Tuesday at four o'clock and have been permitted to appear to you to assure you that revealed religion is the true and only religion by which we can be saved. I am further permitted to inform you that you are with child of a son who, it is decreed, shall marry my daughter; that not many years after

73

the birth of this son Sir Marcus will die; that you will then marry again and that your second husband will make you miserable by his ill-treatment. You will bring him two daughters and afterwards a son, in childbed with whom you will die in the forty-seventh year of your age." "Just Heaven," I exclaimed, "cannot I prevent this?" "Undoubtedly you can," he replied; "you are a free agent and may prevent it all by resisting any temptation to a second marriage, but your passions are strong. Hitherto you have had no trials and do not know their power. More I am not permitted to tell you, but if, after this warning, you persist in infidelity your lot in another world will be miserable indeed." "May I not ask," I said, "if you are happy?" "Had it been otherwise", he replied, "I should not have been permitted to appear to you." "I may then infer that you are happy." He smiled. "But how," I asked, "when morning comes, shall I be convinced that your appearance has been real and is not the mere phantom of my imagination?" "Will not the news of my death", he said, "be sufficient to convince you?" "No," I answered, "I might have had such a dream and that dream might accidentally have come to pass. I wish to have some stronger proof of its reality." "You shall," he said. Then, waving his hand, the bedcurtains, which were of crimson velvet, were instantly drawn through a large iron hook by which the tester of the bed, which was of an oval form, was suspended. "Now", he said, "you cannot be mistaken. No mortal arm could have done that." "True," I replied, "but sleeping we are often possessed of far greater strength than waking. Awake, I could not have done it, asleep, I might; and therefore I shall still doubt." He then said, "You have a pocket book here in which I shall write. You know my handwriting?" I replied, "Yes." He then wrote with a pencil on one of the leaves. "Still," I objected, "in the morning I may doubt. When awake I cannot imitate your handwriting, but asleep it is possible that I might." "You are hard of belief," he said. "I must not touch you, for that would injure you irreparably." "I do not mind a small blemish," I replied. "You are a woman of courage," he said. "Hold out your hand." I did so. He touched my wrist with a hand as cold as marble, and in a moment the sinews were shrunk up with every nerve with them. "Now," he adjured me, "let no mortal eye while you live behold that wrist. To see it would be sacrilege." He was silent, and when I turned to him again he was gone.

'During the time I was conversing with him I was perfectly calm and collected, but the moment he was gone I felt filled with horror. A cold sweat came over me and I endeavoured, but in vain, to wake Sir Marcus. In this state of agitation and horror I lay for some time, when a shower of tears came to my relief. In the morning Sir Marcus rose and dressed himself as usual, without noticing the state in which the bed-curtains remained. When I awoke I found he had gone down. I arose and putting on my clothes went into the gallery adjoining our apartment. I found there a long broom such as in large houses is frequently used for sweeping the cornices, and with the help of it I took down (though not without difficulty) the curtains, the extraordinary position of which would have excited wonder among the servants and occasioned such enquiries as I wished to avoid. I then went to my bureau, locked up the pocket book, and took out a piece of black ribbon which I bound round my wrist. When I came down Sir Marcus observed my agitation and enquired the cause. I assured him that I was well, but that Lord Tyrone was dead, and that he had died on the preceding Tuesday at the hour of four. At the same time, I begged Sir Marcus to refrain from all enquiries concerning the black ribbon he noticed on my wrist. He kindly desisted from further importunities, nor did he ever after ask its cause.

'You, my son, as was foretold, I afterwards brought into the world, and in little more than four years after your birth your lamented father died in my arms. After this melancholy event, I determined (as the only way in which I might avoid the dreadful sequel predicted) for ever to abandon all society and to pass the remainder of my days in solitude. Few, however, can endure to remain for long in a perfect seclusion. I was on terms of intimacy with one family and one only, nor could I then see what fatal consequences were to result from this. Little did I imagine that their son, then a mere youth, was the person destined by Fate to prove my undoing. In a few years I ceased to regard him with indifference. I tried by every possible means to conquer a passion the fatal consequences of which, if yielded to, I knew too well, and fondly imagined I had overcome its influence, when one evening my fortitude broke down and I was plunged into that abyss I had so long been trying to shun. He had often asked his parents for leave to go into the Army, and having at length obtained their permission, came to bid me farewell before his departure. The moment he entered the room he fell upon his knees at my feet, telling me that he was miserable and that I alone was the cause. At that instant my fortitude forsook me and I gave myself up for lost, believing my fate to be inevitable. I thereupon consented to a union which I knew could only result in the greatest unhappiness.

'The conduct of my husband after a few years had passed amply warranted my demand for a separation, but, won over by reiterated entreaties, I was at last prevailed upon to pardon and once more to reside with him. This, however, was not until I had, as I imagined, passed my forty-seventh year. But to-day I have heard on indisputable authority that I have been mistaken about my age and that I am now only forty-seven. I therefore, entertain not the least doubt of the near approach of my death. When that day comes, since the necessity for concealment will be over, I wish you, Lady Betty, to unbind my wrist and to take from it the black ribbon, so that you and my son may witness the truth of what I have related.'

77

At this point Lady Beresford paused for some moments, but resuming her conversation entreated her son to behave in such a way as to deserve the honour he would in future receive from his union with Lord Tyrone's daughter. Lady Beresford then expressed a wish to lie down on the bed and compose herself to sleep. Lady Betty Cobb and her son immediately called her attendants and quitted the room, having first desired them attentively to watch their mistress, and, should they observe any change in her, to call them instantly. For an hour all was silent within the room. Then a bell rang violently. Lady Betty and the boy ran upstairs, but before they could reach the door of the room they heard one of the servants exclaim: 'Oh, she is dead. My mistress is dead!'

Lady Betty then told the servants to go out, and she and the boy approached the bed and knelt down by the side of it. They lifted up Lady Beresford's hand, unbound the ribbon and found the wrist exactly as she had described it, with every nerve withered and every sinew shrunk.

As had been predicted, Lady Beresford's son is now married to the daughter of Lord Tyrone. The black ribbon and the pocket book are in the possession of Lady Betty Cobb, by whom the above narrative has been given. She and the Tyrone family will be found ready to attest the truth of what has been recorded.

This narrative is confirmed by some information given to Lord Halifax by Mr. Beresford Hope. The latter mentioned Gill Hall as the house in which the ghost of Lord Tyrone appeared. After her first husband's death Lady Beresford married a Mr. Gorges, the son of a neighbouring clergyman. On her fiftieth (not her forty-seventh) birthday, a party of friends had called to offer their congratulations. While they were with Lady Beresford her father-in-law came into the room and told her that she was a year younger than she had supposed. Mr. Beresford Hope added that Lady Beresford was so much affected by this information that she took to her bed and died that night or very shortly after.

After the appearance of the first edition of this book, an interesting account of the same incidents was received from Mr. Hugh A. C. Maude of Belgard Castle, Clondalkin, a descendant of Lady Beresford's. Although in its general outline Mr. Maude's account tallies with the foregoing version, many of the names and circumstances are different. It appears that the chronicler was Lady Betty Cobbe (not Cobb) herself; that she was the grand-daughter of Lady Beresford, and could not have witnessed her death; that she had the story from her father, Lady Beresford's son Marcus, and from her aunt, Lady Riverstone, who were both present at Lady Beresford's deathbed and heard her story; and that Lady Betty did not circulate her account until 1806. Even then, in order to avoid giving offence to people still alive, she left a great many of the names blank, and in the account sent to Lord Halifax these blanks were incorrectly filled in. For example, Lady Beresford's second husband was a Colonel (afterwards General) Gorges, and was the brother-in-law, not the son, of Lady Beresford's friend and neighbour. Although there are other discrepancies, the incidents are substantially the same in both versions.

The Passenger
with
the Bag

¶A note by *Lord Halifax* explains that he mislaid his authority for the following story.

A GENTLEMAN WHOSE NAME IS NOT GIVEN WAS LEAVING London one morning by train from Euston. Having with him some papers which he wished to read during the journey, he asked if he might have a carriage to himself. Since the train was not full, the guard found him an empty compartment and locked the door. Just as the train was about to start, an elderly gentleman carrying a bag appeared in a hurry. He turned the handle of the door, which apparently had not, as the occupant of the carriage thought, been locked, and got in. After a little while, the two men fell into conversation, the last-comer informing his companion that he was a Director of the Railway Company and was particularly interested in a branch line which was about to be opened. He added that he was carrying with him seventy thousand pounds which he was to lodge in a local bank for the prosecution of the work.

'Are you not afraid', said the other, 'to carry about so large a sum as you mention?'

'Oh, no!' was the reply.'No one would know. Besides, who would rob me? Not you, just because I have told you. I am not afraid of anything happening.'

They went on talking, and in the course of their conversation the gentlemen with the bag said: 'By the way, I know the house to which you are going. The lady of it is my niece. Will you give her my kind regards and tell her that I hope the next

83

time I come to stay she won't have such a huge fire in the Blue Room as she had the last time? She nearly roasted me out. But here is my station.'

With these words the elderly gentleman rose and prepared to get out. Before doing so, however, he gave his companion his card, on which was the name of Dwerringhouse. He then left the carriage, and his fellow-traveller, settling himself back in his seat, saw him walking down the platform with his bag. At that moment, he noticed a cigar-case lying on the floor close to his feet. Picking it up, he saw Mr. Dwerringhouse's name upon it. Since the train was not due to start for another two minutes, he jumped out and ran along the platform in the hope of catching Mr. Dwerringhouse and handing over the cigar-case to him. He had a glimpse of him standing under a lamp-post and talking to a man at the end of the platform. He noticed that the man's hair was of a sandy colour and could plainly see his face, which was turned towards him. As he drew near, however, he lost sight of both the figures, which had rather unaccountably disappeared. Although he looked round carefully to see where they had gone, there was no sign of them, and when he asked a porter, who was standing by, what had happened to them the man replied that he had not seen any such people and that they could not have passed his way.

The train was now about to start and the gentleman, very much puzzled, had to hurry back to his carriage with no possibility of further enquiry.

Arriving at his destination that evening, he dressed for dinner and found a large party in the drawing-room. During dinner he remembered the message to his hostess, and turning to her said: 'I travelled down with an uncle of yours and he told me to give you the following message.' This he proceeded to do.

The lady appeared to be greatly distressed and put out, and so was her husband, and the gentleman realised that he had said something very unfortunate. What it was or how he could have annoyed his host and hostess he was unable to imagine. However, when the ladies had retired from the dining-room, the husband took him aside and said: 'Very awkward, what you told my wife, when you gave her that message from her uncle. The fact is he has disappeared and no one knows where he is. What is worse, he absconded with seventy thousand pounds. The police are looking for him and, as you can imagine, it is not a pleasant subject in this house.'

It so happened that among the guests were two Directors of the Railway Company. Having overheard the conversation at dinner they approached the gentleman afterwards and asked him if he could give them any further particulars about this man whom he had met in the train.

'No,' he replied, 'I can tell you no more, except that I saw him and talked with him and left him, as I thought, speaking to another man on the platform of the station where we parted.'

85

The Directors continued to press him and eventually asked him if he would mind appearing before their Board and telling his story to them. He agreed to do so and in due course the meeting was arranged. He was in the middle of his narrative when he suddenly exclaimed: 'There is the man I saw talking to Mr. Dwerringhouse!—that man with the sandy hair!'

A man of this description was actually sitting among the Directors. He was the cashier of the Company, and now, taken by surprise, he called out: 'But I was not there. I was away on my holiday.'

This was so strange an interjection that there and then the Directors insisted upon the records being brought in and examined, when it was clear that the cashier had not been away on his holiday, as he had stated. They closely cross-examined him and eventually forced from him a confession. He admitted that he had murdered Mr. Dwerringhouse. He insisted that he had not meant to do so, but had known of the Director's journey and of the money he was taking with him. Having met him at the station, he had persuaded him to take a short cut and, when they were passing through a quarry, had knocked him on the head. He had only meant to stun him and so to get possession of his bag, but in falling Mr. Dwerringhouse had struck his head on a stone and been killed.

The curious episode of the cigar-case was explained by the fact that, owing to some repairs being necessary, the carriage in which Mr. Dwerringhouse had travelled had been out of use from the day of his journey to that of his subsequent appear, ance. It may be added that the guard at Euston was positive that on the day of the appearance he had certainly locked the door of the carriage and that only one gentleman was inside when the train started.

'Marche!'

⁋ This story was apparently sent to *Lord Halifax* by a *Colonel Butler*, of *Plymouth*, who was told it by a *Mr. Roderick Macfarlane*, a chief factor in the Hudson's Bay Company, stationed at *Fort Chippewyan, Athabasca, North West Territory, Canada.*

ON THE FIFTEENTH DAY OF MARCH, 1853, AUGUSTUS
Richards Peers, a fur trader and post manager in the service of
the Hudson's Bay Company, departed this life at Fort
McPherson, Peel's River, in the Mackenzie River district,
North West America. Although he had occasionally com-
plained of ill health, his death at the comparatively early age
of 33, after a few days' illness, was entirely unexpected. He
was of Anglo-Irish origin, an able officer, much esteemed by
his friends and popular among the Indians. During a residence
of, I think, eleven years in that remote district, he had been
stationed for two or three seasons at headquarters (Fort Simpson), and was afterwards in charge of Forts Norman and
McPherson.

In 1849, Mr. Peers married the eldest daughter of the late
Chief Trader, John Bell, who still survives. By her he had
two children, a girl who died in 1863 and a boy now living
in Manitoba. In 1855 Mr. Peers's widow married the late
Trader Alexander Mackenzie, who succeeded her first husband in the charge of Fort McPherson.

Whilst a resident of both Norman and McPherson Forts,
the dead man had been heard to express a strong dislike, in the
event of his decease, that his bones should rest at either spot.
He was believed to have made a will, but if so, he must have
mislaid or destroyed it, as no such document ever turned up.

Having entered the Company's service in 1852, I (Roder-ick Macfarlane) was appointed to Mackenzie River in the following year and reached Fort Simpson five months after Mr. Peers's death.

During the autumn of 1859, at the request of Mrs. Mac-kenzie and her husband, it was decided to carry out, in the course of the winter, the long contemplated transference of the remains of Mr. Peers from their place of interment on the banks of Peel's River, to Fort Simpson, the scene of his earlier residence. Mr. (now Chief Trader) Gaudet, then in charge of Fort McPherson, agreed to convey the body by dog-train to Fort Good Hope, a distance of three hundred miles, while I undertook to take it on to its final destination some five hun-dred miles further south.

Fort McPherson is situated more than one degree north of the Arctic Circle. Owing to the marshiness of the soil, frost is always found a little below the surface of the ground, and on the body of Mr. Peers being exhumed by Mr. Gaudet, it was found in much the same condition as on the day of its burial. It was taken from its grave and placed in a new and unnecessarily large coffin. This was secured by a wrapper and lines on a Hudson's Bay dog-sled, or train. It was an extremely difficult and awkward load for men and dogs to conduct and haul over the rugged masses of tossed-up ice which occur at intervals along the mighty Mackenzie River, especially in its higher and more rapid reaches towards the Northern Ocean.

On the 1st of March, 1860, Mr. Gaudet arrived at Good Hope and delivered up the body to my care. Shortly afterwards I set out with it for Fort Simpson. The coffin was fixed on one team or train of three dogs, conducted by an Iroquois from Caughnawaga, near Montreal, named Michel Thomas. A second train carried our bedding, provisions, etc. I myself led the march on snow-shoes, and after seven days of very hard and trying labour, owing to the unusual depth of snow and the quantities of rough ice, we successfully accomplished the first two hundred miles of our journey to Fort Norman, the nearest point from Good Hope.

At this place the Trader-in-Charge, Mr. Nicol Taylor, was very insistent that unless the coffin was removed and the body properly secured on the train, it would be almost impossible for us to get over the vast masses of ice which we were sure to encounter at certain points between Fort Norman and Fort Simpson. As I had previously covered the same ground twice that winter and had had some experience of the ice, I took his advice—to our future satisfaction.

After one day's rest at Norman, we started on the last and longest portion of our journey. At that time there was no intervening station and very few Indians were to be encountered *en route*. The Iroquois, Thomas, was still in charge of the body-train. The baggage train dogs, and the man from Good Hope were exchanged at Norman for fresh animals, and a new driver named Michel Iroquois joined us. Mr. Taylor also helped me to beat the track, having volunteered to accompany the remains of his former master and friend.

A full description of the mode of winter travel in this country may be learned from the pages of various authors, but it may be briefly stated that we usually got under way by 4 a.m., dined at some convenient spot about noon, and, after an hour's rest, resumed our journey until sunset. We then laid up for the night, generally in a pine bluff on the top of, or close to, the immediate river bank. Clearing away the snow to the ground, for a space of about ten feet square, cutting and carrying brush for the flooring, and collecting a sufficiency of firewood for cooking and warming up, usually occupied us for about an hour. Another hour would see supper over and the dogs fed, and soon afterwards most of the party would be sound asleep. Except on two occasions to be presently mentioned, the train carrying the dead body was invariably hauled up at once and placed for the night in the immediate rear of our camp. Except on the first of these two occasions, our dogs never showed any desire to interfere with the body, or seemed in the slightest degree influenced by its presence.

About sunset on the fifteenth day of March, the seventh anniversary of poor Peers's death, we were obliged to encamp at a short distance above a rock by the riverside, there being no better place within easy reach. The banks here were high, rocky and steep, and we had to leave both trains on the ice. Even so, we found a great deal of difficulty in scrambling up the bank with our axes, snow-shoes, bedding and provisions for supper and breakfast. The dogs were unharnessed and remained below. The weather was calm, and comparatively fine and mild. The bank rose about thirty feet to the summit, some thirty feet beyond which, on a shelving flat, we chose our camp for the night. All hands then set about making the necessary prepara- tions, cutting and carrying supplies of fine brush and firewood.

We had been busy at this work for perhaps ten or twelve minutes, when the dogs began to bark and we concluded that Indians were approaching, this being a part of the river at which it was quite usual to fall in with them. Nevertheless, we continued our work and the dogs went on barking, though not as loudly and fiercely as is usual in such circumstances. Neither the dogs nor the sleds were visible from the camp, but only from the top of the river bank. While I was talking to Mr. Taylor on the subject, we all distinctly heard the word '*Marche!*' (I may remark that French terms are almost univers- ally used to dogs in the North-West). The word seemed to have been spoken by someone at the foot of the bank, who wished to drive the dogs away from his path, and we all left our work to see who the stranger was. When no one appeared, two of us (Thomas and myself) went to the top of the bank, where to our astonishment no one was visible. The dogs were clustered round the body-train at a distance of several feet and were apparently excited by something. We had to call them repeatedly before they broke away and came up the bank to our encampment. Here they stayed perfectly quiet for the night, taking no further notice of the body on the train. It struck me at the time that the word 'Marche' had been more clearly enunciated than I had ever heard it from the lips of an Indian, who can seldom get beyond 'Mash' or 'Masse'.

On the eighteenth of March we had to travel for two hours after dark, in order to find a suitable encampment. Although we eventually discovered a tolerably good place near the head of a large island on the river, it was no easy matter to ascend a perpendicular bank some twelve feet in height. The baggage train being now very light, by tying a line to the foremost dog we managed to drag it to the top. We were able to haul up the dogs of the body train in the same way, but it was beyond our power to pull up the body itself, which we were reluctantly obliged to leave below.

After cutting a road for about thirty yards through some thick willows, we found ourselves on the edge of a dense forest of small pines, where, although dry wood was far from abundant, we made our camp. When most of the work was over, I returned from the spot where I had been collecting wood and Mr. Taylor asked me if I had heard a very loud call, twice repeated, from the direction of the river. I replied that I had heard nothing, but that the thicket was very dense and, owing to the cold, biting wind, my ear-protectors had been closely tied down. The two Iroquois then asserted that they also had distinctly heard the calls.

I said: 'Well, let us see who or what it is. Possibly an Indian has followed our tracks.'

On regaining the river, however, we could neither see nor hear anything. I then decided to haul up the body train, which in spite of the difficulty we succeeded in doing. Early next morning, we had reason to congratulate ourselves on taking this trouble, as on reaching the spot from which we had removed the body train we discovered that a wolverine had been there during the night. Had we left the body on the spot, he would undoubtedly have made havoc with the remains.

Fort Simpson was at length reached without further incident on the forenoon of March the twenty-first, and on the twenty-third the body was duly buried in the graveyard adjacent to the Fort. Shortly after my arrival I recounted everything to Chief Trader R. Ross, the District Manager, who had been an intimate friend and countryman of Mr. Peers. Mr. Ross had an excellent memory and could easily mimic anyone's voice. When he said the word '*Marche*' in what he declared to be the tone of the dead man, it seemed to me to be very similar to what we had heard on March the fifteenth at our encampment near the rock.

During my brief stay at Simpson I shared a room with Mr. Ross. On the first or second night after retiring and extinguishing the light, we were talking about these strange occurrences and other matters, including the supposed disappearance of Mr. Peers's will. I then became overpoweringly conscious of what I can only describe as a supernatural presence in the room. The feeling came on me so suddenly that I instantly covered my face with the blanket. After a few moments, Mr. Ross, who had stopped talking, asked me in an excited voice if I had experienced a very strange sensation. I replied that I had, describing it, whereupon he assured me that this was exactly the experience he himself had just undergone. I know what nightmare is, but it is most unlikely that two individuals, both perfectly wide awake and carrying on a conversation upon a subject of interest to them, should be thus attacked simultaneously. I should add that neither of us had drunk any wine or spirits, which might be held to account for our sensations.

I leave it to others, if they can, to account for the facts I have stated here, but if it be granted that the spirits of the dead are sometimes allowed to re-visit former scenes and their discarded bodies, then, having in mind Mr. Peers's feelings regarding the final disposition of his remains, what more natural course would his spirit have taken in order to prevent the desecration of these? From the position of our camp on March the fifteenth, it may be taken for granted that it was really impossible to have dragged the train up such a steep and rugged bank. Dogs are invariably hungry after their day's work and the weather being fine may have scented the still fresh and uncorrupted body; their barking at and position round the sled would on any other hypothesis be unaccountable. There was, of course, danger from wolves and wolverines, but presumably spirits know more than mortals. On the night of the eighteenth of March the bank was difficult to ascend, and to get up it we had to raise and push the first man until he could catch hold of some willow, by which he could hoist himself up. He then threw us a line. The bank, however, was not insurmountable, and as a most vicious and destructive animal actually visited the spot where the train would have been left for the night, what other course would any spirit be likely to take than to utter those repeated calls which were heard? As to the extraordinary feeling experienced by Mr. Ross and myself at the moment when we were talking of the dead man and his missing will, might not this have arisen from a desire on his part to communicate some information to us, which, through losing our presence of mind, we missed our opportunity of receiving?

The facts I have stated made so indelible an impression on me that the foregoing account, in my opinion, does not differ in any material point from the story which I communicated to Mr. Ross and others at the time and have told repeatedly since.

R. MACFARLANE.

This statement was apparently followed by a letter from Mr. Macfarlane, dated April 24th, 1885, the relevant passages in which are given below:

Since writing out the statement, I have opened your note marked 'Questions: Not to be opened until the story has been written,' and I now beg to reply to these in their order as follows:

1. Mr. N. Taylor, myself, Michel Thomas and young Michel Iroquois, who, if still alive, is with the exception of myself the only survivor of the party, distinctly heard what purported to be the word 'Marche!' I do not think Mr. Taylor made any remark as to the tone of voice, as we all fully believed that an Indian on his way to visit us must have uttered the word; but its clear enunciation struck me at the time. Subsequently, when I heard Mr. Ross imitate the voice of Mr. Peers, I at once recognised a great similarity to the sound I had heard on March the fifteenth. Mr. Taylor also declared that Mr. Ross's rendering of 'Marche!' was very like his recollection of Peers's voice.

2. The sound certainly appeared to us to come from somewhere near the spot at the foot of the river bank where the body train had been left.

3. I have estimated from memory the distance from the encampment of March the fifteenth to the edge of the bank at about thirty feet. It may have been more and there was a further abrupt descent of nearly thirty feet to the body train. As the weather was clear and calm and all of us at the time were listening intently, circumstances favoured the conveyance of sound to our ears, in spite of the almost incessant, but rather low-toned barking of our six dogs. On the second occasion, owing to a stiff breeze which was blowing and the greater dist-

ance (one hundred feet) from the river to the camp, with a drop of twelve feet at the end, no one could possibly make himself heard from below unless he gave a very loud, shrill, and prolonged hail or yell, and this was exactly what Taylor and the other two men asserted having twice heard. I did not myself hear either of the calls, but bearing in mind my position at the time, in the midst of a dense thicket of small pine, with my ear flaps tied down, and the wind rustling among the trees, this is not surprising. Hauling dogs are noted for being remarkably quarrelsome in winter camp, especially before supper, and if I had heard any sounds on that occasion I would naturally have attributed them to these animals.

4. There was no wolverine at or near the body train while it remained on the ice, but we discovered that one had been there during the night.

5. I have had no other supernatural experience worthy of record.

The Man
in a
Silk Dress

¶ *Lord Halifax* gave no authority for this story other than the fact that it was told by the *Rev. Dr. Jessop*, Headmaster of *Norwich Grammar School*.

LITTLE MORE THAN TWO MONTHS HAVE PASSED SINCE MY experience of the supernatural was strikingly enlarged by the occurrence with which the following narrative deals. Already I find that round the original story an accumulation of myth has gathered and that I am in danger of becoming a hero of romance in more senses than one. As I object to being looked upon as a kind of medium, to whom supernatural visitations are vouchsafed, and on the other hand do not wish to be set down as a crazy dreamer, whose disorganised nervous system renders him liable to fantastic delusions, I have yielded to the earnest request of those who have begged me to record my experience in writing. I am told that there are those who busy themselves in collecting similar stories. If so, it is better that they shall hear the facts from me than after they have passed through other channels. The narrative was written at the request of a friend, not many days after the event, when all the circumstances were fresh in my recollection.

On the tenth of October, 1879, I drove over from Norwich to Mannington Hall, to spend the night at Lord Orford's. Though I was in perfect health and high spirits, it is fair to state that for some weeks previously I had had a great deal to think about, some little anxiety, and considerable mental strain of one kind or another, I was not, however, conscious of anything approaching weariness, irritability or 'fag'. I arrived at four o'clock in the afternoon and was engaged in pleasant and animated conversation until it was time to dress for dinner. We dined at seven. Our party numbered six persons, of whom four at least had been great travellers. I myself was rather a listener. The talk, which was general and discursive, amused and interested me greatly. Not for a single moment did it turn upon the supernatural. It was chiefly concerned with questions of art and the experiences of those who had seen a great deal of the world and could describe intelligently what they had seen and comment upon it suggestively. After dinner we played a rubber of whist, and as two of the guests had some distance to drive, we broke up at half-past ten.

The main object of my going over to Mannington was to examine and take notes upon some very rare books in Lord Orford's library, which I had been anxious to get a sight of for some years, but had never been so fortunate as to see up till now. I asked leave to sit up for some hours and make transcripts. Lord Orford at first wished me to let his valet remain in attendance, to see that all lights were put out, but as this would have embarrassed me and compelled me to go to bed earlier than I wished, and as, moreover, it seemed likely that I would be busy till two or three o'clock in the morning, it was agreed that I should be left to my own devices and that the servant should be allowed to retire. By eleven o'clock, busily at work and absorbed in my occupation, I was the only person downstairs.

I was writing in a large room with a huge fireplace and a grand old chimney, and, needless to say, it was furnished with every comfort and luxury. The library opened into this room, and to reach the volumes I wanted to examine I had to pass into it and stand upon a chair. There were six small volumes in all. Taking them down, I placed them at my right hand in a little pile, and set to work, sometimes reading and sometimes writing. On the table were four silver candlesticks with candles burning and, as I am a chilly person, I sat down at one corner of the table with the fire on my left. At intervals, as I had finished with a book, I rose, knocked the fire together and stood up to warm my feet. In this way I continued at my work till nearly one o'clock in the morning. I had got on better than I had expected and had only one more book to study. I rose, wound up my watch, and opened a bottle of Seltzer water, thinking to myself that after all I should get to bed by two o'clock. I then set to work on the last little book. I had been engaged upon it for about half an hour and was just beginning to think that my task was drawing to a close, when, while I was actually writing, I saw a large white hand within a foot of my elbow. Turning my head, I distinguished the figure of a somewhat large man with his back to the fire, bending slightly over the table and apparently examining the pile of books upon which I had been working. The man's face was turned away from me, but I saw his closely-cut, reddish-brown hair, his ear and smooth cheek, an eyebrow, the corner of the right eye, the side of the forehead, and the large, high cheek-bone. He was dressed in what I can only describe as a kind of ecclesiastical habit of thick corded silk or some such material. It was buttoned up to the throat and had a narrow rim or edging, about an inch broad, of satin or velvet, which served as a collar and fitted close to the chin. The right hand, which had first attracted my attention, was clasping without any great pressure, the left hand. Both were in perfect repose, the light blue veins of the right hand being conspicuous.

I looked at my visitor for some seconds, uncertain whether he was real or not. A thousand thoughts came crowding upon me, but I had not the least feeling of alarm, or even of uneasiness. Curiosity and a strong interest were uppermost. For an instant I felt eager to make a sketch of my friend and looked at a tray on my right for a pencil. Then I thought, 'Upstairs, I have a sketch-book. Shall I fetch it?' Sitting there he fascinated me: I was not afraid of his staying but of his going. Stopping in my writing, I lifted my left hand from the paper, stretched it out to the pile of books and moved the top one. I cannot explain why I did this. My arm passed in front of the figure and it vanished. I was simply disappointed and had no other feeling about the incident. I went on with my writing for perhaps another five minutes as though nothing had happened, and had actually got to the last few words of my appointed task when the figure appeared again. I saw the hands close to my own and turned my head in order to examine the man more closely. I was about to address him when I discovered that I did not dare speak. I was afraid of the sound of my own voice. There he sat and there I sat. I turned back to my work and finished off two or three words I had still to write. The paper and my notes, which are at this moment before me, show not the slightest tremor or nervousness. I could point out the very words I was writing when the ghost came and again when he disappeared. Having finished my task, I shut the book and threw it on the table. As it fell it made a slight noise and the figure vanished.

Throwing myself back in my chair, I sat for some seconds wondering whether my friend would come again, and if he did whether he would hide the fire from me. I then for the first time had a dread and a suspicion that I was beginning to lose my nerve. I remember yawning. Then I rose, lit my bed-room candle, took my books into the inner library, mounted the chair as before and replaced five of the volumes. The sixth I took back and laid upon the table, on which I had been writing when the ghost appeared. By this time I had lost all sense of uneasiness. I blew out the four candles and marched off to bed, where I slept the sleep of the just, or the guilty—I know not which, but I slept very soundly.

This is a simple and unvarnished narrative of facts. Explanation, theory, or inference, I leave to others.

The Strange Experience
of the
Reverend Spencer Nairne

¶ This story was sent by *Mr. Wilfrid Ward*, the well-known Roman Catholic writer, to *Lady Halifax*, in September, 1912. The account was evidently written by *Mr. Spencer Nairne* himself.

IN THE YEAR 1859 I WENT ON A CRUISE TO NORWAY, IN A yacht belonging to my cousin. Our party was as follows. James Cowan, M.P. for Edinburgh, Mrs. Cowan, his wife, Miss Cowan, his sister, Miss Wahab,[1] his niece, Robert Watson, his brother-in-law, John Chalmers, his cousin, and myself. The other members of the party were all distant relations of mine, but they being Scotch and I English, I had not previously met them, so that on the day we set out I was among comparative strangers. We were to start from Edinburgh, but the yacht was coming up the west coast of Scotland and we had arranged to join her at Thurso. We all left Edinburgh by steamer at 8.0 a.m. on Tuesday, May 31st, 1859, arriving at Aberdeen at 4.0 p.m. the same day. I had never been there before. We went about the city, seeing its places and objects of interest, and had a high tea together at a hotel about 6.30 p.m. When we had finished we went out again to while away the time until 9.30 p.m., when we were to rejoin the steamer and continue our voyage to Thurso.

We walked up the principal street of the town, which I think is called Union Street. It was about 8.30 in the evening and it was still full daylight (at Thurso there is blue sky at midnight). The street was moderately thronged with people, walking on the footpaths in both directions. I was

[1]Perhaps Wauchope.

arm-in-arm with John Chalmers, and while we were walking and talking there passed me, going in the opposite direction, a lady whom I recognised named Miss Wallis. She was not an intimate acquaintance, but I had known her since my childhood, for some twenty years or more (I was then twenty-six). She had been governess to some little cousins of mine of about my age and had been so much valued and beloved that after they had grown beyond her charge she had lived as governess-companion or visitor in one or other branch of that family. I very seldom saw her, but had a great regard and respect for her and would never have met her without going out of the way to speak to her, as of course I did now. She passed me close enough to touch me. I do not know whether we actually did touch one another, but she was certainly quite close enough for each of us to see clearly and recognise the other. The path being crowded I did not see her until she was close to me. She was walking with a gentleman, holding his arm and talking to him with some animation, and I saw plainly that in the moment of passing she had seen and recognised me.

I at once dropped my friend's arm and turned round to speak to her, quite expecting that she would do the same by me. Not only, however, had she not done so, but so far as I could see, she had completely disappeared. I looked everywhere, up and down the footpath and across the road, walked quickly on in the direction she was going, and then turned back again, but not a sign of her could I see. I also looked into a good many of the shops in the immediate neighbourhood and satisfied myself that she had not turned into any of them.

At ten o'clock we left Aberdeen in the steamer and I did not give much further thought to the encounter. We were in Norway until the 5th of September, sailing on that day from Stavanger. We landed at Aberdeen on Thursday, the 8th September, after dark, and left for Edinburgh by train early the next morning. I had therefore no opportunity of returning to the spot where I had seen Miss Wallis, nor indeed should I have done so, as the incident had almost passed from my recollection.

Some three weeks later I went with my mother to pay a call on some of my cousins who lived in Mecklenburgh Square, London. There I found Miss Wallis, and as my mother was talking with my cousin I had her to myself. Before I could begin she said: 'Now I have a quarrel to settle with you, Mr. Nairne. You cut me in Aberdeen a little while ago.'

I assured her that I had done nothing of the sort, that I saw her and was positive that she had seen me, but when I turned round to speak to her, which I did immediately, she was gone. She replied that exactly the same had happened to her. She had turned round at once and I had disappeared.

I said: 'You were walking with a gentleman and talking to him and I thought that you recognised me just at the moment of passing.'

'Yes,' she replied, 'it is exactly so. I was walking with my brother and called out, "Why there's Mr. Nairne. I must speak to him." When we could not find you, my brother said, "I am so sorry. I have so often heard of Captain Nairne and I should have been so glad to meet him." I replied, "It was not Captain Nairne, but his son, Mr. Spencer Nairne."'

As we could throw no more light on the subject, we dropped it and she began to ask me about Norway, presently enquiring how long I had been there. I replied that my visit had lasted for a little over three months, from June 6th to September 8th.

'Well,' she said, 'but when were you in Aberdeen?'

'On May 31st.'

'But', she objected, 'I was not in Aberdeen then. I spent a week there with my brother in the latter part of July. I have recorded my meeting with you in my journal and if I had the book here with me I could show you the entry. I have never been in Aberdeen before or since.'

She added that her brother lived some distance out of the city, that they never went there in the evening and that her meeting with me took place earlier in the day.

I rejoined that I too kept a journal and that this would prove that the day on which I saw her in Aberdeen was certainly not in July. In fact, I knew it was Tuesday, May 31st. (I may say that in writing this account I have my journal in front of me and it verifies the dates which I have given.)

We could not clear up the mystery. I am sorry that I did not at once write out the story as I have written it here and send it to her for verification and signature. Some years afterwards, on the advice of some friends, I did write it out, but just about that time Miss Wallis died, so that she never saw it. I sent it, however, to Mr. Myers at Cambridge, and so far as I understood his reply I gathered that he had no difficulty in believing that Miss Wallis saw me after I had been on the spot, but a good deal in believing that I could have seen her before she was there.

I can only vouch for the complete truth and accuracy of all that I have written. Miss Wallis was one of the last persons likely to present herself to my mind had I not seen her, and I saw her so distinctly and her recognition of me was so unmistakable that to my mind there is no possibility of explaining the matter away as a case of mistaken identity.

I am not supposed to possess second sight nor am I in the habit of seeing visions. The only other occurrence of the kind within my experience took place when I was at school. I was then aged seventeen or thereabouts and was walking arm-in-arm with a schoolfellow when we passed our headmaster (the Rev. C. Pritchard, afterwards Savilian Professor of Astronomy at the University of Oxford) walking rapidly in the opposite direction. We touched our hats to him, and without looking at us he returned our salute. He passed on, and two or three minutes later exactly the same thing happened again. Astonished, we dropped each other's arms and exclaimed as in one breath, 'Where did he come from?' We were both sure that he could not have played a trick on us by running round some other way; nor was it likely that he would have done so, though I daresay that we, as schoolboys, were quite capable of suspecting him of such an action. These meetings took place in an unfrequented part of the village or town of Clapham in the year 1850 or 1851. We were sauntering slowly, talking, probably about nothing in particular, and both saw him on each occasion. The name of my companion was Henry Stone. He is still alive and lives at Merle Lodge, St. John's, Ryde, Isle of Wight. We never asked our headmaster about this matter, neither did he mention it to us, as I should have expected him to do if he had seen us.

Mr. Spencer Nairne adds certain particulars about himself. He describes himself as of Emmanuel College, Cambridge, sometime Rector of Hunsdon, Hertfordshire, afterwards Vicar of High Wych, Hertfordshire, afterwards Vicar of Latton, Essex, now of Latton, Totland Bay, Isle of Wight.

The Renishaw Coffin

¶ *Renishaw*, about which the following stories are related, is the country house of the *Sitwells*, the well-known Derby-shire family, to which *Mr. Osbert*, *Mr. Sacheverell*, and *Miss Edith Sitwell* belong. It is an old house dating from 1625 and has many ghostly associations.

The first story was probably given to *Lord Halifax* by his friend, *Miss Tait*, the daughter of the *Archbishop of Canter-bury*. The second story was supplied by *Sir George Sitwell* himself, with the addition of a note by his wife, *Lady Ida Sitwell*.

Miss Tait's Story.

IN 1885, SIR GEORGE SITWELL, WHO WAS BORN IN 1860, celebrated his legal coming of age. There was a large party in the house for the occasion, the guests including the Archbishop of Canterbury (Dr. Tait), and one or two of his daughters. Miss Tait was sleeping in a room at the head of the staircase. In the middle of the night she came into the room of Miss Sitwell, Sir George's sister, and declared that she had been awakened by the sensation of someone having given her three cold kisses. Miss Sitwell said she would make up a bed for Miss Tait on the sofa in her own room. She added that she was not willing to go back and sleep in Miss Tait's room, as once she had fancied she had had the same experience when she had slept there.

After the party had broken up, Mr. Turnbull, Sir George's agent, came to talk to him about some business and in the course of their conversation Sir George mentioned Miss Tait's account of what she believed had occurred in the room she occupied. Sir George had thought Mr. Turnbull would be amused, but contrary to his expectations Mr. Turnbull turned very pale and said:

'Well, Sir George, you may make a joke about it, but when you lent us the house for our honeymoon, Miss Crane (sister to Walter Crane, the artist), a schoolfellow of my wife's, came to stay with us, and she had the same room and exactly the same experience'

121

Some time afterwards there was a question of altering and enlarging the staircase. Sir George Sitwell consulted his cousin, Mr. F. I. Thomas, as to how this should best be done and Mr. Thomas recommended throwing the room in question, with the one below it, into the staircase. It was eventually decided that this should be done. When the alterations were begun, Sir George, being anxious to learn anything that was to be ascertained about the ancient plan of the house, left orders with the steward and Clerk of the Works to take note of anything of interest that might be discovered and let him and Mr. Thomas know about it. The work was begun, and one day Mr. Thomas, on opening his letters, found one from the Clerk of the Works. He reported that in removing the floor of one of the bedrooms the workmen had come across something which he thought would interest him. He therefore begged Mr. Thomas to come down and see what they had found.

Mr. Thomas went down and learned that they had discovered a coffin between the joists of the floor of the room in which Miss Tait had slept. From its appearance and the fact that it had no screws but only nails, the coffin appeared to date from the seventeenth century. It was firmly fastened to the joists by iron cramps, but owing to the shallowness of the space between the joists and the floor, there was no lid, the floor boards serving this purpose. There was no trace of any bones within the coffin, but it carried certain marks which suggested that it had once contained a body.

Sir George Sitwell's Story.

Last Saturday two ghosts were seen at Renishaw. Lady Ida had been to Scarborough to attend the Life Boat Ball, at which she had sat up until four o'clock in the morning, returning home in the afternoon. After dinner, the party of six—I was absent for a few hours—sat in the drawing-room upstairs, Lady Ida lying on a sofa facing the open door.

She had been speaking to a friend who was sitting on her left when she looked up and saw in the passage outside the figure of a woman, apparently a servant, with grey hair and a white cap, the upper part of her dress being blue and the skirt dark. Her arms were stretched out at full length and the hands were clasped. This figure moved with a very slow, furtive, gliding motion, as if wishing to escape notice, straight towards the head of the old staircase, which I removed twenty years ago. On reaching it, she disappeared.

Unwilling to think that there was anything supernatural in the appearance, Lady Ida called out, 'Who's that?' and then the name of the housekeeper. When no one answered she cried to those who were nearest the door, 'Run out and see who it is; run out at once.'

Two people rushed out, but no one was to be seen, nor, when the others joined them and searched the hall and passages upstairs, could they find anyone resembling the woman described to them by Lady Ida.

They had given up the search and were returning to the

drawing-room, when one of the party, Miss R——, who was a little behind the others, exclaimed, 'I do believe that's the ghost!' No one else saw anything, but afterwards she described what she had seen. In the full light of the archway below, within twenty feet of her, and just where the door of the old ghost room used to stand, until I removed it and put the present staircase in its place, she saw the figure of a lady, with dark hair and dress, apparently lost in painful thought and oblivious to everything about her. Her dress was fuller than is the modern fashion and the figure, though opaque, cast no shadow. It moved with a curious gliding motion into the darkness and melted away at the spot within a yard of the place where a doorway, now walled up, led from the staircase to the hall.

There is no doubt that these figures were actually seen as described. They were not ghosts but phantasms, reversed impressions of something seen in the past, and now projected from an overtired and excited brain. In both cases the curious gliding movement, the absence of shadow and the absolute stillness of the figures, which moved neither hand nor head and hardly seemed to breathe, point to that conclusion. Such an experience goes far towards solving the ghost problem. Ghosts are sometimes met with, but they are not ghosts.

September 17th, 1909. GEORGE R. SITWELL.

Lady Ida Sitwell's Note.

I saw the figure with such distinctness that I had no doubt at all that I was looking at a real person, while, at the same time, although seated in a well-lighted room and chatting with friends, I was conscious of an uneasy, creepy feeling. I tried to see the features, but could not. Even before I called out, my friends noticed that I appeared to be following something with my eyes. The light in the passage was good and I could see so well that I could distinguish the exact shade of the dress. The figure was that of a woman between fifty and sixty years of age and her grey hair was done up into a 'bun', under an old-fashioned cap. I have never seen a ghost before, nor had I been thinking about ghosts.

The Butler
in the
Corridor

¶ This account of a well-known house in *Yorkshire*, the name of which has been withheld at the owner's request, was given to *Lord Halifax* by his friend, *Sir William Hansell*, *K.C.*, the Diocesan Chancellor, some forty years ago.

A FEW YEARS AGO, EARLY IN JANUARY, MY WIFE AND I
went to stay at A——, arriving on a Thursday or Friday in the
late afternoon. After dinner, our host, who was then renting
the place, told us that the house was said to be haunted by the
ghost of a butler who had destroyed himself. He added that
the ghost had been seen by a sister of our hostess, and that on
another occasion two men staying with them for Doncaster
Races and quartered in adjoining rooms had each accused the
other over the breakfast table of having walked about the passage during the night and opened and shut doors, whereas
neither man had left his room. Our host further told us that
he did not like the matter talked about as the maidservants
were apt to get frightened and to gossip about the ghost.

On the Saturday or Sunday we were shown over the house
and in the course of our tour we were taken into the corridor
which the ghost was supposed to frequent, the room in which
our hostess's sister had seen him, and a large bedroom at the
end of the corridor, which our host said he did not use if he
could help it, as it was said to be a favourite apartment of the
ghost. The bedroom and dressing-room assigned to my wife
and me were some way from this corridor and were reached
by three or four steps and a short passage, which opened on to
another corridor, or longer passage.

I did not think much about the story, but throughout the

129

whole of our visit we slept badly and that night we certainly heard, or thought we heard, odd noises. After the first evening of our visit the only men in the house besides my host and myself were the butler, who was an elderly man with long white whiskers, and a young footman who, I suppose, was about seventeen years old.

On the Monday my host and I walked to and from a neighbouring coal mine, down which we went. Consequently we did not get back to lunch until late, I should think between two-thirty and three o'clock. A transfer of stock or some such matter had arrived and required my attention after lunch; and when I had seen to this I walked alone to the post-office to register my letter. Returning about four o'clock, I went straight to my dressing-room and changed my clothes before tea, and I remember there was just enough light for me to do this without any candle or lamp.

As I was leaving my room, I stumbled slightly on the steps leading into the corridor, and as I did so, I saw, passing along the corridor, a man of medium height and of apparently about forty years of age, with short side-whiskers coming halfway down his cheeks, and wearing a cap and a short, dark coat.

I made some remark to the effect that it was getting rather dark, but got no answer, the man going along the corridor in the same direction as myself, and I following him. At the end of the corridor there was a short staircase, leading down to the smoking-room, for which I was bound, and if I recollect rightly, nearly opposite a baize door leading towards the servants' quarters, and I think also (though of this I am not quite sure) towards the corridor which the ghost was supposed specially to affect. Anyhow, when I got to the head of the stairs I lost sight of the man I thought I had been following, and supposed that he had gone through the baize door and that it was probably the butler who had been out for an afternoon walk.

On descending the stairs, however, and entering the smoking-room, I found my host there with the butler, who was shutting the room up and had evidently just brought in the lamp. It was not until after the man had left the room that it occurred to me that it could not have been the butler whom I had seen, and with that thought the ghost story came into my mind. Still, knowing the story was distasteful to my host, and as my wife had been rather disturbed by the noises in our room at night, I determined to say nothing about it to anybody till after we had left, which we did the next morning. I told my wife about it as we drove to the station.

Some considerable time afterwards we told the story to our host and hostess when we met them in London, but I could not gather that they could provide me with any explanation. I may say that, although the facts I have related are true, I am quite unable either to believe in the ghost or to account for the vivid impression of the scene which still remains with me.

The Telephone at the Oratory

¶ This story is prefaced by a letter to *Lord Halifax* from the priest who had the experience described.

'It is quite true', the priest wrote, 'that I did receive a very mysterious sick call in the night to *Mrs. P——*, but the solution of it I do not pretend to give. Many thanks for your kind invitation, but I am afraid we are not allowed to take meals out of the Community. Perhaps it will answer as well if I call to-morrow (Monday), on my way to *Archbishop's House* at 2.30, and take my chance of finding you at home.'

It would seem that at their meeting on Monday, March 17th, 1919, *Lord Halifax* persuaded the Oratorian to give him a record of his strange experience. The account in the *Ghost Book* is dated April 2nd, 1919, and signed by its author, who declares that 'the above narrative is correctly and truly stated'.

ONE AFTERNOON A SHORT TIME AGO I WAS ASKED TO VISIT a lady (a Mrs. P——), who was ill. The house was in Mont⁄pelier Square, and when I arrived there I was met by the doctor who begged me not to administer the last rites at that particular moment, but to be satisfied with giving the patient a few cheering words and urging her to make an effort to recover; in fact, not to give herself up. I consented, but when I saw the lady I greatly regretted my promise and the fact that the doctor should have made such a request, as I feared the patient was much worse than I had been given to understand. However, the promise had been given, so I arranged that I would come back in the morning and administer the Last Sacrament. Before I left the house, however, I gave the nurse our telephone number and asked her to ring me up if her patient should become suddenly worse.

That night, as usual, the telephone was switched on to the room of one of the Fathers, in case a sick call should come through. I went to bed at my usual time, and in the early morn⁄ing was awakened out of a deep sleep by the opening of my bedroom door. By the light of the moon, shining through the uncovered window, I saw a figure standing by the door. I understood the person to say something about a sick call. I sat up in bed and said, 'Speak more clearly. I don't hear.' As I spoke I saw, as I thought, by the light of the moon, the white collar of the Father⁄in⁄Charge.

This time he spoke more clearly. 'There is no time to lose. There is a telephone message.'

The word 'telephone' brought back to me in a moment my visit of the previous afternoon. I did not, therefore, ask for the address, but sprang out of bed, the door closing as I did so. Turning on the light, I observed it was just a quarter to four. I quickly dressed and went to the Chapel, noticing on my way there that the Father who had called me had forgotten to turn on the light. Going as fast as I could across the space between the house and the gates that shut it off from the main road, I found to my surprise that the gates were locked, so that I had to knock up the lodge porter to let me out. Within a minute or two I was well on my way to the house I had visited in the afternoon.

On arrival I noticed that there were lights in the windows, and after my first ring I looked at my watch and saw that it was five minutes to four. I rang again and again and presently a clock in the neighbourhood struck the hour. Once more I rang, thinking it strange that after they had telephoned for me no one should be there to answer the door. Still no one came, and my regrets of the previous day came upon me with re-doubled force. I banged at the door, making enough noise, as it seemed to me, to waken the whole household. I could see that the electric light was on in the hall and on the staircase, and I remembered that there were only six people in the house, the sick lady in one room, her husband, who was also seriously ill, in another, and the nurses. Evidently, I thought, the two day nurses must be asleep and the two night nurses must be in attendance on the patients. On the other side of the road, at frequent intervals, a cat was squalling horribly.

I still waited on. It was impossible for me to go back after the telephone call, but it seemed more and more strange that I should be kept waiting in this fashion. I again rang furiously, the peals reverberating through the whole house. I looked at my watch and it was twelve minutes past four. At last I thought I would get a stone and throw it at one of the lighted windows, but just as I was about to do this, the cat again made its horrid noise and I threw the stone as hard as I could in its direction.

At that moment, the clock chimed a quarter past four and to my great relief the door opened.

I did not wait to ask any questions, but went straight up to Mrs. P——'s room, where I found the nurse kneeling by the bedside saying some prayers. I noticed that she was startled as I entered and I also heard Mrs. P——'s voice saying, 'I do wish Father C—— would come.'

I was told afterwards that for the space of about half an hour before my arrival she had been expressing a wish to see me and that in consequence the nurse had asked if she should read some prayers. I begged the nurse to leave the room for a few minutes, heard Mrs. P——'s confession, and administered the Last Sacrament.

Within an hour or two she became unconscious and, after reciting the Prayers for the Dying, I was preparing to leave the house when the nurse began to thank me for coming. 'You know, you quite startled me,' she said.

I replied: 'On the contrary, my thanks are due to you for telephoning.'

'But I did not telephone,' she answered.

'Well,' I said, 'somebody did. Perhaps it was Mrs. P——'s sister.'

The next morning, on going to speak to the Father whose duty it was to answer the telephone, I said: 'I am sorry I spoke to you so sharply last night.'

'What do you mean?' he asked.

'Why,' I replied, 'when you came to call me.'

'But I never did call you last night,' he answered.

'Oh yes, you did,' I said. 'You came to my room at a quarter to four this morning and told me there was a telephone sick call.'

He answered: 'I never left my room last night. I could not get to sleep, and as it happens I know that I was awake at that very time as I had my light on. What is more,' he added, 'there was no telephone call last night.'

On enquiring at the telephone exchange I was informed that there was no record of any call to the Oratory on the night in question.

Haunted Rooms

THE STRANGLING WOMAN
'HERE I AM AGAIN!'
HEAD OF A CHILD

THE STRANGLING WOMAN

This story of a haunted room in *Thurstaston Old Hall, Cheshire*, is the first in the book and is in *Lord Halifax's* own writing.

To HIS DYING DAY MY OLD FRIEND REGINALD EASTON, the artist, persisted in the truth of the following story.

One day he had a letter from some people of the name of Cobb, living at Thurstaston Old Hall, Cheshire, asking him if he would pay them a visit and do miniatures of their children. Having accepted the commission, he travelled down to Cheshire to carry it out. The Cobbs, he found, were charming people, and the children were pretty. The house was so full of company that only one room was available for the accommodation of the artist.

Mr. Easton noticed a mysterious sort of muttering passing between his host and hostess, of which he caught the words, 'It cannot be helped; there is no other.' He took it that these words referred to the apartment which was being given him and naturally put a rather unfavourable construction on them, thinking that possibly the room might be damp. This, however, he was assured, was not the case.

Shortly after dinner the household retired to bed. It seemed to Mr. Easton that he had scarcely fallen asleep when he was awakened by a strange intruder in the shape of an elderly lady who stood at the foot of his bed in the full light of the moon.

She appeared to be wringing her hands and her eyes were cast down as though she was searching for something on the floor.

Thinking that she was one of the guests, who had come to the wrong room, Mr. Easton sat up in his bed and said, 'I beg your pardon, madam, but you have mistaken your room.'

His visitor made no reply, but, to his great surprise, disappeared.

'If ever there was a ghost, that is one,' said Mr. Easton to himself.

Next morning at breakfast the mystery of the conversation of the previous night between his host and hostess was cleared up, when in reply to the usual hope that he had slept well he gave an account of his midnight visitor.

'Yes,' said Mrs. Cobb, 'we never use that room if we can avoid doing so, for our friends are sometimes terrified by the apparition of a dreadful woman who committed a murder in that room. She is no ancestor of ours, but came into possession of this property by the murder of the heir to it. He was a child who was the only obstacle to her inheriting the estate. She sent the child's nurse away on a fictitious errand and, during her absence, she strangled the heir, but did it so skilfully that no traces of foul play were discernible. Nothing would have been known of the crime if she had not confessed it on her death-bed. The property was then sold and Mr. Cobb's grandfather bought it.'

'Do you think she will appear again?' enquired the artist.

'Certainly she will, and at about the same time,' was the reply.

At Mr. Easton's request he was furnished with a lamp, the light of which was kept as low as possible, and so on the second night he lay down in bed, with sketching materials by his side, determined to keep awake. Presently the ghost appeared and conducted herself exactly as on the previous night. She must, if capable of surprise, have received a shock when Easton sat up in bed and said: 'I beg your pardon, madam; I am an artist. Will you allow me to make a sketch of you? I shall then convince sceptics of the truth of—' But at that moment, the old lady vanished as before.

Mr. Easton, however, persevered with his portrait, the nightly appearance of the murderess enabling a retentive memory to produce a fair resemblance of what he solemnly declared to me he had seen on each of the seven nights during which he occupied the haunted room.

Mr. Easton lent his drawing of the ghost to Lord Halifax, who copied it. His copy is in the Ghost Book.

'HERE I AM AGAIN!'

Copy of a letter dated July 10th, 1917, from Charles G. S——, Esq., to Lord Halifax.

'DEAR LORD HALIFAX,

'I send you herewith my plain, unvarnished tale, according to your kind request. I may say in confidence that the house was —— ——, Deal, but I would rather that my name and the name of the house should not be mentioned in case you care at any time to give publicity to the story. The only tales dealing with ghostly phenomena which seem to me to be of any value are those relating first-hand experiences. All others are so embroidered that the truth of them is merely a matter of surmise.

'My experience was *horrible*, so much so that I have vowed never to have anything to do with spiritualism in any shape or form. I want no more materializations, which seem to be the goal of all ardent spiritualists.'

The house in question is an old Georgian house in Deal. It was built about 1740 and Nelson addressed many of his letters to Lady Hamilton from there, calling it 'dear —— House'. My host and I had been yachting together, and on our arrival from the sea unexpectedly found the house full of relations who had come to stay. A bed was arranged for me in a dressing-room. On a previous visit I had heard that the house was haunted and that all the daughters had seen the figure of someone they called their great-grandmother gliding about. The servants had been terrified, and in consequence of what they saw had refused to stay. I had forgotten this. I was in rude health after my Channel cruise and nothing ghostly was discussed before I retired to bed.

In the middle of the night I awoke, feeling that something uncanny was about me. Suddenly, there appeared at my bedside the phantom of either an old man or woman, of dreadful aspect, who was bending over me. That I was wide awake is beyond all question. I at once became cataleptic, unable to move hand or foot. I could only gaze at this monstrosity, vowing mentally that if I ever recovered from this horrible experience I would never dabble in table-turning, Planchette, etc., again, for here was a real materialization and the reality was too terrifying for description.

Next morning I told my host privately of what had occurred. He said he was not in the least surprised, as everybody living in the house except himself had, at one time or another, seen something of the sort.

Twenty years passed and I had almost forgotten the incident. I had frequently re-visited the house and had seen nothing. Then one day I was again invited and found my host alone. We played billiards together and retired rather late. I was suffering from toothache and on getting into bed was utterly unable to sleep. The room was in a different part of the house from the dressing-room in which I had slept on the occasion of my first visit.

Suddenly, although it was early summer, I began to feel very cold. I seemed literally to freeze from my feet upwards, and, although I put on more clothes, the cold rapidly increased until I imagined that my heart must be failing and that this was death.

All at once a voice (unheard physically) appeared to be

saying over and over again to me, 'Here I am again! Here I am again, after twenty years.' Once more, in an exact repetition of my feeling twenty years before, I was conscious of the presence of something unseen in the room. I pulled myself together and said to myself, 'This time I will see this thing through and definitely prove whether my former experience was an hallucination and whether there really is such a thing as a ghost. I am wide awake beyond all possibility of doubt and only too conscious of a raging toothache.'

The thing again spoke to me mentally: 'Look round. Look round.'

I now had that unaccountable feeling of horror which all accounts of such manifestations agree in declaring are produced on such occasions. Turning round, I saw in the corner of the room facing me a curious column of light revolving spirally like a whirlwind of dust on a windy day. It was white, and as I gazed, it slowly drew near to me.

'Here I am again!' the thing kept repeating.

I stretched out my hand for the matches at my bedside. As the thing got gradually closer and closer to me, it rapidly began to take human shape. Under my eyes and within my grasp it assumed that very figure I had seen twenty years before. There was no doubt whatever about this, and having reached the limit of my endurance, I shouted out, 'Who's that?' No answer coming, I hurriedly struck a match and lit a candle.

Next morning I told my host what had befallen me. He was greatly interested, and related two weird occurrences in the house, both of which had taken place during the three weeks previous to my visit.

On the first occasion he was in his dressing-room, when a servant came up to say that a friend had called to see him. He ran hurriedly downstairs and, as he turned on the landing for the next flight, he saw the figure of a man rushing upstairs. My friend, unable to stop himself, put up his hands to avert a collision and went right through the figure.

The second occasion had been when one evening an officer of Marines came to play billiards with him and brought his dog, which lay down under the table. Suddenly the dog sprang up and began barking furiously at something invisible in the corner. It went on barking till its mouth foamed and its hair stood on end. They endeavoured in vain to calm it. From under the table it kept making violent rushes at the corner, and then retreating again. Neither my friend nor the officer who was visiting him saw anything.

★

HEAD OF A CHILD

This story was sent to Lord Halifax by Lady Margaret Shelley, daughter of the first Earl of Iddesleigh. Lady Margaret herself had a collection of stories of this nature.

Sir Charles and Lady Hobhouse were giving a party at their place, Monkton Farleigh, and Miss May Hobhouse was

147

talking to one of the visitors, who said, 'I have had a strange and ghostly experience once in my lifetime. It happened when my mother, my little sister, and I were all staying at Sutton Verney. As the house was very full my hostess asked me if I would mind having my little sister to sleep in my room. In the middle of the night I woke up with the distinct feeling that a child's head was resting on my shoulder. I said, as I thought to my sister, "Maudie, why have you come into my bed?" There was no answer and struck I a light, and on looking, saw that my sister was fast asleep in her cot beside me. Presently I dropped off to sleep again, only to wake up once more with exactly the same feeling, but when I put out my hand, there was no child's head on my shoulder. After this I could not sleep and on the following day related my experiences to my hostess. When the same feeling came over me the next night I began to feel very nervous, and for the rest of my stay, to my great relief, I was given another room, in which I had a peaceful night.'

As the girl was telling her story to Miss Hobhouse, another guest, Mrs. L——, came up and said, 'I know you are talking of Sutton Verney. We bought the place and that room became such a difficulty that at last we pulled down the wing in which it was situated. When the men broke up the floor they discovered a cavity in which were the skeletons of five children.'

The
Woman in White

¶From a letter dated December 27th, 1897, it appears that the following story was sent to *Lord Halifax* by *Lord Portman*, whose country estate was at *Bryanston*, near *Blandford*.

ON JULY 25TH, 1837, THREE MEN NAMED ALLEN, ELFORDE and Ball, who had been employed in cutting the weeds in the river Stour, were drowned in a deep hole below the bay at Bryanston. As the then officiating minister of the parish, it was my melancholy duty to take the news of this sad event to the widow of John Allen, who lived in the cottage at the Old Park. On my telling her what had occurred she immediately exclaimed to her sister, who was sitting with her, 'Why, sister, then that must have been poor John's spirit which Polly saw.'

I afterwards enquired what she had meant by this exclamation, and she told me that at about four o'clock in the afternoon, or a little later (as near as I could ascertain, at the precise time that her husband was drowned), her second girl, Polly, a child of three years of age, was playing in the garden in front of the house. Presently she came running in and called to her mother to 'come out and see the tall woman in white who is coming down the hill opposite'.

The mother told the child she was talking nonsense, as whoever saw a woman dressed in white in those parts on a working day? The child, however, insisted that she had seen the figure, adding, 'I saw it come through Bache Gate, and down the hill. It was terribly tall, a great deal taller than you, mother.' I should add that John Allen, when returning from his rounds as keeper, always came through this gate and down the hill by the path, on which the child saw, or fancied she saw, the figure.

In order to pacify the child, Mrs. Allen and her sisters went out to see if there was anyone there, but although they looked in every direction and kept watch for over a quarter of an hour they could see no one. They then returned to the house and thought no more about the incident until I went up shortly afterwards to break to them the news of Allen's death. The mother, indeed, told me that she said to the little girl in joke, 'Why, Polly, I suppose it must have been my spirit'; but she certainly had not the slightest presentiment of coming evil, nor had she any anxiety for her husband's safety beyond what she would naturally have in view of the occupation in which he was engaged and the fact that three years before he had narrowly escaped drowning in the same hole.

The child was afterwards closely questioned as to what she saw, but firmly adhered to her story. My own belief is that what she saw was no human being but the apparition of her father. Even if you accept the theory of a mental or ocular delusion, it is still necessary to account for the impression made on the child's mind at the exact moment when her father was drowning. The child's statement that she saw a woman does not affect the question in any way, since it is probable that any apparition of this kind would appear to a child to be like a woman. It may, however, be observed that she described the

152

woman she had seen as 'terrible tall' and that her father was about six feet in height.

I should mention one further curious circumstance which may or may not be connected with this apparition. Some six or seven months before he was drowned, John Allen came home one night from Blandford in exceedingly low spirits. As soon as he got into the house he sat down and cried bitterly for more than an hour. When his wife asked him what was the matter he replied that he had seen that which told him he should not be long here. He never would describe to his wife what it was that he had seen, but after that evening he suffered periodically from low spirits.

I believe I have given every material particular connected with this appearance, and can vouch for the accuracy of my record.

Prophetic
and
Other Dreams

THE CORPSE DOWNSTAIRS

In the winter of 1889-90 *Lord Halifax* took his eldest son, *Charles*, who was seriously ill, to *Madeira*, where he was told the following story.

DR. GRABHAM HAS JUST BEEN IN AND AFTER HE HAD SEEN the nurse, who has an attack of rheumatism, stayed for some time gossiping with me. In the course of our conversation he told me this story, which struck me so much that, in order to be sure of recollecting it accurately, I am sitting down to write it out exactly as he told it, and immediately after he has left the house.

Some years ago a Mr. Freeland was staying in Madeira. He was not at all well and, as a ball was going to be given at the hotel where he lodged, Dr. Grabham invited him to come up to his house and stay with him for a night or two.

A couple of days later, the Doctor, coming in late, found Mr. Freeland still up and sitting with Mrs. Grabham before the fire. 'My dear fellow,' he said, 'why are you not in bed? You ought to have been there long ago.'

'I could not possibly go to bed,' Mr. Freeland answered. 'I had such a dreadful dream last night that I cannot endure the thought of it. I dreamt that someone was bringing in a dead body and putting it away in the house.'

'What an extraordinary thing!' was Dr. Grabham's reply. 'Not a soul, not even Mrs. Grabham, knows anything about it, but that is exactly what I am proposing to do.'

On being pressed for an explanation, Dr. Grabham told the following story. A certain Professor Clifford, who was staying in the Island, was at the point of death and had often expressed the greatest possible dislike of being taken to any Christian burying place. 'I have been attending him,' said Dr. Grabham, 'and since he is a great friend of mine, I have told him he need have no apprehensions and that I would take care that his wish was respected. "After all," I said to him, "if you don't want to enter any Christian place of burial, no Christian place of burial would care to have you, so as soon as you are dead, I will take you up to my house and keep you there until you can be sent off to England by steamer." I thought', Dr. Grabham added, 'that nobody in the house would know anything about it. There would just be a long, oblong, pack-ing-case stowed away somewhere and everything would have been arranged in accordance with my patient's wishes.

'Mr. Freeland left me the next day, and, in the circumstances I did not encourage him to stop, but that evening, as soon as I was able to persuade him to go to bed, I went straight off to Professor Clifford. I told him there was a man in my house who had dreamt the very thing I was intending to do, in other words, that I had brought in a dead body. Professor Clifford was most interested and began to suggest all sorts of reasons why Mr. Freeland might quite naturally have had this dream.'

The next day or the day after he died. At the end he was so perfectly conscious that Dr. Grabham was able to say to him,

'You will be dead in a couple of hours. Have you nothing you want to write?'

The Professor found some difficulty in replying and Dr. Grabham went on, 'Are you quite content and satisfied? Are you quite sure that death means the end of everything and that within an hour or two you will have ceased to exist? If you have anything to write or to say, or if there is anything you wish done, there is no time to be lost.'

Professor Clifford, however, appeared to be perfectly satis-fied, and although he was very unwilling to leave the world, he neither said nor wrote anything till just before the end, when he asked for writing materials. He succeeded in writing a message for his daughters, which was not to be opened until they were grown up. He also asked that this sentence might be put on his tomb:

'I was not, and was content. I lived and did a little work. I am not and believe not.'

His body was put away in Dr. Grabham's house until it could be sent to England, as had been arranged.

Lord Halifax adds a note: 'Mr. Freeland eventually fell ill at Malta, died on board his yacht, very rich, with nobody to call an heir, and left Dr. Grab-ham £50.'

THE MURDERER'S DREAM

This account of the attempted execution of John Lee at Exeter, was given to Lord Halifax by Lord Clinton, when they were both staying at Powder-

ham Castle, the home of Lady Halifax's father, the Earl of Devon. Lord
Clinton also supplied copies of the letter from the prison chaplain and the
statements of the warders.

On November 15th, 1884, Miss Keyse, an elderly lady,
was found murdered among the burning ruins of her
house at Babbacombe, Torquay. Her butler, John Lee, was
tried for the crime, convicted and sentenced to death at
Exeter on January 4th, 1885. On February 23rd, Lee was
brought out for execution in Exeter Gaol. The rope was ad-
justed, the burial service was read, and the signal was given,
but the drop would not act. Three times an attempt was made
to hang the man, with the same result, and at the end of half
an hour it was decided to postpone the execution. Subsequently Lee's sentence was commuted to penal servitude for
life.

The letter from the Reverend John Pitkin, Chaplain to the
Prison, enclosing a copy of the statement of the warders, was
written to Lord Clinton at his request, when he was staying at
Powderham in the beginning of April 1885, he being at the
time in the Chair at the Quarter Sessions.

The drop was contrived by two doors, secured underneath
by a bolt. The prisoner was made to stand with a foot on each
door, and on the bolt being withdrawn the doors would naturally fall apart. On the Saturday previous to the execution, the
drop was tried five times (twice in the presence of the execu-
tioner, who expressed himself satisfied with it), and on each

occasion it answered perfectly. After the attempted execution, it was again tried, but although there was no weight on the scaffold, it acted successfully. During the execution itself, at each successive attempt, it was found impossible to withdraw the bolt from its socket by the eighth part of an inch.

Letter from the Reverend John Pitkin, Chaplain to Lord Clinton.

HER MAJESTY'S PRISON,
EXETER, *April 8th*, 1885.

MY LORD,

The following are the particulars which your lordship has requested me to supply of the dream of John Lee.

After the attempted execution of Lee on February 23rd, 1885, I went to his cell and spoke to him about the extraordinary event that had happened to him. He replied that on the night before his execution he had had a dream which had shown him what would happen.

At my request he related it to me. He said that in his dream he saw himself being led from his cell down through the reception basement to the scaffold, which was just outside the basement door. He saw himself placed upon the scaffold and efforts being made to force the drop, which, however, would not work. He then saw himself led away from the place of execution, since it was decided that a new scaffold would have to be built before the sentence of the law could be carried out. He told me that when he awoke at six o'clock on the morning fixed for his execution he had mentioned the dream to the two officers who were in the cell with him.

These officers were not present when he told me this, nor had they been with him since the attempt was made. They had, however, reported the dream to the Governor of the Prison, to whom I also made a statement.

I ought to add, my lord, that John Lee did not attach any weight to the dream. Up to the time of the execution he had fully believed that he would be hanged. The dream did not come back to his mind while the attempts were being made, but only after he had recovered from the semi-unconsciousness into which he had apparently fallen.

I am, your lordship's obedient servant,

JOHN PITKIN, *Chaplain.*

Statement of the Warders who spent the night with John Lee, previous to his attempted execution.

At six a.m., when John Lee rose from his bed, he said, 'Mr. Bennett, I have dreamed a very singular and strange dream. I thought the time was come, and I was led down through the reception out to the hanging place, but when they placed me on the drop they could not hang me, for there was something wrong with the machinery of the drop. They then took me off from the drop and took me (instead of the way I had come) around the A. Wing, and back through the A. Ward to my cell.'

162

He told me this in the presence of Mr. Milford, who watched with me through the night.

(Signed) SAMUEL D. BENNETT, *Assistant Warder.*

JAMES MILFORD, *Superior Officer.*

★

The next three stories were all contributed by Lady Margaret Shelley.

THE MAD BUTLER

Not long ago there lived in the South of Devon a comfortable and prosperous married couple. One night towards twelve o'clock, the lady woke her husband in a great state of terror. She declared that she had seen the murder of her old widowed mother, who lived alone in Aberdeen. The dream had impressed her so strongly that for some time she was greatly agitated and her husband had considerable difficulty in persuading her that her fears were foolish and that she ought to go to sleep again.

On the following night the lady had the same dream again and this time became convinced that it was a warning which she ought not to disregard. Accordingly, in the morning she told her husband that she was determined to pay her mother a visit. When he found it impossible to dissuade her, he consented to let her go, though, owing to a previous and pressing business engagement, he was unable to accompany her.

163

The lady, on reaching her mother's house in Aberdeen, and being met at the door by the butler, started, and exclaimed, 'That's the man!' Then, recovering her self-possession, she tried in a confused way to cover up her remark and passed on into the sitting-room, where she found not only her mother, but also two other women who were both great friends of the family.

The lady made some excuse to them for her appearance, carefully concealing the true reason. As the two friends were staying in the house and there was not much room, it was arranged that the mother and daughter should sleep together. Before they separated for the night the daughter spoke to the friends in private, begging them, if they felt any affection for her, to do what she asked without demanding any explanation. She obtained their promise, whereupon she told them that she particularly wanted them both to sit up next night in the room next to hers and to remain awake.

When they agreed, she left them and returned to her mother, and just before they actually got into bed tried to persuade her to lock the door. This the mother refused to do, but as soon as the old lady was asleep, the daughter slipped out and quietly turned the key.

A short time after she had done so, she saw, by the light of the fire, the brass handle of the door turning. She sprang up hastily, calling to her friends, and threw the door open, crying, 'You villain, what are you doing?'

The butler was there with a coal scuttle in his hand. He answered that, fancying he had heard the bell ring, he had brought fresh fuel for the fire. The lady tried to seize him, exclaiming as she did so that he was saying what he knew to be false. At first the man made an effort to escape, but the daughter, with the assistance of her friends, overpowered and secured him. The wretch then declared that he had been prompted by the Devil to murder his mistress, but that Providence had miraculously preserved him from doing so. Next day he went clean out of his mind.

LADY GORING'S DREAM

One night Lady Goring distinctly saw in a dream an old house, which was quite unfamiliar to her. She knew that someone was with her and that she was visiting this house for a purpose; and when she got inside, one special room was fixed in her mind. First, it had a very curious frieze near the ceiling; then the latticed windows were of a peculiar, long, narrow shape and were connected by a striking moulding. In her dream she saw an elderly woman sitting hunched up in an armchair by the fire; but a moment later her attention wandered from her to the door, which was softly opening. She saw a man enter, steal up quickly to the elderly woman, who was apparently asleep, suddenly produce a pistol, place it close to her temple, and fire. When his victim fell over, the

165

murderer tried to arrange the pistol so that it might appear as if it had fallen from her hand. He then noiselessly left the room, shutting the door after him, but a few moments afterwards reappeared and made some further alterations in the position of the dead woman and the pistol. Having done so, he went away and did not return. Lady Goring saw his face so plainly in her dream that it became fixed in her memory.

In course of time she and her husband, Sir Craven, wished to rent a house, and inspected various properties, among others an old manor in Cheshire. The moment Lady Goring entered the manor she felt that the place was strangely familiar to her. Then the truth flashed upon her. 'I have never been here in my life,' she told herself, 'but it is the house of my dream.'

At that moment the caretaker said, 'This door on the right leads to the drawing-room'; whereupon Lady Goring corrected her, saying, 'I am sure you must mean the dining-room.'

The caretaker apologised and replied, 'Did I say the drawing-room? I meant to say the dining-room.'

As soon as she opened the door, Lady Goring recognised the remarkable frieze, the latticed windows and the peculiar moulding. There was also a chair near the fireplace.

The caretaker, on being asked for some information about the house, told the Gorings that the last tenant had not stayed very long and that the family previously in possession had been foreigners. She thought that they were Austrians or Swiss. There were three of them, a gentleman, his wife and his mother-in-law. There had been a sad tragedy in their time because the old lady had shot herself. After this, the husband and wife had gone away to foreign parts and the house had been shut up for some time.

Lady Goring did not take the house, but some months later, as she was walking down Regent Street and idly looking in at the shop windows, she came to a standstill opposite the Stereoscopic. What had stopped her was a photograph in the window. 'Why!' she exclaimed to herself, 'there is the murderer of my dream!' On going into the shop and enquiring who the man in the photograph might be, she found that it was Tourville, who was then being tried for the murder of his second wife in the Tyrol.

★

THE SEXTON OF CHILTON POLDEN

For some years during the last century, the living at Chilton Polden, in Cornwall, was held by a clergyman of the name of Drury. The parish was very scattered and interspersed with rough tracts of moorland. One evening, in April, while returning home, Mr. Drury stumbled on some uneven ground and twisted his ankle very badly. After resting for a short time, he tried to pursue his way and, with many pauses and much difficulty, at last reached the Rectory, from which he sent a message asking the doctor to come round at once. The effort of walking the last mile with his injured ankle had had the effect of increasing the swelling and inflammation to such an extent that the moment the doctor saw it he said, 'There will be no chance, Mr. Drury, of your being able to preach for three weeks.'

'That is dreadful news,' answered Mr. Drury. 'Why, Easter falls in a fortnight and all the clergy round here have more on their hands than they know how to manage. What shall I do?'

'I really cannot say,' returned the doctor; 'but I do know you will not be able either to officiate or to preach this Easter.'

After the departure of the doctor, Mr. Drury thought over the position and at length decided to write to his youngest brother, Frank, who was a curate in Liverpool, to ask if he could come and help him. Very thankful he was too, when in due time a letter arrived from Frank saying that when his Vicar had read Mr. Drury's letter, and understood what had happened, he had been most generous and had given Frank permission to come to Chilton Polden for Palm Sunday and Easter Sunday. Frank ended by promising to turn up in two days' time.

This he did and was delighted to see his brother again, and full of the pleasure at being in the country at so lovely a season, after having spent the winter in the slums of Liverpool. He arrived on the Friday before Palm Sunday.

The next day, when talking to his brother, he said; 'I had a queer dream last night. I thought I was walking around the churchyard here and that I saw an elderly man, with rather long grey hair and a bent figure, as though he suffered from rheumatism, digging a grave close by the south porch of the church. I went up to him and asked him if someone had died lately and for whom he was digging the grave. The man raised himself from his task and looking me full in the face said, quite distinctly, "It is yours, sir." I know it sounds absurd, but the dream gave me a real shock. I had to get up and light a candle and read for an hour before I could sleep again.'

After telling his brother his dream, Frank seemed to forget all about it. In the evening he came in with his hands full of wild flowers, saying, 'I have seen a specimen which I must get to-morrow (Sunday) evening after afternoon service. The plant was growing rather low down under a rock and I had no time to-day to scramble down to it.'

At morning service on Palm Sunday Frank chose for his text, 'Lord remember me when Thou comest into Thy King-dom.' In the middle of his sermon he stopped suddenly and some of the people nearest the pulpit noticed that he had turned rather pale. However, he recovered himself in a moment and went on steadily to the end.

When he got back to the Rectory he said to Mr. Drury: 'Do you know, I have seen the elderly man of my dream in church this morning. The scare came back to me and for an instant I thought I should not be able to finish my sermon. The man was sitting close to the third pillar on the right hand side of the aisle.'

'Yes,' replied Mr. Drury, 'that is just where old Ben, the sexton, always sits, but your dream, Frank, is nonsense. You are only going to be here another ten days and you are in per/ fect health. You must just forget your fright and dismiss the whole episode as a coincidence.'

Frank was young and cheerful by nature. He either suc/ ceeded in forgetting or at any rate appeared to forget. In the afternoon he preached from the text, 'To/day shalt thou be with me in Paradise.' When he returned to the Rectory he made no further allusion to his dream.

After an early tea together Frank gaily started off on his ex/ pedition to get the flower which he had seen and coveted the day before. When supper/time came he had not returned. Evening faded into dusk and dusk into darkness, and still there was no sign of him. Mr. Drury, imprisoned in the house with his swollen ankle, grew uneasy, and at last sent his house/ keeper to tell the village constable. A search, with lanterns, was at once organised, but that night nothing could be found. In the morning, however, when the search was renewed, Frank's body was discovered at the bottom of an old quarry. He held a flower in his hand. That week he was buried in Chilton Polden churchyard.

THE LAST APPEARANCE OF MR. BULLOCK

Mr. H. W. Hill contributed the following experience.

Early one morning, a few years ago, I dreamt that I was in Gatti's Restaurant at Charing Cross one evening getting a meal. As I took my seat at one of the side-tables, I dreamt that I saw the Rev. J. F. Bullock, Rector of Radwinter, near Saffron Walden, a member of the Council of the English Church Union, well known to me and well known to church people as the compiler of the Office Hymnbook. I said to myself, 'Why, dear me, there is Mr. Bullock, and how very ill he looks!'

When I got to the office in the morning, the first letter I opened was one from Miss Bullock, telling me that her brother had had a stroke and was very ill, and would, therefore, not be able to attend to any English Church Union business. At the next meeting of the Council, in making an apology for Mr. Bullock's absence, I told this story.

THE CORPSE THAT ROSE

The Reverend R. A. Kent, who sent Lord Halifax this story, was a grandson of Mr. Reginald Easton, the artist (see page 141).

My grandfather, Reginald Easton, was staying with us at Dinham Hall, Ludlow, about forty years ago, i.e. about 1890, and was sleeping in the bedroom next to mine. There was a door between the rooms. One morning early I was awakened by a voice calling 'Arthur! Arthur!' in desperate tones. I at once went into the next room and found my grandfather sitting up in bed in a very disturbed state. He said that he had had a terrible dream which, at my request, he told me.

He had dreamt that he was staying with an old friend at Breede Hall in Staffordshire. One beautiful day he strolled out through the park, making his way towards the old village church. Passing through the wicket gate and up the pathway between tombstones and monuments, he came to the ancient porch. As he entered, the bell tolled for a funeral. Instead of going into the church, he stepped back on to the pathway, intending, until the funeral was over, to inspect some of the tombstones and memorials in the churchyard. Presently he saw the funeral procession proceeding up the pathway to the old porch. On enquiring the name of the deceased, he was surprised to hear that it was one of his oldest friends, Mr. Monckton, of Summerford Hall, a few miles distant; so he changed his mind and went into the church for the service, sitting at the back. As soon as the coffin had been placed on the bier in the chancel, a little old verger of revolting aspect came up to him and said, 'I understand you are Mr. Monckton's oldest friend. If this is so, will you lead the way to the vault after the service?'

'The service', said my grandfather, 'having been shuffled through by the vicar, whose countenance resembled a withered apple, the coffin was raised on the shoulders of four men to be borne to the vault. The little old verger, again coming up to me, pointed out the way. Descending several flights of steps I was obliged to stoop in order to enter the ancient doorway to the vault, in which was a platform raised to receive the coffin. All around were thirty or forty coffins of members of the family, some of them half broken with age and with skeletons partly hanging out. As soon as the coffin was put on the platform the others filed out, and the little old verger, having crept close to me, knocked the torch which I had been given out of my hand on to the slimy floor. An instant later I heard the door close and the lock click. I was left quite alone in the horrible vault. Wandering round it, I screamed to be let out, but received no reply.

'In this state I was left for half an hour, when all at once there was a violent cracking. On hearing it I said to myself, "Thank God they have come to let me out at last," but to my indescribable horror I saw that I was mistaken and that the noise I had heard was the body of old Monckton wrenching itself out of the coffin. In a moment the body, which was in a state of decomposition, was clear of the coffin and making its way towards me. I dodged round the coffin pursued by old Monckton until at last I fell exhausted on the floor with his putrid corpse on top of me. Planting his nails deep into my cheek, he ripped my face open. I struggled and struggled to force the corpse off me, but without effect. Then I woke up

173

and to my immense relief found the light shining through the window.'

The next day the news came to my grandfather that old Mr. Monckton had died that same night.

The Footsteps
at
Haverholme Priory

¶ Mr. H. W. Hill contributed this story.

On Friday, July 14th, 1905, I went on a visit to Haverholme Priory, near Sleaford in Lincolnshire. The Priory is the property of the Winchilseas, who inherited it about eighty years ago. The tenants, with whom I was staying, were my old friends the Hitchcocks. I dined on the train and got out at Haverholme some time after nine o'clock. It was very hot and I went to bed just before midnight. Mr. Hitchcock accompanied me to my room, which, I observed, was in an old part of the house, apparently on the first floor of the tower, and having a separate entrance from the hall near the front door.

Mr. Hitchcock stayed chatting with me for a little time and I then undressed. Before getting into bed I drew aside the blinds and opened the window which looked out on to a large expanse of park. After I had been in bed for about ten minutes and was still wide awake, I heard someone walking up and down on the gravelled path under the window. I thought it was probably one of the servants and the circumstance made no particular impression on me.

In the morning I asked the son of the house, Hal Hitchcock, if I had been the last to go to bed, and he said that this was so and that he had heard his father leave my room and go to his own. I then asked him where the men-servants slept and he told me that they were all on the other side of the house. In reply to a further question he assured me that when the doors were shut for the night, nobody could get out.

The next day, which was a Saturday, I spent in Lincoln, where I had an engagement to address a meeting of the English Church Union. In the evening I took in to dinner Miss Susan Antrobus, who had been associated with Miss Florence Nightingale in nursing, and was the foundress of the St. Barnabas Guild of Nurses. I asked her to tell me about Haverholme and she mentioned that it was built on the site of a Gilbertine Priory. I remarked how stupid it was of me not to have remembered that, as it now came back to me that the Priory was the very place where St. Thomas à Becket hid himself for a couple of days after the Council at Northampton. She added that the modern interest in the house came from the fact that it was the Chesney Wold of *Bleak House*, and pointing to that side of the house, which contained my bedroom, she added that the 'Ghost's Walk' ran along by it and that footsteps were sometimes heard. It was quite clear to my mind that these must have been the steps which had disturbed me the previous night.

I paid another visit to Haverholme in September 1906, during some very hot weather. On the evening of Saturday, the 8th, I asked who would be going out early to church on the following morning. The nearest church with an early celebration of Holy Communion being at Anwick, on Lord Bristol's property, about half a mile away, I made this enquiry so that I should not occupy a seat in a carriage which might be wanted for someone else. Eventually it was settled that Mr. Hitchcock and some of the ladies should drive to church. I said I would get up early and walk there, while another guest Mr. (now Sir) Cyril Cobb, later Chairman of the London County Council, proposed to ride to church on his bicycle.

When Sunday morning came I was down by seven o'clock and found Mr. Cobb already up and attending to his bicycle. The weather was intensely hot without a breath of wind. Mr. Cobb remarked that I was wise to allow myself plenty of time on such a morning, but that as he was going to bicycle he would not be starting for a while.

I set off, walking through the inner grounds, and crossing the bridge over the river Slea, which runs through the Park. I was then in the long avenue, with elms on either side. On approaching the bridge, which passes over Ruskington Beck, I heard behind me a very loud and fierce whizzing noise. At first I thought this must be Cobb riding furiously, and without turning round, I called out to him, and asked him why he had made such an early start and why he was in such a hurry. No answer came, and although I could see nothing, the whizzing noise seemed to go past me and to disappear in the distance.

In the evening I went with Mr. Hitchcock in the carriage to Evedon Church on the Haverholme property. After the service, having told Mr. Hitchcock beforehand of my experience in the morning, I asked the Rector some questions. He had been tutor to the late Lord Winchilsea and his brother and probably knew more about the place than anybody else. He told me that the long avenue had a bad name and that when he had occasion to visit the Priory at night he neither went nor returned by it. There was, he said, a tradition that the avenue was haunted by a Gilbertine canoness, the point at which she was reputed to have been seen being a particular tree near the bridge over Ruskington Beck.

I was at Haverholme once more in the late summer of 1907, and one evening while I was there, Mrs. Hitchcock went out for a little walk with her maid and one of her dogs, an Aberdeen terrier. They went down the long avenue. Mrs. Hitchcock and the maid neither saw nor heard anything, but just before they reached the bridge in the avenue the dog set up a most pitiful howling and tore back to the house in terror. On returning they had great difficulty in finding him, as he had hidden himself away and for some time refused to come out.

Mr. Dundas's Stories

❡ The first of these stories is recorded as having been told by '*Mr. Charles Dundas of India*, in the library of *Hickleton*, on Tuesday the 21st of December, 1920'. *Lord Halifax* was connected with the Dundases through his sister, *Alice*, who married the *Hon. John Charles Dundas*, son of the first *Earl of Zetland. Mr. Charles Dundas* was their eldest son and a nephew of *Lord Halifax*.

'I WILL PAY YOU ALL TO-MORROW'

I MUST TELL YOU FIRST HOW I CAME TO HEAR THE STORY told. Probably you all know that last year we had a war with Afghanistan. That war was brought to an immediate and sudden end by the fact that we had a very big aeroplane called 'The Old Carthusian' out in India at the time, which was ordered to go and bomb Kabul. This was shortly after the murder of the late Amir,[1] in which the present Amir[2] was supposed to have had a part. The main object of bombing the city was to alarm the mother of the present Amir, a result so sufficiently attained that immediately afterwards a message came in to the effect that the Afghans wanted peace.

Between our outposts and Kabul there is a mountain some 6000 feet high (more than 2000 feet higher than Ben Nevis), and the men in the aeroplane had the greatest difficulty in returning. They only cleared the top of the mountain by ten feet and crashed on the other side, doing themselves a certain amount of damage. The pilot was a little man about 4 feet 5 inches in height, named Hallé, a well-known flying man, and with him was a fellow aviator named Villiers, who had served in France but had retired from the Air Force and was in business in Calcutta. When the war with Afghanistan broke out he had re-joined.

[1]Habibullah Khan.   [2]Now the ex-King Amanullah.

183

Not long afterwards I was coming home to England and met Villiers on board the P. & O. I did not then know that he was a flying man, but about twelve o'clock one day I was talk-ing to him and two senior colonels of the Indian army, acting as brigadiers in Mesopotamia. We were in the Red Sea at the time. The conversation turned on Gallipoli and Mesopotamia, and especially upon the behaviour of the Australian troops in both these theatres.

Villiers then said that he could tell a curious story of the Australian Flying Corps. At that moment, the weather being hot, I suggested a whisky and soda, but he refused, saying, 'If I take it you will certainly not believe the story I am going to tell you.'

He had, he said, been quartered in France at a flying camp next door to an Australian squadron. As everybody knows, most of the pilots in France were young men of from nineteen to twenty-four years of age, and were sometimes even younger than that. The Australian airmen were especially daring, but when they were off duty the pilots and observers led the wildest of lives and spent their time in gambling, drinking and other forms of dissipation, on the principle of 'Let us eat, drink, and be merry, for to-morrow we die'.

One night a game of poker was going on among four young pilots belonging to the same flight, who were all due to go out the next morning. Since they were all heavily in debt, the game was carried on largely upon credit. The heaviest loser was the youngest pilot, who at the end of the evening gave I.O.U.'s for his debts, saying, 'I cannot possibly pay you to-night, but I will pay you all to-morrow.'

Next morning the weather was fair for flying, and the youngest pilot was due to go up first. His machine had hardly got to a height of 300 feet when it suddenly spun into a dive, in a way that was impossible unless it had been forced into it by the pilot; at least, it was not how a plane out of control would normally fall. There was a crash and the pilot was killed on the spot. He was the young man who had said he would pay all the others on the next day.

The next to go up was another of the four poker players. He was flying a double machine with a seat for an observer and dual control, but the observer's seat was empty. When he reached a height of nearly 500 feet, his machine suddenly stalled and crashed to the ground. The pilot was not killed on the spot, although he died a little later. When he was asked how the crash had happened, he replied that the boy who had already been killed was sitting behind him in the observer's seat and had jammed the controls and pulled him down.

The third member of the poker party of the night before went up next. He was alone and reached about the same height as had the other, when the same accident happened to him. As he was killed on the spot it was never known how he had come by his end.

By this time the pilots of the squadron, in the current expression, were 'getting the wind up'. Two men had already been killed outright and one had been mortally injured. The fourth poker player now went to his flight-commander and asked to be excused from taking a machine up that morning. His request was refused on the ground that someone had to go up, and each must take his turn. So he went out, and when he had risen to about 500 feet, for some reason his machine stalled and crashed like the others. He was alive when he was picked up and lived just long enough to tell those about him that the young pilot had been sitting behind him and had wrenched the controls away.

THE HAUNTED BUNGALOW

This story was told on the same occasion as its predecessor and begins with the following note: 'Charlie Dundas, who left here this morning to go to Edwardstone, to shoot with Henry Corry, told me the following story before he left.'

In 1871, a friend of mine in India, named Troward, was on his way to take up an appointment at Hoshiarpur in the Punjab. He and his wife arrived at their destination late one evening. The dak bungalow, where travellers usually put up, not being available, they eventually had to sleep in another bungalow which was hastily got ready for them. They unpacked their camp beds, set them up in one of the rooms, had something to eat, and were going to bed when the servants who

186

were travelling with them came in and said that they did not like the bungalow and were unwilling to spend the night there. They recommended Mr. Troward and the Memsahib not to sleep in the bungalow either, as there was something very wrong about it. Mr. and Mrs. Troward, who were extremely tired, told the servants that they could not change their lodgings and were determined to stay where they were.

They went to bed, and in the middle of the night Mr. Troward was awakened by a loud report, followed by terrified cries and screams from his wife. When he asked her what was the matter, she said that a man in a grey suit had come up to the side of the bed and leant over her, saying, 'Lie still, I shall not hurt you.' He had then fired a pistol or gun across her over the bed.

In the morning the Trowards discovered that a Mr. de Courcy, formerly Commissioner at Hoshiarpur, had shot himself in the bungalow in the middle of the night. Just before he did so he had leant across the bed and said to his wife, 'I shall not hurt you.'

Apparitions

THE MONK OF BOLTON ABBEY

The present *Marquis of Hartington*, when a boy at *Eton*, sent *Lord Halifax* this account of a ghost he had seen at *Bolton Abbey*, the property of his father, the *Duke of Devonshire*. The experience befell him in August 1912, when the late *King* was staying at *Bolton Abbey* for the shooting. Apparently *Lord Hartington* was sleeping, not at the *Abbey*, but at the adjoining rectory.

Statement by Lord Hartington.

ON SUNDAY, AUGUST 18TH, 1912, ON GOING UP TO MY room at The Rectory, at 11.15 p.m., I distinctly saw a figure standing at the door. It was dressed in nondescript clothes and was more or less clean-shaven. I was at the top of the staircase, looking down the passage in which mine was the end room. I went downstairs again and fetched another light, but on going up again the figure had disappeared.

The ghost had been the subject of a conversation that evening at which I had not been present, and I was not thinking of it.

(Signed)   HARTINGTON.
(Witnessed by)   THE KING.
THE DUKE OF DEVONSHIRE.
LORD DESBOROUGH.

Letter from the Duchess of Devonshire to Lady Halifax.

Will you tell Lord Halifax that Eddy (Lord Hartington) will send him an account of his ghost? He seems to be the same man who was seen two or three times by the Vicar, but the Vicar's ghost wore a brown dress and Eddy declares this

man's was dark grey or black. Eddy's ghost had a round face
—no beard, but what he described as a rough face. When we
asked the Vicar afterwards if his ghost had a beard he said,
'No', but that he looked as if he had not shaved for four or
five days, and his face was very round.

Letter from the Marquis of Hartington to Lord Halifax.

I saw the ghost standing in the door of my room, looking
not *at*, but *past*, me, at 11.15 p.m. on Sunday, August 18th. I
was sleeping at The Rectory and saw him when I turned left-
handed from the stairs, which are in three flights, and looked
down the passage some eleven yards long, at the end of which
is the door of my room. While I was going up the last flight,
which consists only of six steps, I thought someone was there
but attached no importance to this, as the Rector often met me
on the stairs.

I thought at once that it was the ghost, but was not frightened of him until afterwards. He was below the middle height
and seemed to be an old man of sixty-five or so. His face was
unusually round, or, rather, broad in proportion to its length,
and was very heavily lined and wrinkled. The eyes were
bright and the face might have been that of an old woman,
but for the fact that there was about a week's growth of grey-
ish stubble on the chin. There was a hood over the head and
he was dressed in a long garment like a dressing-gown. The
hood and shoulders seemed to be grey, but lower down the

colour was black or brown. The light was behind me and I had a candle in my hand, so that his head and shoulders were fairly brightly lighted, while lower down he was in shadow.

I looked at him for a second or two and then went down to fetch the Rector from his study. He was, however, not there and taking the lantern with which I had come across from the house, I went upstairs again, but the figure had gone.

I had heard of the ghost before, but this was the account I gave of him before I heard any description whatever of him. I was not thinking of the ghost when I saw him, but he was being discussed in the house at that moment. There was no question of his being transparent; he was as solid as any actual man.

The wall of my room is the old monastery wall and is seven feet thick.

The habit of the monastery was not brown but white, so that he was certainly not a monk of Bolton Abbey.

THE GENTLEMAN WITH THE LATCH-KEY

The following story was 'told by Lord Falmouth to Lord Grenfell, Lord Methuen, and his son, Paul' (the present Lord Methuen). Lord Falmouth had been told the story by a friend, who had heard it from the man to whom it happened.

A gentleman who had been dining in Phillimore Gardens was walking home between eleven and twelve one night. On turning out of the gardens into a smaller street (possibly Phillimore Street), he found that he was quite alone in it, except for a woman who was walking in front of him, and a man who was a short distance in front of the woman. Presently, the woman walked past the man, and, as she did so, looked up at him, and immediately rushed across the street and down a side turning, shrieking horribly.

The gentleman quickened his pace, wondering what could have happened to make the woman behave as she had done, and by walking fast came up with the man. As he reached him, he saw him take a latch key from his pocket, open the door of a house and walk in. As the man passed inside, the gentleman looked at him and saw, to his horror, that his face was that of a corpse.

After taking the number of the house, he went home, where he spent a troubled night, determined that next day, as soon as his business was concluded, he would try to discover what had happened. He had no difficulty in finding the house again, but saw that since he had been there on the previous night, a notice, 'Apartments to Let', had been put up over the door. This, he thought, will help me. He rang the bell, and when an excited looking landlady appeared, he enquired about the rooms she had to let.

'Yes,' she said, 'yes, I have some rooms to let.'

He asked if he might see them, but she begged him to return another day, as it was not quite convenient at the moment to show him over them. He replied that he was going away from London and was afraid if he could not see the rooms then he would have to give up any idea of taking them.

Accordingly, she took him upstairs, and showed him some very nice, well-furnished rooms, with many interesting and pretty objects lying about in them, such as would be introduced by a man who knew how to make himself comfortable.

'Well,' said the gentleman, 'I think these rooms would suit me all right, but whose are all these things lying about?'

'Oh, they belong to the gentleman who had the rooms.'

'And where is he now?'

At first the landlady was very evasive, but at last she broke down, began to cry, and said, 'Oh, sir, I will tell you all about it. The rooms did belong to a gentleman who has lived with us for years. He was very pleasant and kind, very good to us, and we were all much attached to him and did everything in our power to make him comfortable. Every year about this time he used to go to Monte Carlo, and about a month ago he left us as usual. This morning, at eight o'clock, we had a telegram to say that he had been found there, sitting on a seat, shot through the head and with a pistol in his hand, and that this happened about a quarter to twelve last night.'

This was exactly the time when the gentleman who told the story had seen the dead man enter the house.

THE BORDEAUX DILIGENCE

Lord Halifax supplied no authority for this story, nor, it may be suspected, does any authority exist.

A French gentleman, who had lost his wife and was in much sadness and misery, was walking down the Rue de Bac one day when he saw three men, who looked at him very pleasantly, and pointing to a woman at the end of the street, said, 'Pardon us, sir, but would you do us a favour?'

'Certainly,' he replied.

'Would you mind asking that lady at the end of the street at what time the Bordeaux diligence starts?'

He thought the request odd, but went to the end of the street, and said to the lady, ' I beg your pardon, but could you tell me at what hour the Bordeaux diligence starts?'

She answered hurriedly, 'Don't ask me; go and ask the *gendarme*.'

So he went up to the *agent de police* and put the same question to him.

'What?' said the man.

'At what time does the Bordeaux diligence start?'

At this, the *agent de police* turned round, arrested him, and took him to the police station, where the man was put in a cell and presently brought up before the magistrate, who asked what was his crime.

The *agent de police* replied, 'He asked at what time the Bordeaux diligence starts.'

'He asked *that*, did he?' said the magistrate. 'Put him in the dark cell.'

'But,' protested the gentleman, 'I only asked what time the Bordeaux diligence starts, to oblige some men, who asked me to ask a woman, who told me to ask the *agent de police*.'

'Put him in the dark cell,' was the only reply.

Later on, the gentleman was brought up before a judge and jury, and the judge said, 'What is this man accused of?'

The *agent de police* answered, 'He came and asked me at what time the Bordeaux diligence starts.'

'He said *that*!' exclaimed the judge. 'Gentlemen of the jury, is this prisoner guilty or not guilty?'

'Guilty!' they all cried.

'Take him away,' said the judge. 'Seven years at Cayenne.'

So the wretched man was taken out in a convict ship and kept a close prisoner at Cayenne. After a time, he struck up a friendship with the other prisoners there, and one day they decided that each should tell the reason why he came to be sent to the Island. One said one thing, another another, until it came to the turn of the latest arrival to explain why he had been sent there.

'Oh,' he said, 'I was walking down the Rue de Bac one day, when I saw three men, who asked me if I would ask a lady at the end of the street at what time the Bordeaux diligence started, just to oblige them. I went and asked her and she told me to ask the *agent de police*, but when I asked him he turned round and arrested me and I was taken to the police station, and before the magistrate, and then before a judge and jury, who sent me here.'

When he had finished speaking there was silence, and from that time forward everyone shunned him.

After a while the Governor of the prison came to investigate the crimes of the various prisoners, so that some of them might be let off with easier work. At last the gentleman was brought before the Governor, who asked him what had been the nature of his offence. He repeated his story.

'*That!*' said the Governor. 'Give him solitary confinement.'

The poor man applied for the ministrations of the chaplain, who asked him what his crime had been, but when he repeated his story the chaplain went away and left him.

So he continued in misery and agony for seven years, until at last he was allowed to return home, without money, without relations and without friends. One day, shortly after his return, he thought he would walk down the Rue du Bac once again, and as he did so he saw the same woman at the end of the street, but looking very old and horrible. He accosted her and said, 'You are the author of all my misfortunes.'

She replied, 'Don't touch me, but if you like I will tell you why I asked you to do what I did. Go to the Champs Elysées to-night at twelve o'clock and you will find a hut. Knock at the door and go in and I will explain to you why you have suffered all this misery.'

He went to the Champs Elysées at the time mentioned, identified the hut, knocked, entered, and found the woman inside.

'Now,' he said, 'tell me why I have suffered all this.'

'Give me a glass of cognac,' was the answer.

He took a bottle from the shelf above her head and poured out a glass of brandy, which she drank.

'Now,' he said, 'tell me.'

'Give me some more cognac,' she said.

He gave her some more and she began to speak. 'Put your ear down here,' she said. 'I am very, very weak and cannot speak loudly.'

He put his ear down to her and she immediately sank her teeth into it and fell back with a heavy sigh—dead.

THE APPEARANCE OF MR. BIRKBECK

Mr. W. J. Birkbeck, who appeared in this strange fashion to Mr. H. W. Hill, the contributor of this story, was a close friend of Lord Halifax. He was a well-known authority on the Russian Orthodox Church.

Mr. W. J. Birkbeck of Stratton Strawless, Norwich, is a dear friend, with whom I am in close sympathy and have much in common. About eight years ago (1907), in the winter, I had occasion to write to Mr. Birkbeck a very important letter which I sent to his house at Stratton Strawless. Next day it happened that I was not very well and did not go to the office. I was sitting in my own room in the front of the basement at 9 Bloomfield Terrace, when at a quarter to four in the afternoon, I saw Mr. Birkbeck pass by the window and turn to come up the steps to the front door. I said to myself, 'Oh, I did not know Mr. Birkbeck was in London.' Then I got ready a chair for him, expecting him at any moment to be announced. The minutes passed, however, and he did not come. In order to catch that evening's post I sat down at once and wrote to Mr. Birkbeck at Stratton Strawless, asking him what he had been doing and thinking about that afternoon at a quarter to four. He replied by return that at that hour he had been out shooting and had remarked that he must go indoors presently and get a letter off to me. This, of course, was in reply to the important letter which I had written him the day before.

Mr. Birkbeck was a man of striking appearance, who was unlikely to be mistaken for anyone else.

The Vampire Cat

¶ *Mr. Everard Meynell,* who told the following story in a letter to *Lord Halifax,* was the latter's nephew, being the son of his brother, the *Hon. Frederick Wood,* who changed his name to *Meynell* on succeeding to the estate at *Hoar Cross.*

I REALLY MUST TELL YOU OF A MOST EXTRAORDINARY
story which I have just this moment heard and am putting
into writing at once before I forget any of the details.

I was sitting in my club after dinner, smoking a cigarette
and drinking my coffee, when a friend of mine, whom I had
not seen for some time, came up and began to talk to me on
various subjects. At length he said that he had just experienced a most singular adventure.

It appears that last Sunday he went down to Eastbourne to
stay with some friends for the week-end, hoping to get a little
fresh air and recuperate generally after a period of somewhat
severe work, during which he had been suffering a good deal
from sleeplessness. On the Saturday evening, when he arrived,
he found a cheerful party in the house and was congratulating
himself upon having been able to get away from London.

Before going up to dress for dinner, his attention was
attracted by the behaviour of a large black cat, which rushed
forward to meet him as he came into the hall and began to display violent signs of affection, rubbing itself against his leg and
trying to climb up to his shoulder. This struck my friend as
being most odd, and, in a way that he could hardly explain,
rather repulsive, as he had always had an irrational repugnance
for cats. However, as the animal seemed to be entirely devoted
to him he allowed it to follow him upstairs, but on reaching

his bedroom shut the door against it. When he went down to dinner, the cat was still outside the door and followed him into the dining-room, where its apparent devotion was the subject of much chaff. The same performance was repeated at bed-time, when again he saw to it that the cat was left outside the door of his room. During the whole of Sunday, the cat continued to behave in this strange way, making almost desperate attempts to climb up to my friend's neck. On Sunday evening when he went to bed he had forcibly to prevent the cat from following him into his room.

Benefiting doubtless by the sea air and the quiet surroundings, he at once fell into a deep and dreamless sleep, a thing which he had not been able to do for many weeks. He was awakened very gradually by a curious drawn feeling down one side of him. In his own words he felt as though he 'was breathing only on one side of his body'. At the same time he had a feeling of faintness and languor which tempted him to turn over and go off to sleep again, but a sharp pricking sensation over his heart caused him to place his hand to his side, where he felt something warm and furry. He started up and found the cat pressed closely against him, with its head buried under his arm, and the whole of one side of his night shirt drenched with blood.

He sprang out of bed and said something to the cat, which at once stopped purring, came to the end of the bed, and began to spit and curse at him with a hatred which more than equalled its previous affection. Needless to say, it was the work of a moment to throw the creature out of the room.

Subsequent enquiries explained how the cat had got in. My friend had given instructions to be called early as he wished to catch a train. The footman, however, mistaking the time, had come to his bedroom an hour too soon, at six o'clock instead of at seven, and when opening the door he remembered having let the cat in and having been unable to chase it out again. It was seven-thirty when my friend awoke, so the cat had had about an hour and a half, uninterrupted, in which time it had managed to suck quite a quantity of blood. An extraordinary circumstance was that, although it had drawn so much blood, it must have had to lick through the nightshirt. All the skin on the left side of my friend's body was furrowed up and down, leaving exact marks of the animal's tongue.

It was an extremely unpleasant experience and the cat's immediate discovery of some horrible affinity between it and my friend makes the story the more ghastly. When my friend returned to London he consulted two doctors, who were able to reassure him that the wound was perfectly healthy, and to dispel any fears that he might have of the sanity of the cat.

Lord Lytton
and a
Horoscope

¶ *Lord Lytton*, to whom this story refers, was the first Earl, the poet, diplomatist, Viceroy of India, and son of *Edward Bulwer-Lytton*, the novelist. The story was sent to *Lord Halifax* by *Lady Margaret Shelley.*

MISS JOHNES, OF CORSTOFFY, IN PEMBROKESHIRE, ONCE
went to stay with Lord Lytton at Knebworth. She found him
full of a horoscope he had taken for Lord Beaconsfield, which
had turned out to be a correct anticipation of events. Miss
Johnes begged Lord Lytton to forecast her own future, and
after some persuasion he consented.

He told her: 'You will shortly have a love-affair which will
end disastrously and make you very unhappy. You will then
go out into Society, meet many illustrious people, and have an
interesting time. The tragedy of your life will be connected
with the treachery of a servant. Finally, late in life, you will
meet a man accustomed to command, whom you will marry
and with whom you will be very happy.'

Within a few weeks of this visit to Knebworth, Miss Johnes
became engaged to a nephew of Lady Llanover, but subsequently the engagement was abruptly broken off through her
discovery that her fiancé already had a wife whom he had not
acknowledged. A little later on, she became a friend and correspondent of Dean Stanley and Bishop Thirlwall and spent
much of her time paying visits. On one occasion when she
was away she was summoned home by a telegram bringing
the news of a terrible accident which had befallen her father
and sister. When she returned she found that a tragedy had
taken place. The chef at her home, having been discovered

209

drinking, had been given notice to leave. In revenge, and under the influence of liquor, he had rushed into her father's study and shot and killed him. He had then pursued her sister into the kitchen and shot her too, though not fatally. Finally, he had turned the pistol on himself and blown out his brains. Miss Johnes was broken-hearted over her father's death and the shock to her sister, who never quite recovered, and for a long time she lived very quietly. When, however, she was about forty-eight she met, as a neighbour, Sir Charles Mills, who was a great friend of Lord Roberts and had won the Victoria Cross in India. In ten days' time they were engaged. Soon afterwards they were married and were blissfully happy, living till they were nearly eighty years of age.

Colonel P.'s
Ghost Story

¶ '*Colonel P.'s Ghost Story*' makes no pretence at authenticity, but was of *Lord Halifax's* own invention. For that reason it has an interest and a claim to be included in this book. The house described in the story is obviously Garrowby, *Lord Halifax's* own house near *Kirby Underdale*, in the *East Riding of Yorkshire*.

WHERE ARE THE DEAD—THOSE WHO HAVE LOVED US AND whom we have loved; and those to whom we may have done some irreparable injury? Are they gone from us for ever, or do they return? Are they still amongst us, possessed of that undefined, mysterious, and awful existence which the ancient world attributed to the ghosts of the departed? Are there among the dead those whose love can still protect our weakness? Are there those whose troubled and unquiet spirits are permitted to disturb our peace and avenge their wrongs? Between this world, and that other which escapes our senses, we can neither explain the connecting link, nor admit an impassable barrier. This, however, is certain, whether it be a dream or a fact that the dead still haunt our earthly life, we are all, even the least impressionable, conscious at times of an apprehension of things invisible, and of an undefined fear lest, out of the darkness which surrounds us, powers lurking at our side may suddenly reveal themselves, and we be left helpless in their hands, exposed to all the unknown possibilities of the unseen world. Again, what is that subtle influence of which we are conscious at certain times, and in certain places, which has the power of exciting these apprehensions? and what is it that lies beneath all those beliefs and practices in connection with the dead and their present relation to us, which are confined to no particular time or place, but in varying forms are as widely spread as the human race itself?

213

Is it that, man being a spirit clothed in flesh, an existence constituted in a dual nature, of which the lower, the body, in all that makes up its essential identity is destined, after the temporary separation caused by death between it and the soul, to be again the organ of the spirit, there exists even during the time of this temporary separation a mysterious link? By virtue of the personal identity of the human being which makes of body and soul one man, what connection may be supposed to exist, what relation still to be maintained, between the soul and the earthly remains which it once indwelt, and between the soul and the place where the body rests in expectation of the life it is again to share with the soul? Are words spoken in the neighbourhood of what was once the soul's earthly habitation, a habitation to which, changed no doubt, but with its identity undisturbed, the soul will again return, more likely to reach the ears of the disembodied spirit, to whom that habitation still belongs, than words spoken elsewhere?

Whence comes the almost universal practice of prayers addressed to the departed in the neighbourhood of their graves? How do the ideas which these and similar facts suggest connect themselves with beliefs and practices which can claim the assent of the Christian Church, and, in the domain of superstition and popular belief, with such dislikes and fears as those entertained by Cornish fishermen to walk at night along those parts of the coast where wrecks have taken place, lest they should hear the dead sailors still calling from the sea, or with their belief that the voices of the drowned may be heard on the lonely beaches hailing their own names? Whence comes the belief that the ghosts of the unburied dead, or of those whose bodies have been disturbed, cannot rest in peace, but wander, troubled and unquiet, in the vicinity of their earthly remains? In the well-known case of H.M.S. *Wagner* the shipwrecked sailors unanimously connected their disaster with the body of the man they had found unburied, and which they supposed to be that of a former comrade, murdered by a party who had previously left the island on which they had been cast. It was the same persuasions which influenced the buc- caneers to kill a prisoner or a slave where they had hidden a buried treasure, in the belief that the presence of the dead would secure the spot from the interference of the living.

Do the dead, indeed, make themselves felt in the spots they frequented when alive? Is it they whose tread is heard at night on the stairs, and whose presence at certain moments makes solitude impossible? Have animals a perception of their pre- sence, which is not always granted to men?

What is the connection between life and light, and death and darkness? What is implied in the term the 'nether world'? What are the possibilities suggested by the phrase, 'things un- der the earth'? What underlies the stories so constantly repeated of sounds heard at night within the lonely tumuli on the York- shire wolds? and whence comes the belief that those ancient dwelling-places of the dead are still revisited by the spirits of the departed in the shadowy resemblance of the bodies they once animated, seeking for the remains, the last resting places of which have often been so ruthlessly disturbed? And what explains the tradition of the glimmering lights to be seen at certain seasons round the deserted barrows where rested the bodies of the ancient inhabitants of the land, whose influence, it is said, may still be felt by those who rashly intrude themselves within the sphere of their mysterious attraction?

I had just come back to England, after having been some years in India. I had no reason to be discontented with my past, and was looking forward to meet my friends, among whom there was no one I was more anxious to see than L——. We had been at Eton together, and for the short time I had been at Oxford, before entering the army, we had been at the same college.

It will easily be imagined then, how pleasant it was, two or three days after my arrival in London, to receive a letter from L—— saying he had just seen in the papers that I had arrived, and begging me to come down at once to B——, his place in Yorkshire. 'You are not to tell me', he said, 'you cannot come. I allow you a week in which to order and try on your clothes, to report yourself at the War Office, to pay your respects to the Duke; but after that I shall expect you; in fact, you are to come on Monday. I have a couple of horses which will just suit you [we had both of us hunted a good deal together in our Oxford days], the carriage shall meet you at P——, and all you

216

have got to do is to put yourself into the train which leaves King's Cross at twelve o'clock.' I was just starting on the Monday morning when I received a telegram from L—— to say that, as ill-luck would have it, he was forced to attend a funeral at some distance off and that instead of coming to him I was to go straight to the place of a neighbour, where there was to be some hawking, that he was sending a horse over to meet me, and that I was to ride over to B—— the next day. It was too late to alter the arrangements, even if I had wished to do so, and I arrived at S—— just in time to dress for dinner. There were several people staying in the house, including two or three members of the local Archaeological Society, who, I discovered in the course of the evening, were busy about the exploration of some ancient earth works, and we spent a very pleasant evening.

We were very successful hawking gulls and rooks all the following morning, and it was not till nearly four o'clock in the afternoon that I started to ride over the hill to B——. The first part of my ride was along the high road, about which there could be no possibility of mistake. The first five or six miles were pleasantly got over. Then my instructions were to leave the road, which here crossed one end of Lord N——'s park, and after cutting off a considerable corner, to rejoin the road again at the end of Lord N——'s domain, where it entered a tract of unenclosed grass-land. A little later I was to diverge a second time, and following a sheep track for some distance, to cross two or three open fields, in the last of which I should pass two large mounds covered with trees on the brow of the hill.

I duly reached the point where the road crossed the stretch of unenclosed country, some straggling thorn trees, of which I had been warned, dispelled any doubt as to which sheep-track I was to take, and I began slowly to ascend a slope which was steep enough to make any pace but a walk impossible.

By the time I had reached the top of the hill the sun had set; but there was still a streak of light in the west, and I could see the two clumps of trees I had been told to pass, standing out black against the sky.

As I approached the clumps I saw in the deepening twilight that the trees were of inconsiderable size, but that they appeared higher than they were, from the mounds out of which they grew. The mounds themselves, remembering what I had heard at S——, I supposed to be of British or Danish origin, and I wondered whether these were the identical tumuli the members of the local Archaeological Society were about to explore.

At that moment, though I had not thought of it for years, the recollection was suddenly forced in upon me of a black skeleton, with twisted legs, I had seen as a child in the museum at Z——, which I had been told at the time had been taken from an ancient British barrow on the Yorkshire wolds. I could see that skeleton now, just as it had appeared to me

218

long ago, with the fragments of teeth still adhering to the broken lower jaw, and I found myself wondering again why its legs were so twisted and doubled-up, and as I did so I felt the same awe creeping over me with which the thought of the black skeleton used to fill me as a child at night. The next moment I recollected L—— mentioning a skull taken out of some old earthwork by his grandfather, which, as long as he could remember, had always been kept on the chimney-piece in one of the rooms at B——, and his saying one evening, when we had been telling ghost stories, that he wondered whether it was its former owner that walked in the passages at night. Was it, I wondered, this particular tumulus which had been explored, and was the skull which had so long been preserved on the chimney-piece at B—— the skull of its former occupant?

Foolish as it may seem, I was conscious in the growing darkness of a wish to get away from the tumulus with its black shadows into the comparative light of the high road, and it was with a feeling of relief that I perceived in the growing light of the moon, which was just rising above the hill, that I was not twenty yards distant from the bridle-gate I had been anxious to find. A steep descent, and a further ride of some four or five miles brought me to the park gates of B——.

Some deer, which were feeding close to the road, started away as I entered the park. The approach ascended a slight hill, and, after following it for about a mile, a sharp angle suddenly revealed the house close to me. It seemed a low, gabled structure of no great size, with old-fashioned lattice windows, apparently separated from the park by a terraced garden. There were some high trees at the corner of the house which cast a deep shadow over the road, leaving everything beyond in darkness. As I was hesitating which way to turn, the barking of a dog and the gleam of a lantern relieved my doubt. I passed through an archway into a courtyard. A groom, who was evidently expecting me, came out to take my horse, a door opened, and there stood L——, whom I had not seen for so many years, hardly altered, and with all the joy of welcome beaming on his face. Taking me by both hands, he drew me into the house, got rid of my hat, looked me all over, and then, in a breath, began saying how glad he was to see me, and what a good time we would have together. So saying, he took me through a panelled hall, up an oak staircase, and showed me my room, which, hurried as I was, I observed was hung with tapestry, and had a large, four-post bed with velvet curtains. They had gone into dinner when I came down, but a place had been kept for me next Lady L——. Besides my hosts there were their two daughters, the chaplain, and some others, whose names I do not remember.

Dinner was enlivened, after many questions as to my own life in India, by an animated discussion as to the right policy to be pursued in regard to the Indian frontier, especially in reference to Afghanistan. From these topics we diverged to the real wishes and dispositions of the native races in India, which led up to some Indian stories recently published, which were exciting a good deal of attention, and I was asked whether I really believed, as the writer in question seemed to affirm, that things occurred in the midst of the native populations which it was difficult to account for on any other hypothesis than that of an intervention of spiritual agencies. I expressed my opinion with some hesitation, and related one or two facts which had come within my own knowledge. At this point Lady L—— interfered, and declaring that such stories were very disagreeable, despite the remonstrances of her daughters, summoned the ladies to the drawing-room, begging us at the same time not to stay too long over our cigarettes. The conversation so interrupted took another turn, and reverted to my military experiences on the frontier.

After dinner there was some music in the hall, and a game of whist in the drawing-room, and when the ladies had gone upstairs, L—— and I retired to the smoking-room, where we sat up talking the best part of the night; indeed, I believe it was nearer three than two before we went to bed. Once in bed I slept so soundly that my servant's entrance the next morning failed to arouse me, and it was past nine when I awoke.

Breakfast over, L—— took me for a stroll round the end of the park nearest to the house, the ground of which was much varied and tossed about. After we had come in and disposed of the newspapers, I asked Lady L—— if one of her daughters might show me the house. Elizabeth, the eldest, was summoned, and seemed in no way to dislike the task. It was by no means a large house, though it had the appearance of being much larger than it really was. The house itself occupied three sides of a square, the entrance and one end of the stables making the fourth side. Most of the rooms were panelled, and hung with pictures. Among the latter there was a head of Charles the First, a picture of the Earl of Essex, Elizabeth's favourite, who I was told was in some way connected with the family, and a quantity of portraits, including one of an ancestor who had been beheaded for alleged treason in the religious and political troubles of the sixteenth century.

Beyond the chapel, which had a Jacobean screen supporting a gallery, was a sacristy, in which we found the chaplain busy writing, and opening out of it a narrow, twisting staircase which went up to his bedroom and to a sort of dark attic or lumber-room from which there was no exit. My guide proposed that we should ascend this staircase, and by going through the chaplain's room, which gave access to the gallery of the chapel, pass across it to the other side of the house. We did as she proposed, and as we crossed the gallery she stopped me, saying, 'But you ought to see the long garret,' and opening a door beyond L——'s dressing room, took me up a very narrow staircase, which eventually led into a sort of long panelled gallery running the whole length of the house, with an open timber roof, and containing two very large and deep recesses, the windows of which looked over the garden. There were some bits of tapestry on the wall, two or three oak chests and high-backed chairs, and an old-fashioned bed with carved posts and dark hangings in one corner. A door at one end of the gallery gave access to a panelled room, where, my guide told me, her father kept books and papers, and to which he sometimes retired if he wanted to be alone and undisturbed. I asked if anyone slept in either of the rooms, and she answered, 'No'; the place was not really used except as a play-room, though sometimes she and her sister would take their work up there.

By the time we had completely gone over the house and I had been shown the horses and introduced to the dogs it was nearly one o'clock. We were to have an early luncheon and to drive afterwards to see the ruins of an abbey where there were the remains of a very picturesque gateway. Lady L—— drove, L—— and I rode. It was a very pleasant expedition, and we got back just in time for tea, after which there was some reading aloud. The evening passed much in the same way as the preceding one, except that L——, who had some business to attend to, did not go down to the smoking-room, and I took the opportunity of retiring early in order to write a letter for the Indian mail.

I had finished my letter, which was a long one, together with two or three others, and had just got into bed, when I heard a step overhead as of someone walking along the gallery. It was a slow, heavy, measured tread, which I could hear getting

223

gradually louder as it neared my room, and then gradually fading away as it retreated into the distance. I was startled for a moment, having been told the room was unused, and wondered who it could be, but the next instant it occurred to me that L——, who I knew had some writing to do, had probably gone to fetch some books from the little room upstairs, and I thought no more of the matter.

'How late you were last night,' I said to L—— next morning at breakfast; 'I heard you overhead after one o'clock.'

L—— replied, rather shortly, 'Indeed you did not, for I was in bed last night before twelve.'

'There was certainly someone overhead last night,' I answered, 'for I heard steps as distinctly as I ever heard anything in my life, going down the gallery.'

Colonel L—— remarked that he had often fancied he had heard steps going up the staircase on his side of the house when he knew no one was about, and was apparently going to say more, when his brother interrupted him, as I thought, somewhat curtly. Some orders were given about the time we were to start for our shooting, and I had no opportunity of inquiring further. We only left off shooting at dusk, and by the time we returned home it was quite dark. A carriage was being cleaned in the courtyard as we entered. 'Who can be here?' exclaimed L——. He was answered by a groom, who said that Captain and Mrs. H—— had arrived about an hour ago, and that, one of the horses being lame, the carriage in which they had driven over from Castle —— was to put up for the night. In the drawing-room we found Lady L—— pouring out tea for L——'s youngest sister and her husband, who, as we came in, exclaimed, 'We have come to beg a night's lodging.' It appeared they had been on a visit in the neighbourhood, and had been obliged to leave at a moment's notice in consequence of a sudden death in the house where they were staying, and that their hosts had sent them over to B——. 'We thought', Mrs. H—— went on to say, 'that even if the house was quite full you would be willing to put us up anywhere for a couple of nights.' Lady L—— interposed with the remark that it was all settled, and then, turning to her husband, added, 'but I want to speak to you for a moment.' They both left the room together. L—— came back almost immediately, and making an excuse to show me on a map in the hall where we had been shooting, said, as soon as we were alone, with a look of considerable annoyance, 'I am afraid we must ask you to change your room. I think we can make you quite comfortable in the long garret upstairs, which is the only room available. Lady L—— has had fires lit at both ends, the place really is not cold, and it will only be for a night or two. Your servant has been told to put your things together, but Lady L—— did not like to give orders to have them actually moved before speaking to you.' I assured him that I was delighted to change my quarters; and certainly nothing could look more comfortable than my new lodging when I went up to dress. There was a bright fire at both ends of the room. An armchair had been drawn up to the side of one of them, and all my books and writing things had been put out, with a reading lamp, in the central recess, which gave me quite a separate sitting-room to myself. Indeed, as I looked at the room, I congratulated myself on the change. L—— was necessarily a good deal occupied in the evening with his sister and her husband, whom he had not seen for some time, and when the ladies had retired, instead of going down to the smoking-room, I went upstairs to finish a book in which I was interested. I did not, however, sit up long and very soon went to bed. I must have been asleep for some time, for the moon, which did not rise till late, was shining full into the room, when I suddenly awoke with the impression of having heard a door shut somewhere at the far end of the gallery beyond the room inside mine. I had always been a light sleeper, but on the present occasion I woke at once to complete and acute consciousness, and with a sense of stretched attention which seemed to intensify all my faculties. The wind had got up and was blowing in fitful gusts round the house, and an owl was hooting in the trees close by, uttering now and again a prolonged cry that sounded like the scream of some-one in distress. A minute or two passed, and I began almost to fancy I must have been mistaken, when, as I listened, I heard the noise again. It was louder than before, and I was wondering who could be moving about the house at such a time, and how anyone could have got through my room without waking me, when I suddenly remembered the steps I had heard overhead the night before, and Colonel L——'s remark that he could swear to having heard steps as of someone going up the stairs by his room, when he knew nobody could be about. The next moment I heard the click caused by the fall of the wooden latch which fastened the doors in that part of the house, followed by a creak in the boards as of someone moving in the room within mine. I sat up to listen, and as I did so I heard quite distinctly a step cross the inner room. There was another silence, followed by the sound of something passing behind the panelling, which, owing to the slope of the roof, was a couple of feet distant from the side of my bed, and then, after a minute or two, I heard as distinctly as possible the same noise as before—the click of the wooden latch fastening the door, when pulled up by its string and falling back into the staple— only this time it was the latch of the door which communicated with that part of the gallery in which I slept, and which opened between the bed and the dressing table. A bit of tapestry hung over the door on the side towards my room, and I was sensible of the sort of rustle made by this being pushed on one side, with the slight draught it occasioned as it fell back into its place. The silence which had occurred in the inner room before the door opened was prolonged for a moment after it closed, as if someone had paused, and then I heard the steps slowly proceeding down the far side of the room. There were no shutters to any of the windows of the gallery, and the curtains very imperfectly

227

kept out the moonlight. The window to the left of my bed, beyond the door into the inner room, which looked into the court-yard, was dark, as was the whole space at the end of the room in which the bed stood, but beyond the shadow, the moonlight, streaming in from the windows in the two deep recesses on the opposite side of the gallery, the curtains of which were not drawn close, threw two bright streaks of light half way across the floor, and rendered those portions of the room comparatively light. The rest of the room, with the spaces between the windows, remained in complete darkness, so that on the further side of the gallery I could see nothing, but I could hear, and that as distinctly as ever I heard anything in my life, a slow, heavy tread passing down the room, pausing now and again, and then continuing as before. Opposite the door leading to the stairs the pause was prolonged. I listened still more intently, holding my breath in order to catch the faintest sound. Presently I heard the door into the passage open, and the steps proceed along it towards the head of the stairs. There was again an interval, then the noise as of a falling panel or shutter, and a moment afterwards a duller sound as of some heavy body lighting on the boards, followed by the return of the footsteps along the passage. The door again closed, and the same muffled tread pursued its course down the further side of the gallery. At the end of the gallery the steps appeared to stop. They then seemed to cross the floor, and as they began to return, this time along the opposite wall, I thought I saw for a moment a dark figure crossing the patch of moonlight opposite the further window. It disappeared again into the darkness caused by the shadow between the two recesses, but as the steps seemed to enter the second patch of moonlight in front of the recess nearest to the bed, I had a distinct vision of a tall figure with hollow features and sunken eyes, its teeth clenched together, and with a fur cap pulled over its brows, standing out clear in the moonlight. It was only for an instant, then nothing but the moonlight again, with the step coming nearer and nearer, till I was conscious of something in the darkness tall enough to intercept my view of the moonlight, approaching close to the side of my bed. I threw myself back against the wall, and as I did so, with a cry over which I had as little control as the scream uttered by a sleeper in the agony of a nightmare, I called out, 'Who are you? What are you?' There was an instant during which I felt my hair bristle on my head, as in the horror of the darkness I prepared to grapple with the being by my side, when a board creaked as if someone had moved, and I heard the footsteps retreat, and for a moment saw the same tall figure, with the same fur cap pulled over its brows, standing at the corner of the nearest of the two recessed windows in the full light of the moon, only this time the face was more distinctly turned in my direction, and was looking towards me. The next moment there was a rush up the stairs, the door burst open, and L—— cried out, 'For God's sake what is the matter? What was that scream that rang through the house?' 'There is someone in the room,' I said; 'there, by that recess in the moonlight.' The words were hardly out of my mouth before L—— had struck a light and was searching in the corners of the recess. 'There is no one,' he said; and as he spoke he ran to the window in the corresponding recess at the end of the room. 'You must be dreaming,' he called; 'there is no one here. You have had a nightmare.' He turned and came back, when from what he saw in my face, for by this time I had joined him, or because a sudden thought struck him, 'Stay,' he said, 'it is possible,' and going towards the window, where the wainscoting turned the corner of the recess at the spot where I had seen the figure standing in the moonlight, he pushed back a panel, and disclosed a very narrow passage running between the panelling and the wall past the corner in which the bed stood. 'Stop there,' he said, and lighting a second candle he went quickly through into the smaller room within the one I had been occupying, and which, so far as I knew, had no other entrance. After two or three minutes he emerged from the end of the concealed passage, saying, 'No, there is no one there.' Something, however, still disturbed him, for bidding me follow, he went back into the inner room where he kept his books and papers, and touching a spring in the wall a hidden door slipped back and disclosed the entrance into what I supposed to be a third room, but of which I could see nothing but a looking-glass on the wall opposite, reflecting

230

L——'s face and mine in the darkness. Taking up the candle, L—— stepped through the aperture, and, following him, I saw that we were in a small room hung with faded tapestry, with a picture at one end of it, and on a ledge over the entrance a coffer with an opening cut in front, out of which looked the remains of a skull. The room was large enough to hold some six or seven persons, and going to one corner of it, L—— seemed to look for something which apparently he did not find, for I heard him say to himself, 'It must have been moved; somebody may have got in after all,' but the next minute he exclaimed, 'Here it is,' and taking down a key from behind one of the upright timbers applied it to a keyhole hidden by some of the woodwork. The door, however, if it was a door, was fast secured, for it was a minute or two before L—— succeeded in turning the key in the lock. When he had done so, and satisfied himself that the door had been safely fastened, he put the key back from where he had taken it, saying as he did so, 'You see no one could have got in this way; you certainly have been dreaming.' Without waiting for an answer he retraced his steps, and as soon as we had regained the gallery begged me to come down to his dressing-room. I followed him downstairs, and after he had spoken to Lady L——, who was standing with the door of her room ajar, in a state of great agitation, he turned to me and said, 'You see no one can have been in your room, nobody could have come down on this side without meeting me, and the only other access to the gallery is by the secret door into the attic at the top of the private staircase, on my brother's side of the house, which you saw was locked on the inside, and of which hardly anyone knows but myself. You must have had a nightmare, it can have been nothing else; only,' he added, after a pause, 'I should be grateful if you would say nothing about it: there are people in the house and neighbourhood who are silly enough as it is, and I don't want more stories invented of someone walking about the house at night. But we will talk of all this,' he added, 'in the morning. I see the fire is not quite out; stay here if you do not feel inclined to go to bed, and read. I must go to Lady L——, who is a good deal frightened, and does not like to be left alone.' He went into the bedroom, and five or six minutes afterwards I heard him go upstairs again, to return almost immediately. Sleep, as far as I was concerned, was out of the question, nor do I think that L—— and his wife slept much either, for I heard them talking for a long time together. I turned to the fire, which, as L—— had said, was not quite out. I am not ashamed to say that I had no inclination to go back to my room, and raking the embers together I coaxed them into a flame, and remained where I was, going over and over again in my mind all that had occurred. After a time I took up a book and tried to read, but it was useless: the experiences of the night were too vivid, and the questions they raised too absorbing, to admit of any other thoughts. The leaves were not turned, and my eyes remained fixed on the page, seeing nothing but that dark figure with its hollow eyes and its hopeless look of trouble and unrest standing at the foot of my bed in the moon-light. What was it? Why did it come? Why did it walk through the gallery at night? Was it always there? These and such like questions kept recurring again and again, leaving nothing clear in the whirl of my brain but the vision of the figure with its sunken face and the sound of its measured step on the floor. I sat absorbed in such thoughts till I heard the servants stirring in the morning. I then went up to my own room, left the candle burning, and got into bed. I had just fallen asleep when my servant brought me up a cup of tea at eight o'clock. As soon as he had gone, I got up and looked for the entrance into the passage behind the panelling, and the way into the hidden room. The first I discovered, the second defied all my efforts. At breakfast Captain H—— and his wife asked if anything had happened in the night, as they had been disturbed by much walking overhead, to which L—— replied that I had not been very well and had had an attack of cramp, and that he had been upstairs to look after me. From his man-ner I could see that he wished me to be silent, and I said nothing accordingly. After breakfast L—— asked me if I should feel inclined to go out and look for the hounds. They met a considerable way off, but if they did not find in the coverts they would draw first they were not unlikely to come our way, and if they were lucky we might fall in with them about one o'clock. I welcomed the proposal, and he, his two daughters, and myself—the rest of the party having gone out shooting —started about eleven o'clock for our ride. It was a beautiful day, soft with a bright sun. Our way lay almost entirely over turf, and nothing could be more exhilarating than our gallop. No traces of the hounds, however, were to be discovered; nobody we met had heard anything of them, they must have found at once, and run in the opposite direction; and at three o'clock, after we had eaten our sandwiches, as we were crossing an eminence from which there was a very extensive view, L——, after a careful survey of the country and listening once more for the possible sound of a horn, reluctantly said, despite all the entreaties of his daughters, that we must turn back and go home.

Before we did so, he pointed out two clumps of trees, very conspicuous in the distance, saying, 'Those are the clumps you passed the other evening on your way from S——. They are at the extreme end of the estate, and were planted by my grandfather as a landmark after the barrows, on which they stand, had been explored. You remember the skull I used to tell you about, which was kept on the chimneypiece in my room; it came, I believe, from there.' We turned our horses homewards, and began to descend the hill, when L——, who had been very silent and preoccupied all day, suddenly said, 'My grandfather had some strange experiences in his life. One of the earliest things he remembered was being taken as a child by his uncle—the husband of the lady with the hand,

234

whose picture you may have noticed in the dining-room—to see the execution of five rioters at a time when others were glad to keep out of the way and not identify themselves more than they could help with what was not unlikely to lead to reprisals. As a young man, shortly after he succeeded to the property, he had himself been instrumental in putting down a very serious disturbance in the manufacturing districts, and securing the ringleaders in a way which would have been impossible for anyone but a man of great nerve and resource.' L—— paused, and then added, with a certain hesitation, 'I will tell you a story about him which, though portions of it may have been known, and others guessed, is one which I do not much care to have remembered.'

'My grandfather was in the habit of going round the preserves at night with a young underkeeper, of whom he was very fond, to see if any poachers, whom he looked upon as his natural enemies, were about. The young man belonged to a family that had always lived on the estate, and several members of it, at different times, had been in my grandfather's service and in that of his father before him. One night, as I suppose, for my surmises are only the result of many things put together, my grandfather must have been out with this young man, and in the plantations above the edge of the park, not far from an old chalk pit we passed by to-day, must have come upon a travelling tinker of very indifferent reputation, who was more than suspected of being in league with the bad

235

characters of an adjoining village noted as the resort of all the poachers in the country-side. On the particular night in question my grandfather and the keeper must have caught this man setting snares; there must have been a tussle, in the course of which, as subsequent circumstances have led me to imagine, the man, who was a powerful and desperate fellow, must have been stunned or killed, and my grandfather, for some reason or another, must have gone back to the house unperceived, which he could easily do, as he was in the habit of using a door concealed by the trees at the angle of the house, of which he always had a key, and which, communicating with the private staircase at the back of the chapel, provided a means of exit and entrance entirely separate from the rest of the house. Whether the man had been actually killed by the blow, which had stunned him, or whether he had come to himself, and, finding the keeper alone, the struggle had been renewed with fatal results, I do not know; I imagine the latter, something which once dropped from an old servant entirely in my grandfather's confidence inclining me to think that my grandfather must have left the house and returned to it more than once during the night, but however this was, there can be little doubt that the man was killed and buried secretly in the course of the night not far from the chalk pit I have mentioned. His disappearance, in view of his well-known habits and wandering mode of life, did not for some time excite any surprise, but later on, one or two circumstances having led to suspicion,

236

an inquiry was set on foot, and, amongst others, my grand/
father's keepers were examined before the magistrates. It was
remembered afterwards that the underkeeper in question was
absent at the time of the inquiry, my grandfather having sent
him with some dogs up to the moors, but the fact was un/
noticed, or if noticed, those who observed it preferred to be
silent, and no remark was made. Nothing came of the investi/
gation, and the whole subject would probably have dropped
if it had not been that two or three years later, for reasons I do
not understand, but at the instigation of a magistrate recently
come into the country, whom my grandfather was known to
dislike, a fresh inquiry was instituted. In the course of that in/
quiry, it transpired that a warrant was about to be issued for the
arrest of the underkeeper. My grandfather, who had had a fit
of the gout, was away from home at the time, but on hearing
the news, which was communicated to him by someone who
probably appreciated its importance, he came home at once.
The evening he returned he had a long interview with the
keeper, who left the house to go home about nine o'clock.
The warrant was issued the next day, but in the meantime the
keeper had disappeared. My grandfather gave orders to all his
own people to do everything in their power to assist the author/
ities in the search that was at once set on foot, but was unable
himself to take any active share in it, as he was laid up with a
fresh attack of gout, and obliged to keep his rooms for more
than a fortnight, in fact, during all the time that search was

being made in the immediate neighbourhood. He was never in the best of tempers when he had the gout, and on this occasion he was in a worse mood than usual, and would allow no one to come near him except the confidential servant I have already mentioned. No trace of the keeper was ever found, although at a subsequent period I have been told there were rumours of his having been heard of in America. They were never verified, however, and the man having been unmarried gradually dropped out of remembrance, and as my grandfather never allowed the subject to be mentioned in his presence, I should probably have known nothing about it except for the vague tradition which always attaches to such events, and for two circumstances, one of which strongly impressed itself on my memory as a child, while the other afforded me the clue which has enabled me to piece together the story as I am telling it you. My grandfather had been accustomed to have us much with him in his later years, and would sometimes play with us on a winter's afternoon in the long, panelled gallery, which, as you saw, runs the whole length of the top of the house. One of my earliest recollections is seeing him on one side of the fire, the curate of the parish on the other, and our old nurse sitting a little further off, whilst I and my brothers and sisters played about in the dusk. There is, as you will have guessed, at the far end of the gallery, a concealed communication with the private staircase leading past the chaplain's room to the little door by the corner of the garden;

and at the other end of the gallery there was, and is now, access to a sort of hiding place in the roof, which I and my brothers and sisters discovered one day by accident when the plumbers were engaged on some repairs to a cistern. We mentioned the fact to my mother, who asked my grandfather, in our hearing, to have the place fastened up. "She was afraid", she said, "that the children might get in, and be unable to get out." And I remember being struck by the way in which he answered, "that he would not have the old house touched; places of that sort had been useful before, and might be useful again." The other circumstance which throws light on what happened was that not so long ago, in getting chalk from the pit just outside the corner of the park, the men came upon a skeleton, perfect and entire lying at no very great depth beneath the soil, and which, by the gradual removal of the chalk from the face of the pit, had been exposed in its whole length. I saw the skeleton myself when first found, lying on a ledge of chalk with the soil undisturbed above and beneath it, but I am not sure what became of it. I believe it was covered up again at the time, and if so, as the place has since been planted, I suppose it is there still; but as to its history I have no doubt. I am convinced it is the skeleton of the man who had disappeared some eighty or ninety years ago; and I feel equally sure that my grandfather at the time of the second inquiry succeeded in hiding the keeper in the house at B——on the night preceding the issue of the warrant for his arrest, and in keeping him concealed there, till the immediate search was over, and arrangements had been made for his leaving England from the nearest seaport, which would be easily reached by an able bodied man in a walk of some six or seven hours; that is to say, within the space of a winter's night.' When L—— had finished he rode on for a moment in silence, then taking out his watch, for we were now at the bottom of the hill, he put his horse into a trot, saying, 'We must make haste, or we shall be late.'

On reaching home I found that arrangements had been made for changing my room, and that I had been moved into an entirely different part of the house.

In the course of the evening L——, when no one was about, took me upstairs into the gallery and showed me how the spring worked which gave access to the hidden room beyond. He also pointed out how impossible it was from any spot outside the house to see the window by which the room was lit, and how, communicating as it did by a concealed entrance with the attic at the top of the private stairs, it would be easy for anyone who knew the secret, and had the key, not only to approach the gallery on that side, but also to enter and leave the house unobserved. He begged me, however, to keep this knowledge to myself, which I assured him I would do. Whilst in the secret room, after looking for a moment at the skull in its strange receptacle, 'That,' L—— said, 'is the skull which used to be kept on the chimneypiece in my room, and

240

which I put away here'; he added, with rather a forced laugh, 'I shall certainly have it properly buried now, that no one may say its owner walks the house.'

I have paid many visits to B—— since, though as it happens I have never been there again at exactly the same time of year, no one has ever been sleeping in the long garret, and my room has always been in another part of the house. I have never, however, been able to divest myself of the feeling that there was something about the gallery and the room beyond it which suggested possibilities, not the less disagreeable because absolutely so undefined and incapable of explanation. Others, I found were conscious of the same feeling. Elizabeth L—— once said that, though she could give no reason for it, she and her sister always disliked sitting alone in the long garret after dark. She also told me some years later that the old housekeeper had been very much frightened one evening, when she had gone up to shut a window which had been forgotten, by hearing, as she thought, steps in the garret coming towards her, and that on another occasion she had seen what she declared was the figure of a man crossing the stairs by the door of the unused garret. L——, however, never alluded to the subject again, and his dislike of it was so evident that I never touched upon it either. I have often wondered whether he really believed more than he chose to admit, and connected what I had seen, and the steps heard in the long garret, with the tragic adventure in his grandfather's life. I have sometimes been inclined to think this was the case, and, if so, it would account for his dislike to anything which might tend to revive the recollection of a story which he wished forgotten.

I remained at B—— another fortnight, and gradually got over the impression caused by what I had heard and seen. I sometimes even asked myself, towards the end of my stay, in the face of L——'s professed scepticism, and under the cheerful influences of the happy family life, in the midst of which I found myself, whether L—— had not been right after all, and whether what I had seen and heard might not have been the result of a very vivid nightmare; but the more I tried to convince myself that this was the true explanation of all that had taken place, the more incapable I felt myself of really believing it. A variety of small circumstances and coincidences, insignificant in themselves, but of importance when all taken together, confirmed what was my own conviction at the time, and compelled the belief that I really did see something which could not be explained by any hypothesis of a nightmare, however vivid. What that being was whose step I heard pass down the gallery, and whose face I saw in the moonlight, who shall say? Is it possible to separate a denizen of the spiritual world from the thoughts by which it is possessed? What, indeed, is a Spiritual Existence except intelligence, thought, will, in act? Even in our limited experience thoughts, vividly entertained by one person, seem able to reproduce themselves in the mind of another without words. Are we not conscious of the effect which the mere presence of certain individuals exercises upon those brought within their influence? Are the dead about our path? Do we meet them on our earthly way? Coming within the sphere of their influence, may not the recollections, the thoughts, the passions, which possess them, under certain conditions and in certain circumstances, reproduce themselves in our consciousness, who ourselves are spirits, though spirits linked with clay? Is it indeed the truth that ghosts are the thoughts of the unquiet dead? and that, admitting the presence of spiritual existence in our midst, all else, the possible reproduction in our own consciousness of what possesses theirs, with the consequent vision by us of all the circumstances of the past which that consciousness involves and which determine its character, may not follow as a matter of course? The eye sees what is reflected on the retina at its back. Is it impossible to believe that our souls may be possessed of a similar power of reflection adapted to their immaterial nature, which may render them capable of perceiving, and being affected by existences in that spiritual world to which they themselves belong? The question may not be decided in our present state of existence, nor does the Psychical Society perhaps adopt the most likely way to resolve it. Ghost stories divided into classes, and tabulated under various heads, do not carry conviction. There are regions outside the scope and investigation of science, but at no period of the world's history has the supernatural ever failed to exercise a powerful attraction, even in the case of those who have professed to believe the least in its existence; and a straightforward account of facts within my own experience, given precisely as they occurred, and written down at the time, may not be uninteresting to all who like to read a true ghost story. I need not say that the real initials of the persons concerned, and the names and localities of the places described, have been purposely changed so as to preclude, for obvious reasons, the possibility of any successful attempt to identify either the persons or the places mentioned in this narrative.

VOLUME II

Shrieks in
the West Room
at Flesbury

¶ *Lord Halifax* copied the following story from a manuscript, written by the sister of *John Carnsen*, the child concerned, who died on April 22nd, 1835, aged eleven. He
added the information that 'the house where the events
of this narrative occurred is *Flesbury*, a lonely country
house on the north coast of *Cornwall*. The family who
reside there are the only descendants of the *Carnsens* of
Carnsen, in *Cornwall*.' The names are given as they
appear in the *Ghost Book*, but *Carnsen* should probably be
Carnsew, the name of an old Cornish family, and *Flesbury*
should probably be *Flexbury*, near *Bude*.

A PLAIN STATEMENT OF THE FACTS, AS THEY OCCURRED, without any attempt to embellish or magnify them, will be given.

Early in 1835, my brother John was taken seriously ill, and for many weeks his life hung in the balance. A crisis was reached and passed, followed by a fortnight of mingled hope and despair. At the end of that time his condition showed so great an improvement that the most sanguine hopes for his recovery were entertained by all the family, except his mother and aunt, who continued to be very anxious so long as the doctors were unwilling to give a decidedly favourable opinion.

It was between five and six o'clock on a fine spring evening, towards the end of March. The sinking sun was cheerfully lighting up the West room, where three of John's sisters and his brother William were sitting, having just left their father in the dining-room. Their mother and aunt had returned to John's room. The West room adjoins the principal staircase, which leads up from the entrance hall through the centre of the house. There is a small landing at the door of the West room, the stairs ascending a little further to the principal landing. A second flight leads to the upper landing, on which opened the room occupied by John. Owing to the centre of the house being open, any sound in the hall is distinctly audible on the upper floor. The offices are reached by a long

3

passage behind the hall and the dining-room, so that ordinary sounds from the hall or the staircase cannot be heard there.

The children in the West room were all in the highest spirits. They were no longer feeling anxious about their brother and were even a little inclined to think that their elders had been unnecessarily alarmed. Poor dear Johnnie, they told each other, after all the fuss that had been made, was getting well. To be sure, it was impossible to spoil him; he was such a dear good boy and never made a fuss about himself. But even now Mamma and Aunt would not believe that he was not going to die. In fact, that very day at dinner, Mamma had been actually crying again. The children went on to discuss the two doctors who were attending John. The younger of the two had particularly annoyed them that day in reporting on the state of the patient to their father. While admitting an increase in strength and appetite, he had added, 'Still, I see no improvement.' 'Papa said he was ridiculously inconsistent,' one of the children remarked; and someone went on to say something which raised a general laugh. The laughter had not ceased when a piercing shriek rang through the room. It was as if uttered by someone standing on the landing just outside the open door.

There was silence, and then a second shriek like the first; another silence, and then yet a third shriek, even louder and more prolonged than the others, and ending in a rattling, gurgling sound, as though someone were dying.

The children in the room were struck with horror. None of them is likely to forget that awful sound. As I write, it seems to ring in my ears.

In a moment the door of the drawing-room, on the further side of the hall, was thrown open, and Mr. Carnsen, who had been sitting in the room alone, hurried across the hall to the foot of the staircase. He called in an agitated voice to his daughter, whom he knew to be in the West room: 'Gertrude, what is the matter? Who is screaming in that dreadful manner?'

'Papa,' we answered, 'we don't know. It wasn't one of us, though it seemed quite close.'

'It sounded as though someone were in great distress,' our father said. 'Go down to Grace and ask her if the people in the kitchen are all right, although the noise did not seem to come from there.'

Gertrude went at once and found the housekeeper alone in the big front room. She was standing as if listening and declared she had distinctly heard three shrieks. She was wondering what could be the matter, and though positive that the sound had come from further off than the kitchen, she went there to enquire if the servants knew anything.

When she returned, her usually florid face was quite pale. 'Oh, Miss Gertrude,' she said, 'there is no hope for Master John—that is what it means. What we heard was none of the servants, and no human voice. The servants heard the screams too, but they seemed to come from far off.'

'How can you talk such nonsense!' Gertrude replied. 'A person like you ought to know better. Papa says you *must* find out what it was and let him know.'

The girl then returned to the hall, where she found her father talking to the old doctor, who had just arrived. Mr. Carnsen was saying: 'It was like a woman's voice, screaming as though in the utmost distress. You would have supposed she was being murdered.'

The doctor replied that he had been crossing the lawn at the time, and that if the noise had come from outside the house, he must have heard it.

After Gertrude had reported the failure of her enquiries, her father asked her to tell her mother, who was in John's room, of the doctor's arrival. On her way upstairs, she looked into the West room, where she found that the others had been joined by Ellen, a faithful and attached servant, with the youngest child, then about two and a half, in her arms. Ellen said they had been in one of the rooms on the first landing when they had heard the shrieks, coming, as it were, from the West room or near it. The child asked, 'Who is screaming, Ellen? I didn't scream'; and picking her up the maid had run to the West room to find out what was the matter.

One of the children remarked: 'Poor Johnnie! How frightened he must have been!'

Whereupon Ellen suggested: 'Could it have been Master John seized with a fit?'

6

Struck with this idea, Gertrude ran upstairs. The door of her brother's room was partly open, and when she went in she saw him lying with a very placid look on his face. As she passed the bed, he gave her a look and a smile, but did not speak. Her mother was resting on the sofa and her aunt was reading by the window. Nothing, in short, could have been quieter or more composed than the room and its inmates.

After announcing the doctor's arrival, Gertrude went over to the bed to discover, if possible, without alarming her brother, if he had heard the shrieks.

'Johnnie, how quiet you look!' she said. 'Have you been asleep?'

'No, Gertie,' he replied, 'I was not asleep and I knew the doctor had come; I heard Dash give his little bark'—meaning a short single bark which the old dog, who lay on a mat in the hall, always gave when the doctor arrived. So it seemed that John had heard the bark, but not the awful shrieks which had rung through the house and been heard by everyone in it except himself and those who were with him.

The doctor was now on his way up, and Gertrude, as she left, beckoned to her aunt to follow her. In the West room she told her of their experience, the aunt replying that everything had been exceptionally quiet that afternoon in John's room. He had been lying awake, but without speaking, for some time; and no unusual noise of any kind had been heard.

An immediate search was made, every possible and impossible cause being sought for and suggested; but all was in vain; no explanation was forthcoming.

Next morning, the doctor came to breakfast, accompanied by his brother, the old clergyman, who occasionally visited John; and while they were there, the housekeeper and the farm bailiff were called in and questioned as to the result of the enquiries which, by Mr. Carnsen's orders, they had made. One point was clear: the sounds had been made *in* the house, since no one outside had heard them. The accounts of all those inside the house tallied: there had been three shrieks at short intervals; it was as though a woman's voice were being strained to the utmost; and the noise had ended in a dying rattle. What was most unaccountable was that the shrieks were loudest on the staircase, close to the West room, and therefore should have been distinctly audible in John's room just above; yet everyone there was utterly unconscious of them.

Nothing more could be done. The servants were given strict orders not to allow any report of what had happened to leak out. Mr. Carnsen, who disliked the subject so much that no one ventured afterwards to allude to it in his presence, enjoined a similar silence on the children. The clergyman, after hearing all the evidence, pronounced the incident to be of a kind for which it was impossible to give a natural explanation. He told us that we could not pretend to deny the reality of what we had heard, but must not give way to superstitious

8

fancies. Some lesson or warning, which time would make more clearly known, was intended.

From that day onwards, even those of us who had been most hopeful, found their confidence gone, though for another week John's health continued to show signs of improvement.

After that he took a turn for the worse, and three weeks from the day when the shrieks were heard, he died.

It may be asked whether a similar warning was given on the occasion of the death of any other member of the family. Fifteen years later, John's young sister, Emma, was on her deathbed. In the middle of the night, just before the end, those who were watching in her room heard sounds of hysterical wailing and lamentation passing through the house. The noises ceased as she drew her last breath. A few months later, when the daughters were watching by the deathbed of their mother, they had so strong an expectation of hearing that unearthly voice once more, that they told each other they ought to doubt the evidence of their senses if it came; but it did not come. Nor was any warning given of the deaths of two of the sons in distant lands, or when Mr. Carnsen himself passed away in March 1860, as he knelt in prayer by his bedside.

The Shrouded
Watcher

¶ This curious tale was taken from *Blackwood's Magazine* for January 1891.

IT IS MANY YEARS SINCE THE FOLLOWING REMARKABLE incident in my life took place. For the ordinary commonplace details of everyday experience my memory is generally indiff-erent, but the circumstances in this case were such that they have indelibly fixed themselves in my recollection, as though they had occurred yesterday

At the time I allude to, I was a very raw young ensign, scarcely done with the goose-step. My regiment was quartered in the —— Barracks, situated in a suburb of Valletta, the capital of Malta.

To make my narrative clearer, I will begin by presenting to the reader the chief character in it.

Ralph D—— was a young fellow with an odd history. What brought him to Malta none of us ever exactly knew. He was understood to have been in one of 'John Company's' regiments, but whether horse or foot, I cannot remember. His own account was that he had left the Indian service (for some unexplained reason), and having found his way to Vienna, got himself into a regiment of Austrian cavalry, as not a few British ex-officers managed at that time to do. But, for reasons best known to himself and the authorities, his stay in the Em-peror's service was not of long duration, and when I joined my regiment in Malta, D—— was a well-known character among the English residents and garrison. Not that the

notoriety was altogether conducive to his fair fame; but D——
had a singular way of worming himself into the good graces
of a particular set, and passed for a gentleman of affable manners, much wit, and especially a certain bold *diablerie* that stuck
at nothing, and gave him a kind of popularity among the
more daring spirits in society. How well I can call up his
appearance! Dark, brilliant eyes and black hair; a tall lithe
figure, with a very peculiar but really bewitching smile on
occasions when it suited him to please; and a beautifully
shaped contour of head and profile. He was known to be of
good family, and as he had been in the service, my regiment
had made him an honorary member of our mess; and I
rather think another corps in garrison had given him the
same *entrée* into theirs. At all events, he was on pretty good
terms with some of our fellows, though our colonel and one or
two of the older officers certainly did not encourage him
much, as his example was not considered beneficial to the
juniors.

D—— was a wonderful billiard player. I never saw anyone
to beat him at losing hazards or the spot stroke. As to pool,
our 'lives' were as nothing in his hands; and at all card games
in particular, both the skill and the luck of the man were
extraordinary. Night after night I have seen him at play, and
his winnings must have almost sufficed to maintain him. As
to other traits in his character, I am sorry to say I never heard
of one single good or generous sentiment that could be traced

to him. D——'s talk at the mess table or in the ante-room was of the most cynical flavour it was ever my lot to hear; and though *de mortuis nil nisi bonum* is an excellent and decent moral to abide by, truth compels me to add that some very sinister tales of D——'s influence over the other sex had got about at the time I speak of. What has now come to be digni-fied with the name of hypnotism was unknown as such in those days, but I believe D—— possessed some conspicuous powers in this direction, and I am afraid was not always over-scrupulous in his use of them. Even at this distance of time his portrait stands out clear in my mind's eye, with a kind of Rembrandt-like sheen upon it, by reason of the mysterious shadow in the background which was to loom up and cover it with the blackness of night. I ought perhaps to add, for the better understanding of what is to follow, that for a little while before the *dénouement* came, some ominous whisperings got afloat among us about D——, and the methods whereby so much silver and gold was perpetually being transferred at whist and *écarté* from other people's pockets to his own. For in my long experience of those holding her gracious Majesty's commission, notwithstanding a black sheep here and there, it is not to be denied that scrupulous honour and fair dealing have ever been in the forefront of their traditions.

I now come to the memorable day of the occurrence of the strange incident, to one phase of which I and others—most of them gone now—were eye-witnesses.

The season was Holy Week, towards the end of April 18—. Music has always been a passion with me, and every afternoon preceding Good Friday in that particular week, when I could get off duty from the dust and glare of the white parade-ground and the monotonous bawling of the drill-sergeant, it was my wont to steal away to the Duomo of San Giovanni. And who that has ever sat in that stately cathedral church, and in the dimly lighted atmosphere, odorous with incense, listened to the entrancing strains of the Office of Tenebrae, could ever forget it?

The eve of Good Friday arrived. I had gone over to see a friend on the Verdala side of the Grand Harbour and was returning after dark. The night was still, calm, and cloudless. The air was deliciously soft. As I sat in the stern of the gon-dola-shaped galley, while the dark figure of the boatman silently plied his long sweeps, great grey ramparts frowned on every side, and lights twinkled, flashing back in wavering duplicates from the faintly rippling water. I was soon along-side the low jetty on the Valletta side, and, ascending the great flight of steep stone steps, presently found myself in the strait Strada Reale. Here it was no easy matter threading one's way, for the procession of the Stazione, representing the main incidents of the Passion, was passing up the street. At all times this pageant has seemed to me full of solemnity, not-withstanding that the symbolic figures used are often some-what tawdry. In the intense silence and deep reverence of the

16

spectators, as the wail of the music swells louder and louder; in the sacred form upraised on a colossal cross, flanked by the two malefactors on lesser crosses; in the sudden baring of all heads, as the shrouded platform-bearers go by—in all this one feels the cardinal truth borne in upon one, despite all the gewgaws and evanescent emotion of the scene.

There were reasons why this strange Passion procession on this particular Holy Thursday night should have stamped itself deep upon my memory. Even at the time it seemed to capture me, as I passed up the long narrow street out of hearing of the wild music, and reached the great stone gateway of our barrack square.

The echo of the sentry's sharp challenge, followed by 'Pass, friend—all's well', had hardly died down when I found myself at the door of my quarters, which faced the officers' mess block. By this time the Paschal moon, all but full, was high in the sky, and cast a great shadow from the tall buildings facing the range of barracks across the parade-ground. Though on this night superfluous, a feeble oil-lamp flickered here and there, for gas was a luxury not then indulged in, and the department which was charged with these things loved darkness better than light, because it cost less.

I should here explain that Thursdays were the guest nights of my regiment at that time, and on this evening the regimental band had as usual been playing on the open space just outside, fronting the mess-room windows. It must have been past eleven o'clock when I reached barracks; and although most of the outsiders who were allowed in to hear the music on such occasions were gone, I noticed two or three still waiting about. One in particular, a remarkably tall man in a long dark cloak, was standing under one of the mess windows with his back to me. I sauntered into my room, lit a cigar, and came out again, to muse in the quiet moonlight over the Tenebrae and the Stazione. By this time the loiterers were all gone except the tall cloaked man, who appeared to have never moved or changed his position since I saw him first. The open windows of the mess-room were still aglow, and through the boughs of a row of lank stunted trees along the enclosure wall one could see the distant twinkling lights of the town.

Something in the appearance of this solitary shrouded figure attracted and fixed my attention. To be so attired on a warm balmy night like this, in a semi-tropical climate, seemed peculiar. And I had already been struck by his phenomenal stature, contrasted with those who had been standing beside him. Who could the man be, and what on earth was he waiting there for? It crossed my mind that this must be either one of the dominoed *incogniti* who had been following in the Passion procession, or else one of the Capuchins from a neighbouring monastery; but a friar would hardly stroll in to listen to a military band, and then stand stock-still alone under the windows of the officers' mess. With the passing thought came the sound of pretty loud talking, and occasionally a laugh, from the lit-up ante-room opposite, where it was plain some of our fellows were probably engaged at whist, loo, or some other card game. Why I cannot tell, but along with a feeling of undefinable repulsion towards him, an impulse seized on me to watch the muffled stranger closely, and at the same time I had an awakening consciousness that I had better walk straight over and ask the man what he wanted there at that time of night. As my gaze fastened itself on the motionless figure, whose head seemed in the bright moon-light to be bent a little to one side in an intent listening atti-tude, I became aware of a kind of chill and numbness creeping through my limbs, with that horrible sense of inability to move forward one occasionally experiences in dreams when something dreadful is going to happen which one wants to avert. Yes, whoever the man was, most assuredly he must be watching and waiting and listening for something or some-body in the mess-room, with that strained intentness yet absolute quiescence of posture! But why this vehement and altogether unaccountable foreboding of impending evil borne in upon me?

These thoughts, however, were all the work of a few seconds, when, with eyes still riveted on the mysterious watcher, I heard several voices within the room calling out in excited tones, as though some altercation were going on. One voice above all the others came with a kind of strident harsh-ness through the open window, in which it was easy to recognise D——'s hard and distinct accents. I seem to hear the words rasping out now as I write. 'I tell you, I dealt myself the ace of spades'; then another voice, young N——'s, 'I take my oath you didn't'; and then a terrible imprecation from D——, which I will not repeat, invoking the Prince of Darkness to the ruin of his soul and body, if what he had stated was not the truth.

As the last words struck on my ear, the tall cloaked figure made an instantaneous movement, leaped up with a light swift spring to the window-sill he was standing under, and disappeared through the muslin curtains into the room, for I was unable to see farther into it from my position. Another instant, and an ear-piercing scream rang out—a harsh, appalling cry as of mingled pain, rage, and terror, from one in dire extremity—and to my horror and utter amazement he in the cloak reappeared at the window with D—— gripped in his arms, and half slung over one shoulder, apparently struggling desperately. One instant both faces were visible in the moonlight, D——'s ghastly and convulsed, the other set back in its sombre hood and covered with a black domino, from the eyelets of which I was near enough to catch a lightning flash of fiendish malignancy and exultation. Ere I could collect my bewildered senses sufficiently to rush across to stop them, which I did a moment later, both men had vanished round an angle of the building. After them I rushed, shouting to the gate-sentry to alarm the guard, but on reaching the rear of the block not a soul was in sight. Out turned the guard, and telling the sergeant to take a file and search the enclosure for two men fighting, I ran round to the mess-room. Meanwhile, and before I could reach the entrance-door to the mess, the bell inside was ringing out peal after peal, and an officer came tear-ing out full tilt, nearly knocking me down. 'What is it?' I burst out. 'Where's C——' (our regimental doctor)? 'Is he in his quarters?' he demanded, and away he rushed towards the quarter where Dr. C—— lived. I ran into the ante-room along with one or two of the mess-waiters, helter-skelter. And what a sight inside! There, huddled in a group, with pale scared faces, a whist-table overturned, and a litter of cards strewn all over the floor, were some half-dozen of my comrades of the —th, stooping over the prostrate form of D——, who lay motionless, with lips apart, eyeballs fixed and staring, his head lying back supported by one of our fellows. The surgeon, C——, came in a minute after, tore open D——'s waistcoat and shirt, looked hard at him, knelt down and put his ear to the drawn mouth, felt about the region of the heart, and shook his head. D—— was dead.

As for myself, I could hardly believe my senses. The man I had just seen bodily carried off struggling in the arms of an unknown individual, lying here dead—it seemed an absolute hallucination! I was too taken aback to ask a single question; but as my enquiring eyes went round the circle of assembled officers, I could see in the countenances of all a certain constraint mingled with their horror, but not a syllable was said. It was plain there was a further mystery behind.

The remains of the ill-fated D—— were removed to a spare room in the officers' quarters, and there laid out to await official proceedings on the morrow.

It was not till after the funeral that I learned what had caused the uproar and altercation in the mess-room, which immediately preceded the terribly sudden catastrophe of that memorable night. And even at this distance of time I tell the circumstances with pain and reluctance. D—— had dined with the regiment, and after the band had finished playing, he and some half-dozen subalterns sat down to play *vingt-et-un*. The stakes were high, and it was noticed that D—— turned up a remarkable number of 'naturals'. N——, a not long-joined ensign, had been dealt an ace of spades and 'stood'. At the conclusion of the round, D——, who was dealing, again showed a 'natural', the ace of which proved to be the ace of spades. This, of course, was too much for young N——, green as he was. Hence the indignant remonstrance wafted out to my ears in the barrack square, followed by that awful oath. Whereupon, according to some of the party, a momentary gust of air seemed to shake the farther window-sash, and simultaneously the card-table was stirred—it was, they said, like the tremor of a slight earthquake shock—and straightway D—— threw his hands up and fell back in his chair, gurgling like one in a fit. The rest I have told, and I will say no more upon it.

Needless to say, the officers of her Majesty's —th were for long thereafter chary of conferring upon outsiders the privilege of honorary membership of their mess. We kept our impressions as far as possible to ourselves, though something about them necessarily leaked out through the guard and sentry I had hailed, and from my original statements concerning the pair I believed I had seen so palpably in the moonlight.

When the formal inquiry by the military and civil authorities came on, it was elicited from the non-commissioned officer of the night-guard that no person of the description I gave had been seen to enter or leave the barrack precincts. The certified cause of death was stated to be aneurism, spasm, or something of the heart—what I suppose we loosely call heart disease. The affair was rather hushed up, in deference to the feelings of D——'s relatives, one of whom came out to the island shortly afterwards to make inquiries and settle up the affairs of the deceased.

It may be suggested that what I witnessed in the square was no more than a phantasm of my own brain. I should probably have inclined to such a view myself, but for one circumstance. In the room above mine, and looking out on the square towards the mess-house, was quartered a very dear fellow, rather a favourite with us, although hardly robust enough for a soldier's

23

life. It happened on this very Thursday evening that this man, S——, who had been ailing of Malta fever, was lying on a couch in his room by the open window—the night being so warm—and listening to the band. He was still there when I came into barracks and was arrested by the sight of the tall, solitary figure opposite. When, several days after the event, I touched on the subject, S—— broke in with a very troubled face, and in a serious, urgent voice asked: 'Did you see the man in the long cloak waiting for him?' Then I knew that whatever extra vision had been vouchsafed to me had been shared by him.

Apparitions

THE GHOSTLY PASSENGER

Lord Halifax had this story from a *Yorkshire* friend and neighbour who 'was told it by *Captain Wintour* four years ago'. It was a special favourite, and he used to relate how once, driving in a dog-cart with a *Yorkshire* groom, he told it to his companion, whose comment pleased him greatly. 'There's nothing strange about that, my Lord,' the groom had said, 'because the soul always returns to the body once in twenty-four hours until the funeral.'

ONE EVENING, AFTER A DAY'S SHOOTING AT HOME, I WAS on my way to stay with my friend Marsh at Gaynes Park. I had a drive of some fourteen miles to make and at one point had to cross a bridge over a stream. As I approached, I saw a man leaning over the parapet and looking down into the river below. Noticing that he had a bag by his side and thinking he might be tired, I stopped the dog-cart which I was driving and offered to give him a lift if he was going in my direction. He climbed into the cart without a word and sat there in silence. I made two attempts to draw him into conversation, but gave up trying when he made no sign of responding.

We drove along for some miles together in silence, until we came to a village, where I pulled up, rather suddenly, outside the inn. By this time it was quite dark. The inn was lighted up, some people were standing in front of the house, and the ostler came forward at once to take my horse's head. My companion got down and without one word of thanks to me walked straight into the inn. 'Who is that man who has just climbed

27

down?' I asked the ostler. He replied that he had not seen any-one. 'Well, the man I drove up with,' I said; to which he answered: 'You drove up alone, Sir.'

Feeling very uncomfortable, I went into the inn and sent for the landlord. When I told him of my companion and described him, he looked grave and asked me to follow him upstairs. He took me into a room, and there on a bed lay the man to whom I had given the lift. He was dead, and had been dead for some time; in fact, an inquest had just been held on his body. A day or two earlier he had been found drowned in the stream, close to the bridge where I had seen him.

THE FAWN LADY OF BURTON AGNES

Burton Agnes is a famous *Yorkshire* house, of which many ghostly stories have been told, particularly in connection with the Screaming Skull. The following short tale was sent to *Lord Halifax* in 1915 by *Mrs. Wickham-Boynton*, the owner.

Mrs. Lane Fox[1] tells me that you were interested to hear I had seen the ghost here last month and that you would like to know more about it. We were having tea in the hall, when I looked up suddenly and saw a small thin woman dressed in *fawn* colour come out of the garden, walk very quickly up the steps, and disappear through the front door, which I thought was open, into the house. I imagined it must

[1]Lord Halifax's daughter, now Lady Bingley.

be the parson's wife and remarked to my husband, who had seen nothing: 'There is Mrs. Coutts. Go and bring her in.' He went out at once, but presently came back to say that there was no one there and that the front door was shut.

Then I remembered the old story of a fawn lady who had been seen about the place. Oddly enough, the last time she appeared, many years ago, she was also hurrying up steps into the house; but they were the steps on the east front. My father saw her and followed her inside, but she had vanished. She is probably the Griffith ancestress, A.D. 1620, whose skull is still in the house here, though no one knows exactly where it is walled up. Her sister and heir married Sir Matthew Boynton and so brought Burton Agnes into the family. Of course I am told it was all imagination, but it was very curious.

THE PAGE BOY OF HAYNE

In 1885, when *Lord Halifax* was staying with his father-in-law at *Powderham Castle, Devonshire,* among the guests was a *Lady Ferguson Davie,* wife of *Sir John Ferguson Davie* of *Creedy,* who was old *Lord Devon's* nephew. One evening, when ghost stories were being told in the hall, *Lady Davie* made the following contribution.

Some years ago Mr. Harris of Hayne, in Devon, had a good deal of his plate stolen, and with the plate there disappeared a little page boy who had been for some time in his service. Although every effort was made, neither the plate nor the boy could be traced, and Mr. Harris was so much upset by the whole occurrence that he went away and was absent for a good long while. One night, shortly after his return home, he saw, or fancied he saw, the page boy standing at the foot of his bed. Supposing that he had been dreaming, or that his imagination had played him a trick, he turned over and went to sleep, scarcely giving the matter another thought; the next night he again saw, or fancied he saw, the same figure stand, ing by his bedside, and again he took no notice; but when on the third night the page boy appeared once more, Mr. Harris got up out of bed, and when the figure left the room he fol, lowed it. The boy moved down the passage and the stairs, always a little ahead of him, turning round constantly and beckoning to him, as though he were trying to lead him some, where. At length he passed out of the house altogether, with Mr. Harris still following, and came to a wood close by. Here he disappeared, at the foot of a very large hollow tree.

Next day Mr. Harris had the tree cut down. Inside it were found the remains of the boy and a portion of the plate. The discovery led to the apprehension and confession of the butler, who admitted that he had made away with the plate little by little, as opportunity offered; that he had hidden it in the hollow tree until he was able to dispose of it; and that, find, ing that the page boy had discovered what was going on, he had murdered him, concealing the body in the tree with the plate.

THE GHOST OF LORD CONYERS OSBORNE

Under the date November 16th, 1884, *Lord Halifax* wrote in the *Ghost Book:*

I was staying with the Rev. John Sharp on the occasion of his jubilee, when the Bishop of Winchester,[1] who was also there, told the following stories. George William Frederick, 6th Duke of Leeds, married Lady Charlotte Townshend, daughter of George, 1st Marquis Townshend. Their second son, Lord Conyers Osborne, who was up at Christ Church, was killed accidentally by Lord Downshire on May 6th, 1812. The Bishop had the story from Mrs. George Portal, whose aunt, Lady James Townshend, had married the brother of the Duchess of Leeds. Lady James had told Mrs. Portal that one evening she was sitting writing in her room, when she saw Lord Conyers, wearing a dressing-gown which she had embroidered for him, walk straight through. She rang the bell and asked the butler if Lord Conyers had come. The man replied that he had not, seeming surprised at the question and hinting that Lady James must have been asleep and dreaming. She, however, was so much impressed by what she thought she had seen that, before going to bed, she wrote to Lord James to tell him about it.

Next day Lord Conyers' servant arrived from Oxford. He asked to see Lady James, and when he was shown into her

[1]Bishop Harold Browne, a ghost-hunter after Lord Halifax's heart.

room, told her that his young master had been killed wrestling with Lord Downshire at Christ Church. He begged her to break the news to the Duchess of Leeds, as he did not dare do so himself.

Years afterwards, when Lord James was dead, Mrs. Portal was reading over and tearing up old letters with her aunt; and in a bundle of them, which she was about to destroy, she found the letter to Lord James, describing Lord Conyers' appearance.

★

THE GHOST OF LADY CARNARVON

The Bishop [Lord Halifax went on] also told us this story, on the authority either of Mrs. or Miss Portal, who lived close to Highclere, Lord Carnarvon's place in Hampshire.

Some time ago, Lord Carnarvon's brother, the Hon. Alan Herbert (who was a doctor in Paris) was lying dangerously ill at Highclere. One day, when he was almost unconscious, the nurse saw a lady dressed in black enter the room and draw back the curtains of the bed. She then nodded her head in a very peculiar way. The nurse did not know who the lady was, but supposed her to be some relation staying in the house. Some time afterwards, when Mr. Herbert was getting better, the housekeeper, showing the nurse over the house, took her into Lord Carnarvon's private sitting-room. 'Why,' said the nurse, pointing to a picture over the chimney-piece, 'there is the lady who came into the room and looked at Mr. Herbert.'

It was a portrait of Lady Carnarvon, Alan Herbert's mother, who had died some years before.[1] She always dressed in black and had a peculiar way of nodding her head.

THE GHOST OF BISHOP WILBERFORCE

This story seems to have been collected on the same occasion as the two preceding ones, and the narrator was probably *Bishop Browne*.

The late Bishop of Winchester (Dr. Wilberforce) had often expressed a wish to see Wooton, Mr. Evelyn's place, not far from Guildford. He was particularly interested in a portrait there of Mrs. Godolphin, whose life he had written in his early days. Somehow he had never been able to pay the visit, but on the occasion of his death he was riding with Lord Granville about two miles from Wooton. Mr. Evelyn, the doctor, a Mr. Harvey, and a brother of Mr. Evelyn's were sitting in the dining-room at Wooton when one of the party exclaimed: 'Why, there is the Bishop of Winchester looking in at the window!' They all looked and saw a figure, which disappeared. They went out to see if the Bishop was there, but there was nobody. Half an hour later a servant came in with the news of the Bishop's death. He had been killed by a fall from his horse on his way to Holmbury, where Lord Granville was living.

[1]She was the wife of the 3rd Earl of Carnarvon and died in 1876.

THE SHIP IN DISTRESS

On board a certain ship, the name of which I cannot recall, the words 'Steer to the north-east' were found one morning written on the slate log in the captain's cabin. No one on board would admit to having written the entry, which excited a good deal of wonder and speculation. The mate, however, said he had an idea that he had seen a strange man writing in the captain's cabin. Eventually the captain altered the course of the vessel and steered north-east, as directed, with the result that later on in the day a water-logged vessel with a starving crew was sighted. When the rescued sailors were taken aboard, the mate, looking at one of them, exclaimed, 'That is the man I fancied I saw writing in the captain's cabin.' The man in question was then asked to write the words 'Steer to the north-east' on a slate, without, however, being told the reason for the request. He did so, and the writing was found to be identical with that previously found on the log. On enquiry, it transpired that this particular man had always been certain that he and his mates would be rescued. Early on the morning of the day on which they were picked up, he had fallen into a kind of trance; and on waking up, he had declared that he was more assured than ever that help was at hand.

A similar story was that of a young midshipman, who was drowned on his way home from a foreign station, yet brought a letter from the admiral on the station to his wife. Mr. Church, then Vicar of Hickleton, capped this tale with the information that his grandmother had seen her husband walking in the garden in his uniform, at the very moment when, as was subsequently discovered, he was killed on active service in India.

THE WIDOW IN THE TRAIN

The *Colonel Ewart* mentioned in this story was very possibly the uncle of *Mr. H. B. Ewart,* an old friend of *Lord Halifax. Mr. Ewart* has some recollection of having heard the story from his uncle.

A Colonel Ewart was travelling alone by express train from Carlisle to London. He went to sleep and, when he woke up, found that a lady in black with a crape veil had entered his compartment and occupied one of the corner seats. As he had been asleep for some time, he supposed she must have entered rather quietly and apologised to her for being without his coat and his boots. The lady made no reply, and thinking she might be deaf and had not heard him, he crossed to the other side of the compartment and sat down in the seat opposite to her. But when he repeated his apology, she still did not answer and seemed as though she did not hear him. He thought her conduct strange and was still wondering about it when there came a sudden crash. There had been a collision. Colonel Ewart was unhurt and at once jumped out to see what had happened and if he could be of any use. Then, remembering the lonely lady in his compartment and wondering if she were frightened or injured, he went back. The carriage was empty; there was no trace of the lady anywhere; and the guard declared that the door had been locked, although the collision had forced it open, and that no one could possibly have come in since Carlisle, as the train had not stopped anywhere until the accident occurred.

Later Colonel Ewart learnt that a few years before, a bride and bridegroom had been travelling on the same line and by a corresponding train. The man had put his head too far out of the window to look at something, and it had been caught by a wire, so that the headless body had fallen back into the carriage. At the next station the bride was found singing a lullaby over her husband's body. The shock had driven her completely mad.

KILLED IN ACTION

A certain clergyman had three sons. The eldest was serving in the Crimea, and the two younger ones, who were at school, had come home for the holidays. The boys slept in the same room, their beds, which were on opposite sides of it, facing each other, foot to foot. The window of the room was close to the door and could be seen equally well from either bed. One night one of the boys woke up and saw the figure of his brother, then in the Crimea, kneeling at the window in an attitude of prayer. He called out to his sleeping brother, asking him if he could see anything; and he, waking up replied, 'Yes, I see Arthur kneeling at the window.' As they spoke, the kneeling figure turned and gave them a sad and loving look.

The boys were frightened and wondered how they could get out of the room without passing by the kneeling figure. At last they made a rush past the window, reached the door, roused their father, and told him what they had seen. He went up to their room and, finding nothing there, concluded they must have been dreaming. He told them, however, to say nothing to their mother of what they thought had appeared to them.

Two or three weeks later news came from the Crimea of an attack upon the Sandbank Battery, in which Arthur had been killed. One day, after the end of the war, when the troops had come home, the family had a visit from the chaplain attached to the regiment in which Arthur had served. He told them that, though a stranger to them, he had felt so great an interest in their son that he was impelled to come and see them. He went on to say that on the night before the attack on the Battery their son and a few other officers had asked to be given Holy Communion; that Arthur was quite certain that he would be killed; and that, while expressing no particular wish to live, he had said he would have liked to see his two brothers again.

The Troubled Spirit of Tintern Abbey

¶ This story was privately printed in 1910 and sent to *Lord Halifax* apparently by the author, who subscribed himself *'E.B.'*

IT WAS, I THINK, IN THE SPRING OF 1895 THAT MY WIFE and I went for a bicycling tour along the Wye. In due course we arrived at Tintern, where we proposed to stay for a couple of nights. After luncheon we inspected the ruins, and paid them a second visit after dinner, as it was a delicious evening with brilliant moonlight.

My wife has at times the power of writing automatically. She rarely exercises it, as she somewhat mistrusts herself and therefore prefers to leave these matters alone. However, that evening the beauty and mystery of the ruined Abbey impelled me to ask her if she had any psychic feelings. She replied that she had. We sat down upon a block of masonry, and almost at once her right hand was controlled as it were by an invisible agency which made it rap repeatedly on her knee. She asked that the action should be moderated, and I suggested that if anyone wished to communicate with us, three taps should be given for 'yes' and one for 'no'.

Her hand at once rose and fell three times, more gently than before, and we established communication by the tedious but usual process of going slowly through the alphabet until a rap announced that the right letter had been reached. Many questions and answers resulted in our receiving the following information.

The personality or control in communication with us purported to be that of a Saxon soldier who had died fighting for King Henry II. On my expressing surprise that a Saxon should have been defending a Norman king, he maintained that his account of himself was nevertheless true. He had fallen in the neighbourhood of the Abbey and had been buried without any prayer being said over his body; and although, like most people, he had been neither very good nor very bad, and was not unhappy in his present state, he would be in, finitely easier if a Mass could be said for him. When I re, marked that the Abbey, near by which he said he had been buried, did not exist in the time of Henry II, he replied that there had been an earlier abbey on the same spot, a statement which I was not in a position to dispute. I then asked how it was that, after the lapse of many hundred years, he should apply for assistance to a couple of Anglicans whose Church did not include prayers for the dead among its doctrines. He answered that he had frequently, but without success, tried to communi, cate with his descendants and others, that the difference of religion did not affect the question, and that he would be most grateful if we would have a Mass said for him. This we promised to do; whereupon he thanked us and bade us goodnight.

My wife's arm was released from the control and we went home to bed greatly interested but not in the least excited. Either that night or the following morning I wrote to an old friend of mine, Father A—— and, without going into details, told him that, as the result of a strange experience, I was anxious to see him in order to arrange, if possible, for Masses to be said for the repose of a soul. I added that I was uncertain whether his Church would allow such Masses when there was no means of identifying the person for whom they were to be said.

We visited the Abbey again in the daytime but nothing unusual took place; but that night the same phenomenon occurred, my wife's arm was at once controlled, and a message was given expressing gratitude for what we had done. I asked if we could be of any further help, but was assured that if two Masses could be said, the spirit would never trouble us again. The control then ceased and we went home.

On reaching London a few days later and referring to Green's *History*, I found that the amalgamation between Saxons and Normans had made great progress by Henry II's reign, and, indeed, that the Saxons, having accepted their foreign kings, were the more loyal of the two races, frequently supporting the monarch against his turbulent barons.

Presently I heard from Father A——, giving me an appointment and adding that his Church gave full power to the priesthood to say Masses for the unknown departed. I told him the whole story, which greatly interested him, and he promised to say four Masses for the troubled spirit of the Saxon soldier. In the following year he died. I did not expect to hear anything more of our friend at Tintern, but ten years later, in 1905, he gave us the following reminder of his existence.

43

One evening in November of that year, having several friends to dinner who were interested in so-called spiritualistic phenomena, we agreed to have a sitting round a table. About seven people were present, among them two ladies known to be possessed of remarkable psychic powers. One of them was an intimate friend; the other we had met that evening for the first time.

We sat down. It was not quite dark, for a fire was burning. At first a number of messages from acquaintances who had passed away were delivered in the usual way by raps or the tilting of the table, until the power seemed to be exhausted and the manifestations ceased. Thereupon our new acquaintance grew impatient and pressed with some heat for further messages to be given. My wife protested, pointing out that we should not try to force the power; whatever it might be, it should be treated with courtesy. The table immediately tilted towards her and slowly rapped out the words 'Very many thanks'. We thought she was being thanked for her remonstrance, but the taps continued. The whole message was 'Very many thanks for the Masses said'. Afterwards the two psychic ladies, who were sitting on either side of my wife, said that they had seen standing behind her the bearded figure of a handsome middle-aged man, dressed in strange close-fitting clothes of a grey material. Some years before, we had told our story to one of the two ladies, but it was not known to anyone else in the room.

44

Labédoyère's
Doom

¶ This story appeared in the January number of *Fraser's Magazine*, 1882. The author was *Canon Malcolm MacColl*, a well-known priest with whom *Lord Halifax* was personally acquainted.

OF ALL NAPOLEON'S VICTORIES, THE BATTLE OF Marengo is considered by military critics to have been, on the whole, the most brilliant in conception that he ever fought, as it certainly was one of the most fruitful in its results. Yet, after all, it may be said to have been won by a fluke. The passage of the Alps by the First Consul took the ever-unready Austrians completely by surprise. Their forces were scattered among the fortresses of Lombardy and Piedmont, and their generals were disconcerted by the sudden apparition of Napoleon, and by the unexpected tactics which he pursued. Masséna, with a small French and Cisalpine garrison, was shut up in Genoa by an Austrian army and blockading squadron; and both he and the Austrians expected that Napoleon would march to the relief of the besieged. Meanwhile the Austrian commander-in-chief, the Baron de Melas, was in Turin hurriedly collecting his forces.

But, instead of marching on Genoa, Napoleon turned to the east and placed his army between the Austrians and their own fortresses. He entered Milan and seized the passages of the Po and the Adda without firing a shot. Piacenza fell an easy prey, and in a few days Melas was completely cut off from his communications north of the Po. The Austrian commander was thus reduced to the dilemma of cutting his way through the French lines or making his escape to Genoa,

Masséna having in the interval surrendered on condition of being allowed to retire with all his garrison.

The besieging force, being thus released from Genoa, hastened to join Baron de Melas at Alessandria. Even then the Austrians could only muster 30,000 men out of the 80,000 which they had foolishly scattered in weak detach/ments all over Lombardy. Napoleon, whose force was also about 30,000, had his centre half/way between Piacenza and Alessandria. He made sure that Melas would retreat rapidly on Genoa, and despatched accordingly the divisions of Desaix and Monnier to intercept him. But Melas did not retreat. He made up his mind to give Napoleon battle, and quietly awaited his approach at Alessandria. As soon as he discovered the mistake which Napoleon had made, he issued from his stronghold and flung his whole force against the weakened French line, first at Montebello, and then at Marengo.

After seven hours' fighting, the French, in spite of Napol/eon's exertions and Murat's brilliant charges, in spite also of the heroic stand made by the grenadiers of the Consular Guard, were driven into a narrow defile where they were exposed to the Austrian artillery and almost surrounded by the Austrian infantry and cavalry. Having made his dis/positions and secured, as he thought, his prey, the Austrian commander returned into Alessandria to take a little rest before summoning the French to surrender. So certain did he feel as to the issue of the battle that he sent out despatches announcing a victory.

Meanwhile, however, the sound of the cannonade behind them had reached the ears of Desaix and Monnier and caused them to hurry back to Marengo. They were met by a multitude of panic-stricken French fugitives, who declared that the battle was lost. 'Then we will win another,' gaily replied Desaix. The fugitives immediately turned back with him. The French, thus reinforced, renewed the fight: the Austrians, completely off their guard, were thrown into confusion by the suddenness of the onset; and Murat completed their overthrow by one of his impetuous charges.

The victory was dearly bought by the death of Desaix, but the prize which it yielded was magnificent. The Baron de Melas, utterly stupefied by so great a disaster after so signal a victory, sued for a truce and agreed to purchase it by the surrender of Genoa and all the fortresses of Lombardy and Piedmont. Probably he had no alternative, for he was completely severed from his communications and his army was broken and demoralised.

The battle of Marengo was thus a turning-point in Napoleon's career. The fortunate return of Desaix at the critical moment saved the First Consul from surrender or death. What a change in the map and history of Europe those few hours made! Napoleon knew well the importance of securing to himself in the estimation of the French the sole credit of the victory of Marengo. He collected and destroyed every document which told the true story of the battle and wrote his own account of it in a despatch which ascribed all the glory of victory and its stupendous consequences to his own genius and courage. To possess the French mind with his own story of Marengo was in fact to establish his ascendancy beyond the reach of all competitors.

How was this to be accomplished? It did not take Napoleon long to decide that question. He had a favourite young *aide-de-camp*, Labédoyère by name, on whose zeal and devotion he could thoroughly rely. To him he entrusted the task of bearing the Napoleonic version of the battle of Marengo to Paris. Relays of fresh horses were ordered along the road, and Labédoyère was directed to ride by way of Genoa and the Riviera de Ponente, and proclaim along the coastline the last splendid achievement of the First Consul's genius.

The battle of Marengo was fought on June 14th, 1800, and on the morning of the following day young Labédoyère started for Paris. His ride, as far as Avignon, took him through some of the most splendid scenery in Europe, but he had little time to admire it. His orders were to have Napoleon's despatch published *in extenso* in Paris within nine days of his parting from the First Consul, and to communicate a summary of its contents to the proper authorities in the principal places *en route*. This involved desperately hard riding. From Genoa to

Nice the young *aide-de-camp* only paused once, except for the purpose of refreshment and changing horses; and that one pause nearly cost him his life.

The shadows of evening were falling as he passed through Mentone, and before he had reached the summit of the mountain that separates Mentone from Nice, the light of day had completely vanished. A bend of the road brought him in sudden view of the sea lying far beneath him and gleaming tremulously in the light of the moon and stars. An ejaculation of delight escaped from his lips and he stopped to contemplate the scene.

His reverie was rudely and almost fatally broken. His horse took fright at something and made a violent bound, which threw its rider clean out of the saddle and over the parapet. With no worse injury than some superficial scratches, he regained the road, where he found his horse standing quietly, though still trembling from the fright.

On the morning of June 23rd, Labédoyère reached Paris. He had accomplished his long ride well within the prescribed time. As he passed Notre-Dame about eight o'clock in the morning, the door of the cathedral was open and the interior looked cool and refreshing, in striking contrast with the glare of the streets and the aching of his tired limbs. Seized by a sudden impulse to refresh himself in the coolness, and at the same time to return thanks to God for the safe accomplishment of his journey, he dismounted, handed the bridle of his horse to a bystander, and entered the church with his despatch-bag slung over his shoulder.

He was, as far as he could see, the only occupant, but after a while a priest came out of the sacristy and began to say Mass at one of the side altars. He was a venerable-looking old man, with scanty locks of white hair falling almost down to his shoulders. In figure he was tall and thin, but the most striking part of his person was his face. It was handsome and noble, but wore an expression of such hopeless yet unrepining sorrow as to impress Labédoyère with a vague feeling of mingled sympathy and terror. The old man's pensive grey eyes, too, when they turned in the direction of Labédoyère, seemed to be gazing so intently at something beyond, that the young *aide-de-camp* could not help looking instinctively behind him. But there was nothing but the empty floor and the dead wall of the cathedral. And the voice of the priest, even in the low tone in which he said Mass, had a weird, musical, pathetic wail in it. Altogether Labédoyère felt fascinated, whether by attraction or repulsion he could hardly tell.

Meanwhile, the priest, having administered the Sacrament to himself, looked round to see if there were any intending communicants present. Labédoyère was the only person in the church, and he, still under the spell of those sad grey eyes, moved, half mechanically, towards the altar, knelt down in front of the old priest, and received the Sacrament. Then, just as he was rising to return to his seat, the old man whispered in his ear: 'Young man, the soldier's calling is not favourable, in these days especially, to the vocation of a Christian. All the more do I rejoice that the darts of temptation, to which a soldier's life is so perilously exposed, have thus far glanced scatheless from your shield of faith and purity.'

As he said this, a look of great pain flitted across the old man's face. But he continued: 'I have been struck with your simple faith and unaffected devotion—qualities, alas! too rare nowadays in men of your years and calling. Is there anything I can do for you? For I should like to serve you.'

Labédoyère, taken utterly aback, stammered out: 'No, there is nothing.' But instantly, observing the priest's disappointed look, and being unwilling to hurt his feelings, he asked: 'But what do you mean? What kind of service do you speak of?'

'I have the gift of foretelling future events,' said the old man. 'Is there anything you would like to know as to your future life? Any danger which timely knowledge might avert? Any obstacle in the way of legitimate desire which I might help you to remove?'

Labédoyère, more for the sake of saying something than from any other cause, answered: 'Well, if you can really see into the future, will you tell me how long I have to live?'

All this time the old man's eyes had a fixed, absent, anxious look, as if watching for some expected apparition. On hearing Labédoyère's question, he started and waved his arms violently as if repelling some advancing object, while at

53

the same time his face betokened extreme terror. In a moment, however, he recovered his composure and said to Labédoyère, in a slightly agitated tone of voice:

'I wish you had not asked me that question. And yet, perhaps, it is best as it is. Yes, yes; no doubt you have been sent to me for the very purpose of receiving this warning. You wish to know how long you have to live. I am commissioned to tell you that on this day twelvemonth, at midnight, you will die. And now, my son, since this is a danger which no foresight can avert, you must prepare yourself to meet it. You think me cruel'—this was in answer to a look half of terror, half of reproach, on the face of Labédoyère—'no, my son, the message you have received through me has been sent to you in love. Think how many are called suddenly out of this life without a moment's preparation. Not that I would have you suppose that sudden death is necessarily in itself an evil, or that a sure warning of the day and hour of one's death is necessarily in itself a blessing. Warning of death is a distinct disadvantage to a being on probation unless it works a fundamental change, not simply in his conduct, but in his principles and motives. The best preparation for death is diligence in the task allotted to us. Go home, therefore, my son, and remember this day twelvemonth at midnight. But in the meantime neglect not the duties of your daily life.'

The old priest then finished the service somewhat hurriedly and disappeared into the sacristy.

Labédoyère remained kneeling on the altar steps, dazed and stupefied. The disappearance of the priest recalled him to himself. He rose and moved slowly to the seat where he had left his cap and despatch-bag. Kneeling down, he buried his face in his hands and made an effort to recall his wandering thoughts and assure himself that it was not all a dream. Satisfied on that point, he next tried to persuade himself that the old priest was crazed, and had mistaken the aberration of an eccentric imagination for the inspiration of a Divine message. But there was that in the voice, look and manner of the old man which would not square with this theory, something which Labédoyère felt, though he could not explain it, and of which he could not shake off the impression. He had a vivid presentiment that it would be perilous to disregard the warning so mysteriously given. 'After all,' he said, 'my prudent course is to assume that the doom just pronounced on me will be fulfilled. Let me see; I have a year before me. If the old man spoke truth, I need not fear death in the interval. That, at least, is some compensation. I will divide my year into two equal portions. The first half I shall devote to seeing what I can of life; the life of a great city; the life of women and children, of gaiety and brightness, as well as of soldiers hacking each other to pieces for the sake of glory. But I should like to see the old priest once more. I must get his address, for he may be of use to me.'

But the old priest had left the church and Labédoyère could not discover anything about him, not even his name.

The verger said he was a stranger who had 'asked for an altar at which to say his Mass'; and no one knew whence he had come or whither he had gone.

Labédoyère rode straight to his *appartement*, not far from Notre-Dame. After breakfast and a short nap, he sallied out to arrange for the publication of Napoleon's despatch on the morrow. His next step was to resign his commission and leave the army.

The Parisians have always shown a wonderful alacrity in passing from the deepest despondency to the utmost gaiety. At this period, Paris was just emerging out of the gloom and agony of the Reign of Terror. It was but six years previously that Robespierre had closed his career on the scaffold to which he had sent so many others. But all that was forgotten in the buoyancy of spirits caused by the wonderful success of the arms of France across the Alps and beyond the Rhine. Paris was enriched by the spoils and forced contributions of the conquered. She was thus wealthy and gay and proud when Labédoyère plunged into the vortex of her pleasures. For a season he enjoyed them with all the zest of inexperienced youth. The image of the old priest soon vanished from his memory, and with it the predicted doom. Presently, however, they returned with added and tragic force.

Labédoyère, as was natural to a man of his age and susceptible temperament, had fallen in love. Whether it was natural that he should have fallen in love with a woman considerably older than himself, by no means handsome, and remarkable for nothing in particular except an extremely shrewd intellect, a caustic wit, a diminutive body, and a splendid head of hair, is more than I can tell. She conquered Labédoyère through his vanity, of which he had a considerable bump. Within three weeks of his first meeting Mdlle Oudinet, he was as helpless in her toils as Samson in the arms of Delilah when the locks of his strength were shorn. She was the orphan daughter and only child of a worthy butcher who, from humble beginnings, had amassed a large fortune by means of army contracts. Uneducated himself, he had bestowed on his daughter the best education that money could purchase. Her wealth, her tact, her wit and talent for conversation had made a sort of reputation for her, and her company was sought at the tables of even the most exclusive houses. For it had become known that any party at which Mdlle Oudinet was a guest would at least not be a dull one. While enjoying her social success, she knew that the admiration which she extorted was hollow, and that the proud ladies who sought her company did so from the same motive for which they hired their cook, to make their dinners attractive. Some of them hated her cordially; for she had a rare gift for impromptu epigram, and her shafts were always barbed and found their mark. No woman offended her without paying the penalty of being made the laughing-stock of every *salon* in Paris for the next few days.

What Mdlle Oudinet wanted was not love but admiration. She was clever enough to know that her wit and brilliance could not secure till the end of the chapter the homage that was now paid her. She was only in and not of the society in which she mingled. The butcher's daughter must merge her name in that of some ancient house.

She had formed this resolution about the time she met Labédoyère. He was poor, though possessing a sufficient income for a bachelor, and he was noble. She was plebeian, but rich and sought after in society. Were they not made for each other? Paris was hankering for the pageantry of a court and there were signs that ere long its wish would be gratified. The wife of Citizen Labédoyère would then be the Marquise de Labédoyère. The young man, too, was just then one of the 'lions' of the city. His name had been mentioned more than once in despatches for conspicuous gallantry, and he was known to be a special favourite with the First Consul. Nor was he at all injured in the public estimation by the resignation of his commission. It was believed that he had a secret mission in Paris under the orders of Bonaparte, and would soon receive some important appointment. In every way young Labédoyère was a prize well worth hunting down.

Nor did the hunt last long. The inexperienced young soldier fell an easy prey to the artful flattery of a woman whom all the men admired and all the women feared. But his engagement was succeeded within a few weeks by serious misgivings as to the wisdom of his choice. His *fiancée* made the mistake of imagining that a conquest so easily won could be as easily maintained. Labédoyère soon woke to the consciousʹ ness that he had foolishly allowed himself to be made the tool of a designing woman. But what was he to do? He was an honourable man, and Mdlle Oudinet took good care to give him no pretext for quarrelling with her. As his coolness increased, so did her devotion to him.

Aid came at last in an unexpected way. The First Consul saw the blunder the Republic had made in arraying against itself all the religious sentiment of France and lost no time in permitting the churches to be opened again for the worship of God. One Sunday evening, Labédoyère chanced to pass the open door of a little church in a byʹstreet in the Quartier Latin. He went in and found a crowded congregation lisʹ tening with uplifted faces to an impassioned sermon by a preacher whom Labédoyère could not see from the place where he was standing, but whose voice instantly arrested his attention. The preacher was finishing, and his words fixed themselves so indelibly in Labédoyère's memory that when he went home he had no difficulty in reproducing them in his diary. The text was: 'Every idle word that men shall speak they shall give account thereof in the Day of Judgment.' Nothing, the preacher warned his hearers, that was spoken was ever lost; it remained imprinted on the tablets of the memory, and by it a man would one day be judged.

The preacher finished, and then descended among the people to collect his alms. He was no other than the old priest of Notre-Dame. His eyes and Labédoyère's met, and as the latter bent forward to drop a coin into the bag, the priest whispered in his ear, 'Remember midnight on the twenty-third of next June.' He then passed on.

When the service was over and the congregation had dispersed, Labédoyère made his way into the vestry, where he found the old priest on the point of departure. He paused on seeing the young man, but kept his hold on the handle of the door, as if impatient to be off. After a hurried apology for his intrusion, Labédoyère begged to be permitted to call on the priest. 'I have no home,' replied the old man, 'and my time is not my own. To-day I am here, to-morrow gone; and I know not from hour to hour whither I may be sent by Him Whose unworthy servant I am. I cannot therefore make appointments, because I can never be certain of being allowed to keep them.'

Labédoyère asked that at least he might be told his name.

'I am dead to the world,' said the old man, and his voice resumed that weird wail and his eyes that distant look, which Labédoyère remembered so well before the altar of Notre-Dame. 'In religion I am known as Brother Antonio. Ask me no more questions. I have already delivered my message and I have no commission to satisfy an idle curiosity. Remember the twenty-third of June at midnight. Time is short. Eternity is long.'

And the old priest, bowing courteously, passed out, closing the door behind him.

Next day Labédoyère sought an interview with Mdlle Oudinet. A few days ago he would have welcomed any pre-text for breaking off his engagement; now, with this reminder of his doom, he could tell his *fiancée*, quite truthfully, that for her own sake she must be released from her engagement. She, of course, would scarcely listen to him and rallied him on the folly of believing the ravings of a crack-brained old priest. When raillery failed, she tried tears; but Labédoyère was in-exorable and cut short the scene by abruptly taking his leave.

It was the first time that Mdlle Oudinet had found herself jilted by a man, and something in Labédoyère's manner told her that he had found her out. 'A woman either loves or hates,' says the Roman proverb; 'there is nothing between.' With her, love had been changed to hate. 'I will anticipate the priest's prediction', she told herself, 'and save Fate the trouble of fulfilling her decree on the 23rd of June.'

Accordingly, she sent a note to one of her rejected lovers, whom she had still kept dancing attendance on her, even after her engagement to Labédoyère. He was a young man of good family, shady character, broken fortune, and expensive tastes, to whom an alliance with a rich heiress was of prime impor-tance. He had been hopeful of success until Labédoyère crossed his path and carried off his prize. Naturally, therefore, his feelings towards his rival were far from benevolent. Equally naturally, this fact was not hidden from Mdlle Oudinet. But an even greater recommendation in her eyes was the circumstance that Picard was reputed one of the best swordsmen in Paris. It was easy to give him a version of her quarrel with Labédoyère which at once portrayed herself as an innocent victim and served to revive the hopes of her old suitor.

Picard took in the situation at a glance. If only he could get rid of his rival, his ambition would be realised. He left the lady's presence in great glee and soon found an opportunity of forcing a quarrel upon Labédoyère. A sneering insinuation at an evening party, in the other's hearing, that a lack of cour- age had led him to leave the army, was enough. Labédoyère also was a dexterous swordsman, but out of practice and spirits—two great disadvantages where quickness of eye and strength and suppleness of wrist are so requisite. His antagon- ist, on the other hand, was in daily practice and his spirits rose. Probably, however, Labédoyère's depression was of great service to him on this occasion. He had become so per- suaded of the fulfilment of his doom on the twenty-third of the following June that he had come to regard his own death before that date as an impossibility. He knew of his opponent's skill of fence, though he had never witnessed it, and he had no mean opinion of his own; so, believing in his immunity, he appeared on the ground with his head as cool as if he were sitting down to a game of chess.

Picard's head was not nearly so cool, and he made, moreover, the fatal mistake of despising his adversary. A few passes, however, showed him that he would need all his skill and nerve. In fact, they were so evenly matched that, after fighting for ten minutes without either touching the other, by mutual consent they paused to rest. On renewing the contest, they fought for some time without advantage to either side, until Picard lost patience, and attempting to pass Labédoyère's guard with a rapid thrust, his foot slipped on the dewy grass, the point of his sword flew up, and he fell heavily forward, transfixing himself on his opponent's weapon. The wound was fatal, and before Labédoyère fully realised what had happened, he was gazing horror-struck on the corpse of his foe.

Thrusting his reddened blade into the ground, he broke it, and as he did so, through the stillness of the morning air a well-remembered voice uttered in low but clear tones: 'We shall meet at midnight on the twenty-third of next June.'

The voice sent a chill to Labédoyère's heart. He rushed in the direction from which it had seemed to come. A high hedge separated the field where the duel took place from the road which, at a distance of some two hundred yards, entered a dense wood; and just as Labédoyère looked over the hedge, he saw a tall, dark, slim figure, with flowing white locks, disappearing into the wood. Hastily dressing himself, and leaving the body of his late foe with the seconds and surgeon, Labédoyère pursued the mysterious priest, but failed to overtake him—which was not surprising, since the wood was intersected by many paths and Labédoyère evidently missed the right one.

He now resolved to leave Paris and await his doom elsewhere. He would have liked to rejoin the army, but that was impossible. He had deeply offended the First Consul by retiring, and Napoleon was not the man to forgive an offence of that kind. In the end he made up his mind to go to Palermo, where he knew he would receive a warm welcome from the Marchesino San Juliano, whose acquaintance he had made in Italy, and whose father, the Marchese, had large estates on the island.

Labédoyère arrived in Palermo on a bright afternoon at the beginning of April. At the Palazzo San Juliano he found all the family out; but the servant told him that he would probably meet the Marchesino in the public gardens by the roadstead. There, among a throng of loungers, Labédoyère found his friend and his family, who greeted the young Frenchman with genuine hospitality. With them he now spent some delightful weeks, first at Palermo, and afterwards at their villa near Taormina.

About three weeks after his arrival at Taormina, Labédoyère made a solitary excursion to the marble quarries on

Monte Ziretto. Returning, he missed his way and found himself at nightfall skirting the rocky peak of Lapa. Then he knew where he was, for he could see Taormina not very far off. At that moment, however, he was startled by the sound of a shot fired close above him, while at the same time a gruff voice cried, 'Bocca a terra!' He had been in Sicily long enough to know that he must throw himself face downwards on the ground and let the brigands seize him, on pain of being instantly shot. Six guns were pointing at him from a distance of about ten yards, but since, for another month, he bore a charmed life, he disregarded the challenge and rushed down the mountain. The brigands did not fire, and he was beginning to think he had escaped them when he was thrown violently to the ground. A powerful bloodhound was standing over him, and before he could recover himself, the brigands were on him and overpowered him.

For some hours they led him blindfolded over the mountains. When they unbandaged his eyes, it was quite dark and he had no idea where he was. Towards the following afternoon the band arrived with their captive at a cave which was evidently their lair and where they had tolerably comfortable quarters. They set food and wine before their prisoner, who partook of them with a sharpened appetite. He was then told to write a note to the Marchese demanding a handsome ransom, on receipt of which by the brigands he would be conducted in safety to the neighbourhood of Taormina. In vain

Labédoyère explained that he had no claim whatever on the generosity of the Marchese; in vain he defied his captors to shoot him. The chief brigand told him in the blandest tones that they never shot a captive; after the ransom became due, they sent a piece of his body at intervals, while life lasted, to quicken the zeal of his family and friends. Labédoyère shuddered. Death he could face, but not piecemeal mutilation. He wrote the note to the Marchese and awaited the issue with all the stoicism at his command.

During the day the band was augmented by the arrival of four more brigands, who had been on an unsuccessful expedition in another direction. At first Labédoyère took no particular notice of the new arrivals, but presently he was conscious of being an object of curiosity to one of them, whose eyes he found steadily fixed on him whenever he looked in that direction. He had a feeling that he had seen the man before, and all at once it flashed on him that the new arrival was a Genoese soldier who had been badly wounded on the field of Arcola. Labédoyère had happened to be passing just as the wounded man was about to be thrown into a pit with the dead bodies and, finding that his pulse was still beating, had had him carried to his tent. Thanks to Labédoyère, the man recovered and was set at liberty. He now contrived to slip into his benefactor's hands a paper on which were scrawled the words: 'I shall be one of your guard to-night and will help you to escape. But beware of the hound.'

So it fell out. During the afternoon the chief went off with the band, leaving two men, of whom the Genoese was one, to guard the prisoner. In the course of the night the other man fell fast asleep. The Genoese proposed to kill him, but Labédoyère would not consent. He agreed, however, that they should bind and gag the sleeping brigand and then make their escape.

The man was soon overpowered and the two fugitives fled. It was lucky for Labédoyère that he was not alone, as he had not the least idea which way to turn on leaving the cave. His companion, however, knew the way to Taormina, and they hurried as fast as their feet could carry them, in the hope of being beyond the reach of capture by daybreak. Whenever they came to a stream, they waded through it for a considerable distance in order to throw the hound off the scent in the event of their being pursued.

Towards daybreak they were following the course of a wide but shallow mountain stream, whose banks were covered with brushwood, when the quick ear of the Genoese caught in the distance the deep baying of the bloodhound. Quickly they waded to a rock, covered with scrub, where they hid themselves, dripping as they were. The hound was then so close that they could see the swaying of the bushes on the bank of the stream, as he made his way through them. At length he reached the spot at which they had entered the water, ran up and down the bank and plunged once or twice un certainly into the stream. He had lost the scent, and after a while stood still and bayed aloud his disappointment. Half an hour later the chief and four of the brigands arrived. They searched diligently both sides of the stream, passing and re-passing within a few yards of the men for whom they were searching. Fortunately it never occurred to them to visit the rock, and at last, cursing the dog, they gave up the chase. The fugitives stayed in hiding until it was quite dark and then, resuming their flight, arrived in the early morning at the Villa San Juliano.

Here Labédoyère was greeted as one risen from the dead. The Marchese had sent to his banker for the ransom money, but that was no longer necessary. The mail had arrived during Labédoyère's absence, and among his letters he found, to his surprise, one from the old priest summoning him to Paris at once.

Despite the dissuasions of his friends, he started the following day, taking the Genoese ex-brigand with him. On arrival in Paris, he went without delay to the address which the priest had given him, but found the old man had gone out of town. He had, however, left a note behind him, telling Labédoyère he would call upon him *at midnight on the twenty-third of June*. It was now the seventeenth. Labédoyère accordingly invited two of his closest friends to dine with him on the twenty-third, adding in a postscript that they would oblige him by retiring at ten o'clock.

The day arrived. At ten Labédoyère was left alone, as he thought. He sat in an armchair and began to read Pascal's *Pensées*, with occasional glances at the clock on the mantel-piece opposite. Eleven struck, and he fancied that a numbness was creeping over him. Telling himself that it was only nervousness, he tried to go on reading. Half-past eleven struck and he felt his pulse, which was certainly slower than it should be. A quarter to twelve, and he closed his book and sat with his eyes fixed on the clock and a finger on his pulse. There was no doubt now: it had almost stopped. A deadly chill settled on his body. Then the great clock of Notre-Dame began to toll out the hour of midnight, and as the echo of the last stroke of the hammer was dying away, he fell back in his chair, half-unconscious. How long he remained in that state we know, for a pair of keen eyes were earnestly watching him; and before life had quite departed and while he hovered, as it were, in the borderland of this world and the next, a heavy hand fell upon his shoulder, and a hollow voice, as from the tomb, spoke in his ear: 'Awake, for I am going—*to shut up the church.*' Labédoyère opened his eyes slowly and saw, standing before him, key in hand, the beadle of Notre-Dame!

Haunted Houses

EXORCISM AT ST. DONAT'S CASTLE

The following story was sent to *Lord Halifax* by *Mr. Charles G. Stirling*. During 1917 *Mr. Stirling*, while staying in Scotland, met a *Mr. X——*, a well-known Faith-healer, whose real name is divulged in the letter but is better withheld from publication. 'He is an unassuming man of much piety and obvious sincerity,' *Mr. Stirling* wrote. 'He told me astounding tales of his experiences in exorcising haunted houses in various parts of the country. The enclosed is a literal version of what occurred at *St. Donat's Castle, Glamorgan-shire.* . . . You may rely on its being an unembroidered and precise account, as I had it from *Mr. X——'s* lips.'

St. Donat's Castle is a picturesque building on the *Glamorganshire* coast, rather over two miles west of *Llantwit Major*. The present hall dates from the sixteenth century and provided a sanctuary for *Archbishop Usher* after the ruin of the Royalist cause at *Naseby* in 1645. He was invited to take refuge there by the *Dowager Lady Stradling* of the day, and the little chamber in which he lived for upwards of a year may still be seen.

FOR SOME TIME THE INHABITANTS OF ST. DONAT'S Castle had been greatly alarmed by a variety of ghostly phenomena which appeared by day as well as by night. The materialisations which occurred scared not only the servants and the children of the house, but also the owner and his wife. The situation at length became so intolerable that the owner, a retired naval officer, decided to let or sell the place, which accordingly was advertised in *Country Life*.

At this juncture, however, he happened to hear of the fame of Mr. X—— as an exorcist. Mr. X—— is a remarkable man, born in one of the Dominions, who at the age of fourteen discovered that he possessed extraordinary powers of healing. His record of cases is amazing. He devotes his life to healing the sick and to casting out evil spirits from individuals and from haunted houses.

Informed of Mr. X——'s gifts, the owner of St. Donat's wrote to him and invited him to pay a visit to the Castle and investigate the phenomena which were giving such trouble. Mr. X—— consented, and in due course arrived. He found that the principal manifestations were as follows:

(1) A panther was repeatedly seen by the household in the corridors.

(2) A bright light appeared nightly in one of the bedrooms, having the semblance of a large, glaring eye.

(3) A hag of horrible appearance was seen in the armoury.

(4) The piano, even when closed, was played by invisible hands.

Having received this account of the manifestations, Mr. X—— retired to the bedroom, in which the light had been reported, to pray and grapple with the Powers of Darkness. He requested the owner of the house to sit meanwhile in the hall, with the front door wide open, while the process of exorcism went on. After a while, as though to mark Mr. X——'s triumph over the evil forces of the place, a great gust of wind suddenly blew out from the room where he was praying, swept down the main staircase and all but carried the owner of the Castle into the garden.

From that day and hour the ghostly disturbances completely ceased. All was peaceful in the Castle, which is no longer to be let or sold.

★

WHAT THE GARDENER SAW

This story was sent to *Lord Halifax* by *Mrs. J. Rawlinson Ford* of *Yealand Conyers, Carnforth, Cumberland*. She added in a postscript: 'Of course I could give the name of the lady and the house, but am not sure that I may; the present occupiers may not know about the ghost.' The letter was written in February 1914.

A curious instance of an appearance just before or at the moment of death took place some years ago at a place about thirty miles or so from here (Carnforth).

One day the gardener at this place was at work in the garden when he happened, for some reason, to turn round. To his great surprise he saw his mistress coming towards him, apparently in distress and wanting his help. His astonishment was the greater as at the time she was very ill and he believed her to be in bed. As he hurried towards her, she unaccountably disappeared; and when, in bewilderment, he went on to the house and made enquiries, he was told that she had just died in her room upstairs.

There was a sequel which may be held to explain the apparition. Years afterwards the lady's maid, on her deathbed, confessed that she had murdered her mistress. Having discovered that the lady had left her some money in her will, she had given her poison. Thereafter the lady was supposed to haunt the house. I stayed there more than once and always felt—as people say—'eerie' on the staircase and landing, but not when I was in my room. On the death of my host, his wife and child left the house and it went out of the family.

Not very long ago, I was speaking to my former hostess about ghosts and asked: 'Which was the actual room at the Hall where the lady was murdered?' She replied that it was the one in which I had slept. Since I had never had any uncanny feeling while in it, I suppose that my discomfort on the landing and staircase must have been caused by the old pictures and furniture and the dark corners, and that the ghost of the murdered woman had nothing to do with it.

★

THREE IN A BED

Three in a Bed was evidently an old favourite with *Lord Halifax*. In the early days of his marriage, when he lived at the *Moult* in *Devonshire* he used to tell the story to his visitors with great effect. Towards the end of his life he must have found that he could not recall the details, as he seems to have written to one of the visitors of those early days and asked her to refresh his memory. In complying with his request, she reminded him, 'how you used to make us shudder when you related the story; what particularly haunted me was the fear afterwards of touching something cold.'

A certain Dissenting minister and his wife took a large house near a town in one of the Eastern counties. After they had been there a little while, they were disquieted to observe that, although they were not using the upper floor of the house, often when they came home at night after evening service, they used to see lights in the upper windows.

One day, an old friend came to stay with them for a few days, and since there was no other accommodation for him in the house, they put him to sleep in one of the rooms on the top floor, at the end of a passage. On the morning after the first night of his stay, the visitor came down to breakfast looking very pale and harassed. He found, he told his hosts, that he had to leave at once, and although they pressed him to remain, nothing would shake his determination to depart without delay; nor, although they questioned him, would he give any explanation of his sudden change of plan.

A little later on, a young couple arrived as guests. They were given the same room as the previous visitor had had. When they retired to bed there was a bright fire burning and there was nothing to disquiet them. They settled themselves for the night and soon fell asleep. Presently the man awoke with a start and a strong feeling that he was lying between two people. So certain was he of this that he dared not put out his hand on the side opposite to that on which his wife was lying. Instead, very cautiously, he roused his wife, and persuaded her to get out of the bed on the far side. He followed her, and then, looking back, they both distinctly saw, by the light of the fire, the bedclothes heaped up, as it were, round a human form which lay in the bed.

As they stared, they heard footsteps coming slowly and softly down the passage outside. They reached the door and stopped. After a moment's pause, the brass handle turned and the door, which had been locked, swung gently open. The unfortunate couple hid their eyes in terror, so they saw nothing of what immediately followed. But they heard the footsteps pad softly across the room. There was silence, and then a dreadful gurgle; and looking at the bed once more, they saw the clothes twitched suddenly right off it on to the floor. Once more the footsteps retreated to the door and died away down the passage.

The rest of the night was spent in fear and watchfulness; and when, next morning, the maid arrived with their hot water, the door was still locked. Coming down to breakfast in great agitation, they told their experience to their host, who wrote off at once to his previous visitor. In his reply, the latter admitted that he had had a precisely similar experience. No explanation of any kind was forthcoming, and, needless to say, the house was given up.

THE SIMLA BUNGALOW

The story of *The Simla Bungalow* was sent to *Lord Halifax* in 1925 by his sister, *Mrs. Dundas*, who had had it from her grand-daughter in *India*.

The other day, while I was staying with friends at Simla, I met a very charming Mrs. Giles. She had been a Miss Fordyce, and before her marriage had lived up there with her mother and stepfather, in a house now occupied by an American doctor. It was an old building, and after a little while they began to have complaints of nocturnal disturb, ances. Two of their guests, a man and a girl, reported that the most extraordinary noises had prevented them from sleeping; and although Miss Fordyce assured them that what they had heard must have been rats scampering about, they were quite unconvinced by the explanation and continued to be very much upset.

A little while afterwards, Miss Fordyce and her mother, who was not at all well at the time, were alone in the house. One night Miss Fordyce was awakened by the agonized whimpers of her fox terrier, which always slept near her bed. The dog jumped up on to the eiderdown and seemed to be trying, in terror, to crawl under it. Miss Fordyce always kept a light burning, and she sat up in bed at once and looked round to try to see what could have frightened her dog. The room, as is quite usual in India, was an inner one, with a dressing, room leading out of it. The dressing room door was open, and looking through it she saw, standing on the step in the outer doorway, an old man leaning upon a stick and staring at the floor. As she looked, he vanished. Curiously enough, in spite of this alarm, she was able to lie down quite calmly and go to sleep again.

Next day, however, thinking over her adventure, she felt

79

very frightened. Owing to her mother's illness, she did not like to tell her what she had seen, and felt obliged to continue sleeping in the room. But the fox-terrier would never enter it alone again, and if it happened to get shut in there, would howl terribly until released.

Long afterwards, when she was at a luncheon party, Miss Fordyce found herself sitting next to a young man who told her that his parents had once lived in that identical house and that it was haunted. He was also able to explain the haunting. An old man, he said, had once lived in the house with a young wife, and one night, in a fit of jealousy, he had murdered her. Many people had heard noises; some had even seen the ghost of the young wife running along the covered verandah crying; but as far as is known, Miss Fordyce is the only person who ever saw the old man.

THE CARDINAL AT WAVERLEY ABBEY

Waverley Abbey is close to the *River Wey*, about three miles from *Farnham*. Founded in 1128, it was the first Cistercian establishment in *England*, though little of the original buildings now remain. The 'Cardinal' of the story may have been *Peter de Rupibus*, the famous *Bishop of Winchester*, of whom it is recorded that his heart and bowels were buried in the Abbey church, while the rest of his body lies in *Winchester Cathedral*. What was supposed to be his heart was discovered in 1731, within two leaden dishes soldered together; its subsequent fate is unknown.

The following story was sent to *Lord Halifax* in 1925 by *Mrs. Anderson*, the owner of *Waverley Abbey*.

Mrs. Dundas[1] left us this morning. She has been staying with us for the last week and made me promise to write you the following little story of what occurred here during the War, when our house was turned into a hospital for wounded men.

We had beds here for two hundred and fifty wounded. The Bishop of Winchester, Dr. Talbot, was our chaplain, a Father Robo looked after the Roman Catholics, and the Dissenting Minister from Farnham attended to the Nonconformists. I always made a point of sending the Roman Catholics in to the church at Farnham for Mass, but the little room that used to be my sitting-room was also turned into a chapel for the use of those who were unable to make the journey. Father Robo could come here as often as he liked. He always had lunch with us in the Staff Room and we became great friends.

One Easter he told me that he wanted to have High Mass in my little sitting-room. This had never previously been allowed in a house belonging to Church of England people, but he had obtained permission for the service from the Pope, in recognition of what we had done for the Roman Catholic wounded.

It had always been supposed that the Abbey was haunted by the ghost of a Cardinal, whom some declared they had seen walking about the place. He was one of those who had

_____
[1]Lord Halifax's sister.

81

been buried in the old Cistercian building and should have been prayed for in perpetuity. He frequently appeared in the large drawing-room, where we had eighteen beds for the wounded. They and the nurses continually saw him; and this happened when they were all together, so that the apparition could not be explained away as proceeding from the imagination of a single person. The general belief was that the Abbey was under a curse, as having been the property of the Church and stolen from her.

The priest had invited me to be at Mass that Easter morning and consequently I heard the address which he gave to the men after it was over. He told them that he had had a message from the Pope through the Archbishop of Westminster (Cardinal Bourne). His Holiness had sent word that, in appreciation for what we had done for his flock, he had removed the curse from Waverley Abbey; that we were to pray for the Cardinal, which thereupon we did, after which his soul would rest in peace. This happened seven or eight years ago, and since that day the Cardinal has not been seen again.

I was in Rome last April. The present Pope knows all about the story and graciously sent for me to have an audience with him, which I much appreciated.

Ghostly
Guardians

'SOMEONE BY HIS SIDE'
BISHOP KING'S ESCAPE

'SOMEONE BY HIS SIDE'

Mrs. Ford of Carnforth had this story from her mother-in-law.

ONE STORMY NIGHT A MAN, KNOWN TO BE OF GREAT help to those who were distressed in body or mind, was startled by a loud ring at his bell. Going to the door, he found a messenger from an invalid living some miles off who was in grave trouble and begged for this man to go and see him. (I have forgotten the invalid's name and am not sure whether or not he was a relation.)

The first man dismissed the messenger, saying he would go as soon as he could. As he was starting off, he hesitated and even thought of giving up the journey. It was a terrible night, and the storm had increased to such a pitch that there was a risk of his lantern light being blown out. However, he went. What with the intense darkness and the wind and rain, he had some difficulty in walking along; but presently he had a curious feeling as of someone by his side. He could neither see nor hear anyone, but the sensation that he had a companion was extremely strong and continued until he arrived at his destination, where he stayed for some time.

On his way home the storm was as bad as ever, but he again had the feeling of being accompanied. Yet, mysterious and unaccountable as it was, he was not in the least afraid.

Many years afterwards, he had a request one day to visit a

85

prison where a man was condemned to be hanged. He was not surprised at receiving such a message, as he often called at that particular prison to bring comfort and help to its inmates. He found the man who had sent for him, and the prisoner said that he did not wish to die with any crime unconfessed, whether or not it had been actually carried out. 'Do you remember', he asked, 'walking along a dark lonely road in a storm several years ago?' The visitor replied that he did. 'I knew you had been sent for to a dying person,' the prisoner went on, 'and that you always wore a valuable watch and might have money on you. I lurked under a hedge prepared to attack and rob you, but as you walked along, someone else was walking with you, so I waited for your return. But when you came back, the person was still there, walking by your side, and I did not dare to attack two people.'

BISHOP KING'S ESCAPE

The story of the escape of *Edward King, Bishop of Lincoln,* was sent to the present *Lord Halifax* by *Miss A. E. Nash.* It is so similar to the preceding tale that very possibly it refers to the same incident. The *Bishop* told his story at tea one day to *Canon Perry,* his daughters and *Miss Nash's* sister.

I do not know if you ever heard of our dear Bishop King of Lincoln's experience. He told it to Canon Perry, when my sister was staying with him and the Bishop came to tea, as at that time he often did in order to consult him on Canon Law, when those creatures were prosecuting him.[1] When the Bishop was a young man, he was curate in a village. One wet cold night he had come home very tired and had just got his boots off, when his landlady came in and said that a farmer, living three miles off across the fields, had met with a serious accident and wanted King to come at once. She did not know the messenger, and he refused to come in because he was so wet. King put his boots on again and started off; but it was very dark and he missed the man who had brought the message. When he reached the house to which he had been summoned, the door was opened to his knock by the farmer himself, hale, hearty, and much surprised to see his visitor. No message had been sent, and, greatly mystified, King went home. The man who had summoned him had gone, and the matter remained unexplained.

Some years afterwards, in another county, King was ministering to a dying man in hospital, and the man said: 'Don't you remember me, Sir?' The Bishop could not recall him until he gave his name, which was that of a very bad character who had lived years ago in that village where King was a curate. The man went on: 'It was lucky for you that you brought a friend with you that night when you thought you had a call to the farm. I meant to murder you, only I couldn't, as there were two of you.' The Bishop had seen and heard nothing, but the man was certain that he had been

[1]The famous trial of Bishop King before Archbishop Benson in 1890.

accompanied by a second great-coated figure walking beside him.

A similar occurrence was told me by a young priest who was working in a mining district in Canada. He had to go a long ride through thickly wooded country. He did not relish the job, as there were plenty of undesirable characters about; but duty called and he went, returning in perfect safety. Some little while afterwards he was called to see a dying man in hospital, who told him that he and a 'pal' had been so furious with him for his interference with their doings that they had determined to kill him. Knowing of his journey, they had lain in wait for him in the loneliest part of the way, but, to their great annoyance, two other men were riding, one on each side of their proposed victim, so that they could not get a shot at him. Like Bishop King, the priest thought that he was alone.

Two Friends

¶ This story was told to *Lord Halifax* by his friend, *Mr. Augustus Hare*, author of *Memorials of a Quiet Life*. *Mr. Hare* claimed to have had it from *Lady Blomfield*, who in her turn had heard it directly from the man to whom the experience happened, but who did not wish his name to be disclosed.

TWO BOYS AT A PUBLIC SCHOOL WERE ABSOLUTELY devoted to each other. They did everything together and in the manner of boys swore eternal friendship. In order to seal this promise, each made a cut in the other's arm and signed a paper in blood to the effect that which ever of them should die first would appear to his friend at the moment of death.

The boys spent all their holidays together, and great was their despair when their schooldays ended and young B——, who was to be called to the Bar, went up to the University, while his friend, who was going into the Indian Army, was sent elsewhere to undergo his military training.

Of course, they promised faithfully to write to each other, and indeed began by writing twice a day; but presently twice became once, and once a day became twice a week. After the young soldier had gone to India, the correspondence further languished, until at last it ceased altogether. The old friendship died. B—— became an eminent barrister in London, his friend pursued his Indian career, and for many years they held no communication with each other.

On a certain Saturday, just before Christmas, B——, who had been overworking and felt that he wanted a little country air, resolved to run down to Virginia Water for the Sunday. On arrival there, he put up at the Wheatsheaf, and after dinner sat over the fire in the entrance hall smoking his pipe. As he sat, a curious uneasiness came over him. He felt restless. Then he fancied he saw a face looking in at the window, and what vaguely troubled him was that he seemed to know the face, yet could not put a name to its owner.

At length, on the pretence of re-lighting his pipe at the gas bracket, he got up and walked slowly past the window. Undoubtedly there was someone there; undoubtedly, too, the face was familiar. But who was it? He could not remember, and, a good deal disturbed, he went past the window a second time. Then the truth flashed upon him: it was not the face of the boy he had known at school, but was, as it were, the development of that face into that of the man he would probably have become.

A little uncertain whether what he had seen was real or not, he sent for the landlord of the Wheatsheaf and told him, 'There's a man looking in at the window.' The landlord went to see, but came back shaking his head. 'Oh no, sir, there's no one there. The yard gate is locked at ten o'clock and nobody can get in at this time of night.' B——, however, was not satisfied. He was sure that he had seen something, though of what it was he was not sure. At any rate he could not leave the puzzle unsolved. 'I must go,' he told the landlord, 'and get a breath of fresh air.' 'Better not, sir,' replied the man. 'There's an east wind blowing fit to cut you to pieces.' 'I can't help that,' said B——. 'I am stifling. Go out I must.'

TheWheatsheaf Inn lies close to the edge of VirginiaWater, and as B—— stood at the door of the inn he looked out into what seemed to be impenetrable darkness. Gradually, however, as he gazed, the darkness appeared to concentrate and gather itself together, until it was focused upon one spot, as it were the mouth of a tunnel, and out of this tunnel came a lighted train. The picture grew clearer. In one of the middle carriages B—— saw two men apparently engaged in a deadly conflict, one forcing the other back towards the door of the carriage. All at once the door fell open and the man underneath the other fell out, face upwards, at B——'s feet. It was the face he had seen a few minutes before looking in at the window of the inn, the face of the man into whom the friend of his boyhood had grown. Then, in a moment, train and tunnel and face all vanished, and B—— was alone in the darkness.

With a cry of horror, he staggered back into the hall of the inn. 'I am ill!' he cried to the landlord. 'I don't know what is the matter, but I have been seeing visions, terrible sights. I must get home at once; I cannot be laid up here. I must go back to London this very night.'

Fortunately, there was a last train which he could catch, and so he got to his London house, went to bed tired out, slept soundly, and awoke next morning completely recovered. His vision of the previous night ceased to trouble him; the change of air, he thought, had after all done him good; and some interesting work was awaiting him, so that he was kept occupied most of the day.

Going for a stroll late in the afternoon, he was in Picca-dilly when he saw, on the other side of the street, the brother of his former school friend, a man with whom he had a slight acquaintance. This encounter brought back to him, with a sense of shock, his vision of the night before, and he hurriedly crossed the road and greeted the man. 'What news have you had of Willie?' he asked. The other looked very grave and sad. 'Bad,' he replied, 'very bad, I am afraid.' 'He is dead?' 'Yes.' 'Was he killed?' B—— asked excitedly. 'Thrown out of a railway carriage?' 'Yes, he was,' said the brother, pro-foundly astonished. 'But how on earth have you heard? We only got the telegram this morning.'

Dreams and Portents

THE SPANISH KNIFE

The *Rt. Hon. A. Beresford Hope*, who told *Lord Halifax* this story, was a well-known member of Parliament and Anglo-Catholic. The *Lord Waterford* referred to was probably the 3rd Marquess. A footnote adds that the story is referred to in the record of the Limerick Jury.

LORD WATERFORD, HIS GAMEKEEPER, AND THE MAN who kept the local inn were one day in the church at Curraghmore. The gamekeeper reported that a man had been 'found murdered in the mountains'. 'It must be the little one,' the innkeeper at once and unaccountably exclaimed. He went on to explain his remark by telling the other two of a dream he had lately had. In it two men, one big and one little, had come to his inn, and he had seen the big man kill the little man by stabbing him with a knife of a kind he had never seen before.

In the morning the innkeeper had told this dream to his wife; and in the course of the day, sure enough, two men, one big and the other little, had arrived at his house. So vivid was the impression of his dream that he refused to admit the men; but later, his wife, unwilling to lose their custom, had let them in by the back door. Some little while afterwards, when he was taking some refreshments into the room in which the men were seated, he had noticed lying on the table a knife of peculiar and outlandish shape, such as he had seen in his dream. Presently the men had paid their bill and taken their departure.

The body of the man who had been found murdered in the mountains was brought in. It was, as the innkeeper had surmised, the smaller of his two visitors; and he had been stabbed to death. A description of the murderer was published and circulated round the country, a strict watch being set in particular on the bridge at Carrick, which was the most likely point at which the wanted man would try to cross the river Shannon; and there he was eventually caught and arrested. On investigation, it transpired that he and his companion had been employed in the cod fisheries off Newfoundland. In his possession was a Spanish knife. It was of a very peculiar make, such as was quite unknown in Ireland, and there was no doubt whatever that it had caused the wound in the body of the murdered man.

'TURN TO THE RIGHT!'

A man once had a vivid dream in which he was travelling in a wild and unfrequented part of the Black Forest. Two ruffians suddenly emerged from the trees and attacked him; he fled for his life and they pursued him. After a while he came to a point where the road forked, and while he was desperately wondering which of the two arms was the more likely to bring him to safety, and the robbers were coming up behind him, he heard a voice close to his ear, which told him, 'Turn to the right!' He did as he was told, and quite soon he came

98

to a lonely house, which turned out to be an inn, where he was taken in and was safe from pursuit.

Twenty years passed and he had almost forgotten his dream, when he chanced to be travelling in Germany and passing through the Black Forest. Just as had happened in the dream, two robbers sprang out on him and attacked him; and again as in the dream, he came in his flight to a fork in the road. He could hear the robbers in hot pursuit and was undecided which of the two tracks to choose when, in a flash, his dream came back to him. He turned to the right, and soon found safety in the inn.

PRESIDENT LINCOLN'S DREAM

The story of *President Lincoln's* dream on the night preceding his murder is well known. *Gideon Welles*, one of the members of his Cabinet, has left on record his recollection of what the President told his colleagues:

'He [*Lincoln*] said it was in my department, that it related to the water, that he seemed to be in a singular and indescribable vessel, but always the same, and that he was moving with great rapidity toward a dark and indefinite shore; that he had had this singular dream preceding the firing on *Sumter,* the battles of *Bull Run, Antietam, Gettysburg, Stone River, Vicksburg, Wilmington,* etc. . . . Victory did not always follow his dream, and the events and results were important.'

The version in the *Ghost Book* is more detailed and dramatic. How *Lord Halifax* obtained it he does not divulge.

Several years ago, Mr. Charles Dickens, as we know, went on a tour to America. Among other places he visited Wash- ington, where he called upon his friend, the late Mr. Charles

Sumner, the well-known senator who was present at Lincoln's deathbed. After talking of various matters, Mr. Sumner said to Dickens: 'I hope that you have seen everybody and everything that you wanted to see, that there is no wish unfulfilled.'

'Well,' replied Dickens, 'there is one person whose acquaintance I greatly wish to make, and that is Mr. Stanton.'

'Oh, that is very easily managed,' Sumner assured him. 'Mr. Stanton is a great friend of mine. Come and meet him here.'

So it was arranged, and much conversation passed. Towards midnight, before the three men separated, Stanton turned to Sumner and said: 'I should like to tell Mr. Dickens that story about the President.'

'Well,' said Sumner, 'the time is very suitable.'

Stanton proceeded as follows:

'During the war, as you know, I was in charge of all the troops in Columbia, and as you may imagine, I had my hands pretty full. One day there was a council ordered for two o'clock, but I was pressed with business and could not get there till twenty minutes past. When I entered, most of my colleagues were looking rather grave, but I thought nothing of that, nor of the words that fell from the President as I entered: "But, gentlemen, this is not business; here is Mr. Stanton." Business proceeded and various matters were discussed and settled. When the Council broke up, I walked away arm in arm with the Attorney General, saying to him as we left: "Well, we have really done some work to-day. The

President applied himself to business, instead of flitting about from one chair to another, talking to this and that man." "Ah," said the Attorney General, "but you were not here at the beginning; you do not know what passed." "What did pass?" I asked. "When we entered the Council Chamber to-day", resumed the Attorney General, "we found the President seated at the top of the table with his face buried between his hands. Presently he raised it, and we saw that he looked grave and worn. He said, 'Gentlemen, before long you will have important news.' We all enquired, 'What, sir, have you had bad news? Is it anything serious?' He replied, 'I have heard nothing; I have had no news; but you will hear to-morrow.' We again pressed him to tell us what had happened, and at last he said, 'I have had a dream; I have dreamt that dream three times—once before the battle of Bull Run, once on another occasion, and again last night. I am in a boat, alone—on a boundless ocean. I have no oars—no rudder—I am help-less. I drift! I drift!! I drift!!!' "

'Five hours afterwards the President was assassinated.'

JOHN ARTHINGTON'S ESCAPE
This story was sent to *Lord Halifax* by *Mrs. Ford* of *Carnforth*.

The following is the story as I remember it being told to me by my mother-in-law, Mrs. Ford.

Among the many family stories which my grandmother Whitelock used to tell, I have more than once heard her relate how the life of her uncle, John Arthington, was saved by a dream. He had to take a journey to some place which he had never visited and by a road unknown to him. As he rode along on horseback, it struck him that the way was familiar, a thing which puzzled him considerably. At last he came in sight of a ferry-house, at the door of which stood a man looking out for passengers. Instantly it flashed across John Arthington's mind that a few nights before he had dreamed the whole scene, and that in his dream he had got into the ferry boat, that it had sunk, and that he had been drowned. He was so strongly impressed by this memory that he asked the owner of the boat if there were no other way of crossing the river. The man replied that there was a bridge two miles further up, but people generally preferred to cross by the boat.

John Arthington, however, said he would ride forward to the bridge and did so. On his return journey, which he also made by way of the bridge, the man at the ferry-house stopped him to say that it was very fortunate for him that he had chosen the bridge, for when the boat reached the middle of the river, it had turned over and all on board had been drowned.

TWO SUBMARINES

The following story, though written in the third person, was apparently sent to *Lord Halifax* by *Ruth, Countess of Chichester.*

During the War, an old nurse who came down from Scotland to visit Lady Chichester, told her that one night recently she had had a dream about the Forth Bridge, and that in the dream she had seen what she described as whales, with castles on their backs, circling round the third pillar of the Bridge. On the following night exactly the same dream had occurred again. So impressed was she by the dream and its recurrence that she wrote to her nephew, who was employed at the time in work on the Bridge, told him of her experience, and asked him if he thought it had any meaning.

In due course, the nephew replied. 'What you saw', he wrote, 'is not whales with castles on their backs, but submarines with their periscopes showing above the water.' He told her that at the time when her letter arrived, they were engaged in protecting the Bridge against submarine attack, by surrounding the pillars with concrete, against which the shock of a torpedo would spend itself. Every pillar had been so protected, except the third pillar, work on which was only half completed. The nephew had accordingly shown his aunt's letter to his foreman, a shrewd old Scot, who was sure that something was intended by it, remarking at once, 'We had better take measures to make everything safe.'

Some of the men were kept back and, by working day and night, finished concreting the third pillar. At the same time a hint of some sort was passed to the naval authorities that submarine attacks were to be expected.

On the day after the Bridge was made safe, two German

submarines actually appeared in the Forth and attacked the Bridge. They were unable to do any damage and one of them was eventually taken.

★

THE FIGHTING ROOKS AND THE BLACK MOUSE

The following stories were sent to Lord Halifax *in* 1880 *by his uncle, the* Rev. the Hon. Francis R. Grey, *son of* Lord Grey *of the Reform Bill and for many years* Rector of Morpeth.

A former curate of mine, F. Howson, is spending this week with us. Last year he was one of the curates at All Saints', Margaret Street, and is now with Chadwick at St. Michael's, Wakefield. Yesterday he told us two stories, for the truth of which he vouches.

Some time ago, before there was telegraphic communica-tion with India, a lady was sitting one spring day in her garden in the Isle of Wight, when she saw a duel in the air between two rooks, one of which fell bleeding at her feet, so that her white gown was sprinkled with blood. She got up in great alarm, declaring that she was certain she would shortly hear bad news of her only son, who was in India. She forthwith re-tired to her room, where she wrote on the window shutter the date, day and hour of her experience. The days passed, the poor woman awaiting in great anxiety the arrival of the Indian mail. When at last it came, it brought her a letter announcing that her son had been killed in a duel. When dates and times were compared, it was found that he had met his death on the very day and at the very hour when his mother had witnessed the duel between the rooks.

The other story is of a clergyman attending the deathbed of a man who had led a very evil life. In company with the wife of the dying man, the clergyman was watching by the bed, when a jet black mouse crept on to the counterpane. They tried to frighten it away, but there it remained; they tried to catch it, but it always evaded them. In spite of all they could do, the mouse stayed on the counterpane until the man died, when it disappeared as suddenly as it had come.

The dead man left behind him a son, whose life was as wicked as his father's had been. When, some years after his father's death, the young man too was dying, it happened that the same clergyman was watching by the bed with the mother. Once more the black mouse appeared, could not be dislodged, stayed until the young man was dead, and then disappeared.

I think Howson told me he had had this story from the clergyman who was at both deathbeds.

LORD DECIES' RING

Mr. Beresford Hope (see p. 97) told *Lord Halifax* this story on the occasion of the latter's visit to him at Bedgebury in December 1874. *Mr. Beresford Hope* had had the tale from his uncle, *Lord Decies*.

Some years ago, while travelling on the Continent, Lord Decies had come across a Mr. Lionel Ashley, son of the sixth Earl of Shaftesbury. Mr. Ashley appeared to be very much out at elbows, but was wearing a peculiar ring with a skull and crossbones engraved upon it. On Lord Decies showing some curiosity about the ring, Mr. Ashley told him that it had been given to him by a celebrated French mesmerist and conjuror. The same man had given a similar ring to two or three other men, predicting in each case that the man would die before he was twenty-five. All the other men to whom rings had been given had duly died in accordance with the prediction. Ashley alone remained, but he was only twenty-two at the time. Having told his story, he presented Lord Decies with the ring, and during the next few weeks the two men met constantly. Some little while later, Lord Decies was sitting in his room—Mr. Beresford Hope did not say where—when Ashley appeared. Lord Decies would never disclose what actually passed between him and his visitor, but presently rang the bell. He was alone in the room when the servant arrived, and he asked him if he had let Mr. Ashley in. 'Mr. Ashley, my lord!' replied the servant. 'Mr. Ashley died yesterday!' The young man was twenty-three at his death.

Lord Decies always wore the ring he had been given by Ashley and told his nephew the story of it more than once.

THE DEATH OF LORD HASTINGS

A note explains that '*Aunt Maria* sent me *Miss Copley's* account of *Lord Hastings*' ghost story.' '*Aunt Maria*' was the wife of *Henry, 3rd Earl Grey*. The *Lord Hastings* of the story was the 4th and last *Marquess of Hastings*, the notorious gambler who lost £120,000 over *Hermit's* Derby. He died in the following year, overwhelmed with debts.

It appears that Lord Hastings, before starting in his yacht for Norway, was entertaining at Donington a party of men, of whom Colonel Gordon, son of Lady Francis, was one. After dinner one evening, Lord Hastings suddenly got up from the table and rang the bell. When the servant came, he said, 'Go and find out who has called at this time of night: I heard a carriage drive up to the door.'

After some time had elapsed, the servant returned and reported that there must have been a mistake, as no one had called and there was no trace of wheels on the drive outside.

Lord Hastings was apparently satisfied, but a few minutes later he jumped up again and rang the bell. 'I have heard another carriage drive up,' he told the servant on arrival. 'Go and find out what it means and who it is.'

This time the servant was absent for still longer. When he returned, he said, 'My lord, I have been round to the stables and everywhere. There is no sign of any carriage and no one has called.' Whereupon Lord Hastings threw up his hands and exclaimed, 'Then I am a dead man before the end of the year.'

His companions at table thought his conduct very strange, some of them supposing that their host must have drunk too much. Noticing their surprise, Lord Hastings explained his conduct. There was, he told them, a tradition that when the head of the Hastings family, sitting at his table, twice heard a non-existent carriage drive up to the front door of the house, he would die before the end of the year.

Next day, Colonel Gordon wrote to his mother. At the end of his letter, he asked, 'By the bye, is there any legend attached to the Hastings family?' He was careful to give no indication that he was referring to any particular incident that had happened. Lady Francis replied by return of post: 'You ask about a legend in the Hastings family. Surely you must have heard that when the head of the house, sitting at his own table, twice hears a carriage drive up to the door, and no carriage is there, he will die before the end of the year.'

I have told the story [added Miss Copley] as I heard it from C. Walrond, only I am not sure whether the carriage was to be heard by the head of the house only, or if the other guests, without knowing the story, also shared the delusion. If they heard nothing, it is possible that Lord Hastings was drunk, or if sober, was suffering from a bad conscience. When I told the story the other day, someone who was present and already knew about it, added the information that Lord Hastings had taken a bet about his death. 'With whom?' I asked. 'With a friend—that he would not be dead. And he cannot lose. If he lives, he wins; and if he dies, he can't pay: nor need his successor, since debts of honour are not transferable. I can believe anything of him. The legend certainly exists. The scene in the dining-room at Donington certainly occurred. There are still four and a half months before the 1st of January, 1869.'

Lord Hastings died on November 10th, 1868.

The Rustling
Lady of Lincoln

and other stories

¶ *Miss Nash,* a lady in *India,* sent the following stories to the present *Lord Halifax.*

MY GRANDFATHERS EACH HAD A PROPHETIC DREAM. MY father's father, Dr. Nash (one of those whom Dean Church in his book on the Oxford Movement calls 'the precursors' of that revival) had been in Scotland and intended to start on his return journey, by coach, of course, on the following day. During the night he dreamed that the coach capsized and that all the outside passengers (of whom he meant to be one) were killed. So vivid was the dream that he put off his journey. The coach was wrecked and all the outside passengers were killed.

My mother's father, after leaving school, was offered by the father of a schoolfellow a clerkship in the Linen Hall in Dublin. He accepted it, to the indignation of his own father, who probably wanted him to sit down and bemoan the folly of his grandfather in running through his property and leaving his family a paltry two hundred pounds a year on which to live. One night, my grandfather dreamed that he was sent to the bank for money (a duty which, as he was a junior clerk, he had never been given before), and that while he was there a man came in and presented a cheque, the signature on which he knew in his dream to be forged. He whispered his information to the cashier, the man was detained, and the forgery was discovered. Next day, all happened as in the dream. The young clerk was sent to the bank; the man came in with a cheque; and he presented it to the cashier next to my grandfather. Almost involuntarily the latter whispered the information that the signature had been forged; and so it turned out to have been, my grandfather gaining much kudos. But he used to say that he would never forget the terror which swept over him when he realised that, on the flimsy evidence of a dream, he had brought a serious charge against a complete stranger.

★   ★   ★   ★

My father was for ten years in Western Australia, where at one time he was looking after his brother's station up-country. Mr. X., a settler in the district, who had been doing well, often spoke of going home for a holiday; so that no one was surprised when another friend, riding over to see X., was told by the overseer that he had gone for two years, leaving him in charge. Shortly afterwards, however, this same friend happened to pass by again and was greatly astonished to see X. sitting on a fence. 'Hullo, X.,' he called out, 'I thought you had gone home.' The other made no reply, but got down from the fence, walked a short distance away, and apparently vanished. The friend, after discussing this experience with some of the neighbours, returned to the place with some native trackers, who examined the place and reported, 'White man's brains.' They then followed the tracks to the spot where X. had disappeared and said, 'Dies'. A little below the surface of the ground, the body of Mr. X. was found. The overseer was arrested, and, of course, everyone, including my father and my uncle Richard, went to the trial. At first the man protested his innocence, but when the story of the appearance of X. and the finding of the body was related, he confessed in open court. He said he thought he would have two years in which to feather his nest and before he need disappear. Both my father and my uncle were present when the murderer confessed, and this is their account.

★   ★   ★   ★

Canon Charles Gray of Retford and Blythe (Notts) told us that his brother, who was solicitor to the York Chapter, once lived in an old house in the Close. He had a small son, and soon after they had moved into their house, the child began to talk of 'my old gentleman' who visited him in the nursery when no one else was there. At first they thought he was imagining or dreaming, but he was so sure of what he had seen that the father, after getting from the child as well as he could a description of the old man, went to the Cathedral library to enquire into the history of the house. He found that it had once been inhabited by the uncle of Laurence Sterne, and a portrait in the library showed him dressed just as the child had described.

★   ★   ★   ★

At one time we lived in Lincoln. My Uncle Perry was at Waddington, four miles away, on Lincoln Cliff. He married my mother's sister and wrote a *Students' Church His-*

tory and other books. Four miles further along the Cliff was Harmston; and I remember as a child, when staying at Waddington, going for a walk to Harmston Hall and thinking what a desolate place it looked. The owner, a crony, I think, of George IV, had fled the country for some unknown reason, and the place was in Chancery. Some years later, when we went to Lincoln, I used to go out once a week to Waddington to study Latin and early English with Uncle Perry. One day, he told me that long ago he had been over to Harmston as a witness, I think, when officials opened the room which had been locked by the wicked squire when he fled thirty years before. Nothing much had been done while he lived abroad, and Uncle Perry said the room looked as if the guests had suddenly jumped up from the table: chairs had been knocked over, glasses were lying on the floor, there were mouldy, dusty remains of food, all as if something frightening had happened. The story was that the squire suddenly informed the company that his wife had run away with his best friend, sent them all off, locked up the room, and went abroad the next day. Uncle Perry, however, said it looked more as though something dreadful had caused their flight. However it may have been, neither friend nor wife was ever heard of again.

My sister had started a school in Lincoln, and I, being just trained, and about to be given the headship of a High School, had to give up everything and join the others in Lincoln.

While we were there, two of the boarders, nice girls, daughters of a gentleman farmer living at Harmston, once asked M—— and me to come out to tea in the holidays. We went for a long afternoon and found they were living in Harmston Hall, as the farmer was farming the land. The mother told us that the house was haunted, though she had had no idea of it when she went there. The first night, just when the clock in the hall struck eleven, she heard a loud shriek of terror and someone rushed down the passage and fell against the door. She thought one of the children had been frightened by a dream in the strange house and ran to the door and opened it; but there was no one there. Every night as eleven struck the same thing happened, and she got quite used to it. I, thinking of old stories, asked, 'Why did they not raise the hearthstone of that room?' It seems they never thought of doing that and anyhow it had all happened years before. Perhaps the wife and friend of the old squire were murdered and buried under the hearthstone of the locked room. The old squire's son came back and lived and died in a Waddington cottage, regarded as uncanny by people, I believe. Several persons tried to live in the Hall, but it was never long before they left. One manufacturer made a good many alterations to the house, but his wife went out of her mind and they departed. At last the old owner died and the place was sold to a Lincoln ironfounder. I do not know how he got on or if there were any more appearances.

★   ★   ★   ★

My sister had been told that the house she had taken in Lincoln was haunted, but none of us nor of the servants knew this till after we had left. It was built in 1107 and the lower part was Roman brickwork, roughly L-shaped, a lovely place. My mother turned a small room, entered by two steps down, into a bathroom. There was a long corridor leading to the panelled drawing-room. A passage ran west, passing one bedroom and, on the other side, the bathroom, and ending in a large bedroom with a powdering closet off it. Beyond it was a small room in which I slept, and a flight of stairs went up to the servants' bedroom and down to the oldest part, where M——, my eldest sister, was sleeping. Soon after we had moved in, N——, the youngest of us, said to me, 'Alice, I wish you would sit on the bathroom steps and talk to me when I'm there.' (She and I took our baths at night.) We laughed, but I did as she asked. One night in the holidays I was in the bathroom and everyone else was in bed, when I heard someone with rustling skirts run past the bathroom door and into the end bedroom. As soon as I could get out, I went into the room, but no one was there. One of us always stayed with my mother, who was over seventy, and one day when I was at home with her and the others were all out, she sent me to shut the windows as it was beginning to rain. My own room was the furthest off, and while I was in there, close beside me and quite plainly, I heard a deep sigh. That was not the only occasion on which I had heard things, and after we had left the house, N—— confessed that she had asked me to sit on the bathroom steps and talk because, when she was having a bath, the rustling lady would be about. She said she had seen the lady three times, twice going into a bedroom and once into the powdering closet. Once she had chased her into the bedroom, thinking it was the new charwoman going the wrong way, but when the lady reached the other door she vanished. My mother and my other sister saw nothing and heard nothing, though the sister lived in the most haunted room.

The lady we saw was supposed to be Lady Deloraine, one of the Scrope family (the drawing-room panelling was bordered with the arms of Berkeley and Scrope), and was said to have been passionately devoted to the old house. She was a plucky and vigorous woman, for they say that she threw stones out of the window at Cromwell's soldiers when they came to pull down Lincoln Cathedral.

Some Curious Stories

THE BLOODY HAND
THE 'TWEENIE'
WARNING FOR A SUBMARINE

THE BLOODY HAND

IN A CERTAIN VILLAGE ON THE SOUTH COAST, A WIDOW and her two daughters were living in a house standing rather apart from its neighbours on either side. It was situated on a wooded cliff, and about a quarter of a mile from the garden was a waterfall of some height. The two daughters were much attached to each other. One of them, Mary, was very good-looking and attractive. Among her admirers there were two men especially distinguished for their devotion to her, and one of them, John Bodneys, seemed on the point of realising the ambition of his life, when a new competitor of a very different disposition appeared and completely conquered Mary's heart.

The day was fixed for the marriage, but though Mary wrote to the Bodneys to announce her engagement and to ask John to be present at her wedding, no reply was received from him. On the evening before the day, Ellen, the other sister, was gathering ferns in the wood when she heard a faint rustling behind her and, turning quickly round, thought she had a momentary glimpse of the figure of John Bodneys; but whoever it was vanished swiftly in the twilight. On her return to the house, she told her sister what she thought she had seen, but neither of them thought much of it.

The marriage took place next day. Just before the bride was due to leave with her husband, she took her sister to the room they had shared, the window of which opened on to a balcony from which a flight of steps led down to an enclosed garden. After a few words, Mary said to her sister, 'I would like to be alone for a few minutes. I will join you again presently.'

Ellen left her and went downstairs, where she waited with the others. When half an hour had passed and Mary had not appeared, her sister went up to see if anything had happened to her. The bedroom door was locked. Ellen called, but had no answer. She called again more loudly; there was still no answer. Becoming alarmed, she ran downstairs and told her mother. At last the door was forced open, but there was no trace of Mary in the room. They went into the garden, but except for a white rose lying on the path, nothing was to be seen. For the rest of that day and on the following days, they hunted high and low. The police were called in, the whole countryside was roused, but all to no purpose. Mary had utterly disappeared.

The years passed by. The mother and Mary's husband were dead, and of the wedding party only Ellen and an old servant were left. One winter's night the wind rose to a furious gale and did a great deal of damage to the trees near the waterfall. When the workmen came in the morning to clear away the fallen timber and fragments of rock, they came upon a skeleton hand, on the third finger of which was a wedding ring, guarded by another ring with a red stone in it. On searching further, they found a complete skeleton, round whose dried up bones some rags of clothes still adhered. The ring with the red stone in it was identified by Ellen as one which her sister was wearing on her wedding day. The skeleton was buried in the churchyard, but the shock of the discovery was so great that a few weeks later Ellen herself was on her deathbed. On the occasion of Mary's burial, she had insisted on keeping the skeleton hand with the rings, putting it in a glass box to secure it from accident; and now, when she lay dying, she left the relic to the care of her old servant.

Shortly afterwards the servant set up a public house, where, as may be imagined, the skeleton hand and its story were a common topic of conversation among those who frequented the bar. One night a stranger, muffled up in a cloak and with his cap pulled over his face, made his way into the inn and asked for something to drink.

'It was a night like this when the great oak was blown down,' the publican observed to one of his customers.

'Yes,' the other replied. 'And it must have made the skeleton seem doubly ghastly, discovering it, as it were, in the midst of ruins.'

'What skeleton?' asked the stranger, turning suddenly from the corner in which he had been standing.

'Oh, it's a long story,' answered the publican. 'You can see the hand in that glass case, and if you like, I will tell you how it came there.'

He waited for an answer, but none came. The stranger was

leaning against the wall in a state of collapse. He was staring at the hand, repeating again and again, 'Blood, blood,' and, sure enough, blood was slowly dripping from his finger tips. A few minutes later, he had recovered sufficiently to admit that he was John Bodneys and to ask that he might be taken to the magistrates. To them he confessed that, in a frenzy of jealousy, he had made his way into the private garden on Mary's wedding day. Seeing her alone in her room, he had entered and seized her, muffling her cries, and had taken her as far as the waterfall. There she had struggled so violently to escape from him that, unintentionally, he had pushed her off the rocks and she had fallen into a cleft where she was almost completely hidden. Afraid of being discovered, he had not even waited to find out whether she were dead or alive. He had fled and had lived abroad ever since, until an over-powering longing led him to revisit the scene of his crime.

After making his confession, Bodneys was committed to the county gaol, where shortly afterwards he died, before any trial could take place.

THE 'TWEENIE'

This story and the next were sent in 1920 by *Commander Francis Cadogan,* grandson of the *5th Earl Cadogan* who was at *Eton* with *Lord Halifax.*

Mrs. Chilton (the real name is a little different), the wife of a captain in the Navy and a very sensible matter-of-fact sort of person, took a couple of rooms on the third floor of a tall house near Palmerston Road, Southsea. Her husband was away at sea at the time, but as she went out a good deal and had a latchkey, she asked the landlady not to trouble to wait up for her. Nevertheless, for a time the woman disregarded her request; and when Mrs. Chilton returned for the night, she would find the landlady sitting up for her, coming forward with a candle, and insisting on escorting her upstairs.

One night, however, the landlady was not there. Mrs. Chilton returned about half-past twelve, let herself in, found and lit a candle, and started upstairs. When she was about halfway up the zig-zag stair-flight she had a feeling that someone was following her, and, looking round and down, she saw what was apparently a small 'tweenie' maid. As she had never noticed her about the place before and it was rather strange that she should be up and about at that time of night, Mrs. Chilton hurried on to the next flight of stairs. When she got there, she looked round, and there was the 'tweenie' just behind her. Mrs. Chilton now turned right round, holding the candle well before her, to confront the girl, who clutched the banister with her hands, and sinking nearly to her knees, gave an imploring look. Mrs. Chilton, by now a little frightened, scurried on up to her room and neither saw nor heard any more that night.

Next day, when she questioned her landlady, she was given the most unsatisfactory answers and decided to leave the lodgings at once. Subsequently she heard that other people who had stayed there had had uncanny experiences, and that the house was known to have a bad name.

★

WARNING FOR A SUBMARINE

Francis Cadogan wrote to *Lord Halifax* that this story was 'general knowledge among the senior submarine officers and was told me by the officer commanding the *Mediterranean* flotilla in 1919.'

Among the commanders of submarines operating during the War from the south-east coast of England was an officer whom we will call Ryan, a man of striking appearance and charming personality, a great favourite in the mess of the Depot ship, and the sort of fellow who made everybody present cheer up when he came on the scene.

It was the custom for these vessels to leave for an observation patrol of from two to three weeks' length, usually off the Dutch shoals and the entrance to Jade Bay. They worked on the surface at night, but in the daytime, owing to the numerous German aircraft patrols, they were generally submerged, coming up at intervals to have a good look round through their periscopes. Ryan's ship left on one of these cruises, and when she never returned, it was taken for granted that she had met with bad luck and been sunk, either by the Germans or by some accident.

Some seven or eight weeks later, another submarine was operating in a similar fashion and on approximately the same beat as Ryan's. She was proceeding at slow speed and had

128

just broken surface with her periscope, through which at the time the second-in-command was observing. Care was necessary, since to emerge even to this extent had been proved from experience to be a dangerous and often a fatal hazard. It was a bright, sunny day, and as the officer was searching the seas with his periscope, he was heard suddenly to cry out, 'By Jove, there's jolly old Ryan waving to us like mad from the water!'

He immediately blew the tanks to bring the submarine to the surface, the commander and all aboard feeling that it was worth while taking a risk. Some of the men crowded into the conning tower and out on to the deck with life-lines, while others stayed below and prepared restoratives for Ryan when he should have been rescued. But when the submarine came up, still keeping a little way on, not a sign of Ryan was to be seen, though the day was quite clear and a thorough search was made. Yet the officer was quite positive that it was Ryan whom he had seen and no one doubted him. Ryan was a man of such distinctive appearance that a mistake could hardly have been made; nor had there been lately any talk of him to set imaginations at work.

After a short while an object was discerned in the sea right ahead and on the course the submarine was steering. As she came up with it, it resolved itself into two mines, which the submarine would undoubtedly have struck, if Ryan had not waved to warn her off.

The
Restless Dead

¶ This story was taken from *Blackwood's Magazine* for December 1892.

FIVE YEARS BEFORE THE DATE OF THIS STORY, GEORGE Woodfall, a wealthy and respected citizen of Sydney, beloved of all classes for his uprightness and benevolence, suddenly vanished, leaving not the faintest trace. His disappearance caused the most profound sensation, and as his affairs were found to be in perfect order, foul play was for a time suspected. No clue, however, was forthcoming, and after two years a monument was raised to the man who had earned the right to be called a public benefactor.

My name is Power—the Rev. Charles Power. I am the incumbent of the parish church of St. Chrysostom, Redfern, Sydney; and, though a clergyman, I have never so far been led to suspect myself of being in any way a weakling, or given over to vain imaginings. I am forty years of age, and un- married. My life has been uniformly practical and I cannot remember to have ever been the prey of any morbid sentiment whatever. Hitherto I have utterly disbelieved in apparitions of any description, regarding them as illusions presented to a temporarily, though slightly, disordered brain; and I am free to confess that, had I alone been the witness of the apparition herein described, I should have felt bound to set aside my own impressions as unworthy of serious attention, on the grounds already stated, nor should I have further investigated the mat-

133

ter; and thus what is now known might never have come to light, and, for all we know, rest and peace might have been denied to a long-tortured soul. Thus much of myself.

Of my friend, William Rowley, I may say that he is a man of like mind unto myself; that as a scientist—famous throughout the world as the man who planned and carried out the canal system of New South Wales—his education has not been such as to render him fanciful, even did his natural instincts turn in that direction, which they do not. In a word, he is a hard-headed, shrewd, and utterly unimaginative man.

One thing must be stated at the outset. The exact locality in which the events here recorded came to pass we have concealed, fearing lest some too curious hand might disturb that lonely grave among the mountains, where lies all that remains of a man who, if he sinned, surely also suffered.

With what amazed horror the inhabitants of the city of Sydney will learn the fate of George Woodfall we can well imagine. When a man respected and beloved among us for twenty years departed suddenly from our midst, the whole community mourned for him as for a father. And now, when the veil is rent and he whom we believed a saint stands revealed the opposite of all we once conceived him to be, amazement is only natural. But, lest that feeling should change in the minds of some to that of scorn, I would say, 'Judge him not; for you know not how he was tempted. Judge him not, until you have been tempted even as he was; and then, if you resist, still judge him not, because of the awfulness of his doom.' The actual narrative of our experiences I shall leave to William Rowley, whose powers of description, as I find on comparing our two separately compiled statements, considerably surpass my own.

In the month of September last year, my friend Power and I were shaking the cobwebs from our brains and enjoying a short holiday among the mountains of the Great Dividing Range. I shall not, as Power says, indicate more nearly the precise locality to any but those who may have a personal or public right to the information. We had been out about a fortnight, and Power, who is an enthusiastic botanist, had already made several new discoveries among the Australian flora, while I, gun in hand, contented myself with bringing down that particular section of the fauna most directly concerned with our breakfast and dinner. One evening—it was the 20th, and the date is indelibly engraved on my memory—when we were in the very heart of the lofty ranges, we began to cast about for a spot where we could camp for the night. Not far away we could hear the thunder of a waterfall, and judging that we should find what we wanted somewhere in its vicinity, we pressed on, descending deeper and deeper into a long gully, the sides of which were thickly covered with tall trees and tangled undergrowth. On reaching the bottom, we walked forward till we came upon a pretty glade, formed by clumps of tall fern-trees, or rather tree-ferns, fringing a deep pool, which was formed, in part at least, by the water which poured incessantly from the heights, and constituted the head of a small creek, which flowed away, and was soon lost to sight among the dense foliage through which it forced its way.

This was the very spot for us, and during our supper we found leisure to observe the formation of the waterfall, exactly opposite to which we reclined. It was very curious. From the top of the cliff, the water, projected by some force, the nature of which we could not divine, sprang sheer out from the brink of the precipice, and descending in a mighty and unbroken arc, poured with a never-ceasing roar upon a great ledge of rock which jutted out some forty feet below. Here, after being collected, as it were, in a vast reservoir, it continuously overflowed and rushed down the black face of the rock in a torrent of silver foam.

Scarcely had we finished our supper, and, piling a few logs on the fire, lit our pipes for a yarn, than suddenly, as it seemed, the clear starry sky became overcast; a violent gust of wind rushed shrieking through the gully, scattering our fire in all directions, ceased, and for a few moments all was still. Then drip, drip, fell splashing a few heavy drops of rain, and, almost before we could reach the shelter of the nearest clump of ferns, a tremendous storm burst upon us with a fury which, notwithstanding my long experience of tropical storms, I have never seen surpassed. The wind had died away, but the thunder rolled and crashed and reverberated in an awful manner. All the time, writhing and coiling and darting with forked tongues about the topmost summits, gleamed the electric fires, like a multitude of blazing serpents let loose upon the blackness of the night.

From the shelter, such as it was, where we crouched, Power and I watched the progress of the storm. So pitchy dark had it grown that, though touching, we could not see one another, and though we heard its never-ceasing rush, even above the fury of the storm, the great white mass of falling water immediately in front of us had become invisible.

Suddenly, a levin-streak flashed out of the gloom, struck, for one instant, the face of the cliff with a broad blaze of light, then vanished, leaving all once more in darkness. No, not all, for through the intense blackness there arose, just in the position of the watery arc, a soft and luminous mist. Faint and shadowy at first, it rapidly increased in density, becoming clearer to the sight, till at length it hung, as it were, a great white pall, suspended between heaven and hell. Crash! and another stunning thunder-roll shook the air, while again the forked flame darted its fiery shaft upon the face of the cliff. Then darkness once more, save for the misty veil, now no longer white, but suffused with a pale pink glow, delicate and fleeting as the first faint flush of dawn. Swiftly it deepened to

137

an exquisite tint, while thousands upon thousands of rosy drops were flung hither and thither, as the spray from the ledge was splashed and dashed in all directions.

But, beautiful as this was, scant time was left us to admire it. Another crash; another flash; a roaring, rumbling noise, as if an earthquake was upon us, and once again the scene was changed. There was one brief interval of perfect stillness; and then, in an instant, the pink glow went out. Darkness, while one might draw breath; and then a blood-red glare, so intense, so lurid, that it required but little imagination to suppose a torrent of blood descending on us where we sat. Out curved the great arc, in a vast sheet of crimson, and down the black face of the cliff poured the red stream in all manner of fantastic shapes. But now the light was not confined to the water alone, for the whole mountain glared and glowed and the giant trees seemed to reel in desperate conflict. Then, as suddenly as it had come, the glorious display vanished, and thick darkness settled once more upon everything.

Hitherto we had watched in silence, too absorbed in the grandeur of what we saw for speech. But now I turned to Power with a light remark about our good fortune in having witnessed such a phenomenon. As I spoke, I felt him grasp my arm convulsively. 'My God!' he said, in a voice so unlike his own I scarcely knew it, 'what is that?'

'What?' I exclaimed, rather startled by the tone in which he spoke.

He did not answer, but his grasp tightened on my arm. I looked in the direction of the waterfall. Heavens! what was it? Out of the gloom, high up in the midst of the arc of water, appeared a human hand. It was the hand of a dead man, long and lean, with the blue decaying flesh shrivelling on the fingers. And, as it waved and beckoned, another hand, withered and gruesome like itself, grew before our eyes, and the long thin fingers twined themselves together as if in supplication. Struggling, as it were, into material shape followed the arms; and then, as I sat, my mouth agape with horror, and every nerve tingling, there, in ghastly complete/ ness, stood a man. But what a man! He had been dead for years; on his bones the flesh had shrunk and dried, and in some parts rotted off; it was a man, yet not a man, a skeleton, yet not a skeleton, a horrid corpse endowed with life, or at least with the semblance of life. And now a great blaze of crimson light burst forth again, and all over the figure, and about and around it, seemed to flow streams of blood. The awful thing writhed and rocked in what seemed to be a deadly paroxysm of anguish, now standing erect, and flinging its weird arms above its head as though invoking curses; now falling on its withered knees in an agony. I could bear no more, and hid my face in my hands. When I looked again, the ap/ parition had vanished. 'Power,' I said, falteringly. There was no answer; he had fainted.

When he came to, the moon was again shining high in

the heavens, there was no trace of the recent storm, and the cataract was a broad and gleaming sheet of silver, as though nothing had ever happened to disturb it. Power stretched himself, rubbed his eyes, and then sat up and looked about him in a bewildered way. At last he spoke.

'Rowley,' he began hesitatingly, 'I have had a very curious dream. I—'

I thought it best to cut him short. 'It was no dream, Power,' I said; 'for I saw it too.'

He looked at me for a moment incredulously, then covered his face with his hands. 'You saw it too!' he gasped. 'Then, my God! what can it mean?'

Power is a cool and remarkably self-possessed man, and before very long his nerves recovered their balance and he spoke to me again. 'Of one thing I am firmly convinced,' he said. 'So terrifying a spectacle would never have been allowed to appear to us without some reason. What do you suppose it to be?'

'Really,' I answered, 'I have no idea and prefer not to imagine. We must go up there and try to find out.'

'My own thought,' he said, rising to his feet. 'Come.'

'What, now!' I cried in astonishment. 'Surely you will wait till morning! There is nothing to be gained by such haste, or to be lost by a little delay.'

'That may or may not be,' he replied firmly. 'All I know is that I am going to try to get behind that veil of water to-night. Could you sleep', he added with a faint smile, 'while there was a possibility of that ghastly thing appearing to us again? I could not.'

'There is not much chance of that,' I admitted. 'To tell you the truth, I rather wish it would, for then we might arrive at some scientific explanation of it. I was so taken by surprise when the gentleman made his first appearance that I—'

'Rowley,' he interrupted, 'don't jest. We do not agree on all points, and your belief in the unseen is much weaker than I would have it. But here we have both of us had evidence of the most startling and convincing kind. Believe me, there is a meaning in this, and it is our plain duty to discover it if we can. Let us go now, while we have the moon to light us.'

'All right,' I said, 'go ahead.' And so we began the ascent together.

There is no need to set down all the details of that weary climb. It was about half-past nine when we began it, and eleven when we reached the level of the rock on which the arc of water broke. A chasm lay between us and it, looking across which we could see a dry wall of rock receding away from the water and leaving a wide passage, along which we could see from one end to the other.

'That looks like a cave of some sort,' said Power. 'Can't we reach it?'

'Not without jumping that chasm,' I replied, 'a feat I for one am not going to attempt. Let us see what can be done from the top.'

It took us another hour to reach the summit, and once there we seemed no better off than before, for the water flung itself with a furious rush over the brow of the cliff, while on each side the sheer face of the precipice precluded any idea of descending that way.

'There must be an entrance somewhere,' I said. 'Let us set to work to find it.'

I then cut down a stout young sapling and began to lay about me with a will.

'Whatever are you doing?' cried Power.

'Knocking down the brushwood and trying to find the entrance, if there is one, to that cave.'

'Nonsense! If there were a hole you would have fallen through it long ago. Depend upon it, if there is any entrance at all from above, it is much farther away than this.' With that, Power turned his back on me and disappeared among the rocks which covered the summit. Presently I heard him coo-ee. I answered, and following the direction of his voice, found him less than a hundred yards away, and almost in a straight line from where we had been standing.

'Well,' I asked, 'have you found anything?'

'Yes,' he replied; 'but I don't know how much it means,' and he pointed to a blaze on a fallen iron-bark tree by which he stood, under which a broad arrow pointed directly down-wards.

'A government surveyor's mark, probably,' I said. 'However, we'll see.' Once again I set to work, beating down the brushwood with my sapling. It took some time to clear away the bushes that had grown up under and over the arch of the fallen tree, but at last it was done and, stooping down, I began a thorough examination of the place. Beginning at one end of the tree, I went carefully towards the other, thrusting my pole in all directions. When I had covered about two-thirds of the distance, I gave a sharp exclamation. 'Give me the lantern,' I cried.

'What is it?' asked Power, his voice trembling with excite-ment, as he hastily unslung and handed me a small bullseye lantern which he carried, and for which, on account of the brilliance of the moon, we had hitherto found no use.

'I'll tell you when I know myself,' I answered; and taking the lantern I flashed the light into the mouth of a great hole my attack on the shrubs had laid bare, Power leaning over me and trying to peer into it.

'That is the way down,' he said.

'Not a doubt of it,' I returned. 'Come along.'

He started back. 'You're never going down there!' he gasped.

'Yes, I am,' I answered. 'I'm going to see this thing through now that we have got so far. Come on, you don't mean to let me go down alone?'

'Of course not,' replied Power, pulling himself together. 'But how are you going to get down? You don't know the depth of the hole.'

'No, but I'll soon find out. Look here.' All the time I had been talking, I had been clearing the undergrowth from the mouth of the hole and thrusting my pole down to find, if possible, its depth. This I could not do, but struck by the fact that something hard projected at regular intervals from one side of the shaft, I concluded that the descent must have been made by a series of stakes driven into the earth. I verified this by leaning over the hole and thrusting my arm down, till my knuckles came into contact with the first rung of the ladder, if it may be called so. I pointed this out to Power.

'Well, what are you going to do now?' he asked.

For answer, I laid my sapling across the mouth of the hole, and swinging myself into it, found, as I expected, that my feet rested on a second support about half my own length lower down. Another step, another and another, and my feet touched ground so suddenly that I fell in a heap, with an involuntary shout.

'Are you all right, Will?' asked Power anxiously from the top.

'Yes; at least I think so. But pass the light down.'

Power tied his handkerchief to the strap of the lantern and lowered it down to me, joining me himself a moment later.

'We're in for it now, Will,' he said.

'Yes,' I replied, 'we'll not go back; but the sapling may be useful.' And, swinging myself up once more, I drew in the long staff, and planting it on the ground below, sprang down

144

again to Power's side. He flashed the light hither and thither, and we could see that we stood at the beginning of a long and fairly broad passage, the extent of which we could not guess.

'Listen!' said Power, suddenly. 'What's that?'

I am not a very nervous man, but that startled ejaculation was somewhat trying in the circumstances, and so I told Power.

'But I did hear something, Will,' he said apologetically.

'Of course you did,' I replied, 'but it was only the water-fall.' This was true, for we could distinctly hear the thunder of the water. I was leading with the lantern, and feeling doubt-ful of Power's nerves, I suggested leaving him behind and going on alone. 'How do you feel, Charles?' I asked him. 'If you wait here, I'll go on by myself.'

This suggestion had the effect of bracing his nerves. 'Thank you,' he replied. 'I don't feel very happy, I admit, but anything is better than being left here by myself. We can't see anything worse than we've seen already. Go on.'

We went forward cautiously, till presently we were brought to a standstill by what seemed to be a solid wall of rock bar-ring our further progress. We soon saw, however, that what appeared to be a complete wall was merely a partition be-tween the passage in which we stood and another passage, or perhaps a cave, beyond. The communication was established by means of a natural archway, more than large enough to admit a man crawling on his hands and knees.

Power went through first, while I guided his movements as well as I could with the lantern. Presently he called out.

'Are you through?' I cried, almost immediately behind him.

'Yes,' he answered, 'and I've found something too.'

'What is it?' I asked.

'I don't know exactly. It feels like a bundle of sticks tied together.'

As soon as I had crawled through, the lantern settled the question. What Power had found was a bundle of torches.

'This decides one point,' I exclaimed, drawing one out. 'We are not the first to visit this mysterious place. Let us light a torch and see better where we are.'

The first few torches, being damp and mouldy with age, refused to light, but at last I succeeded with two from the centre of the bundle. We each took one, holding them high above our heads. For a moment we were dazzled, and then a wonderful sight met our eyes. We were in a vast cavern. In front of us rose the grandest array of stalactites and stalagmites I ever saw, stretching away in innumerable aisles, as it were the nave of some mighty cathedral. From the roof, between the great pillars, depended the most exquisite tracery of quartz. From prisms here and there the light from the torches was flashed back in many coloured waves.

For a while we stood silent. At last Power said, in an awed voice: 'We shall never see anything more marvellous than this.'

'Let us go on,' I replied.

We had moved forward for perhaps a hundred yards, the sound of the falling waters increasing at every step, when what was, as it were, the nave of the cathedral, with its rows of pillars, came to an abrupt end, and in front of us at right angles ran another row of columns, resembling an exquisitely wrought choir screen.

'Wonders will never cease,' remarked Power. 'It really would not surprise me to find an altar on the other side of that screen. Isn't it beautiful?'

'Very,' I replied, 'and very annoying too; it completely bars our way in this direction.'

'Perhaps there is an opening somewhere,' he suggested, and moved off to the left.

I took a few paces in the opposite direction and presently cried out: 'You're right. Here is the opening, and it's an artificial one.' I pointed to a large and ragged hole in the screen. 'Look at that. It has been smashed to pieces with a hammer or some such instrument.'

'Not a doubt of it,' Power agreed. 'But it must have been broken long ago, for there are traces of a new formation in progress. What is beyond?'

'Another cave, not so large,' I replied, having already passed through the aperture. And beyond that is the waterfall, not sixty feet away. There is nothing here; I can see all round. Let us—oh!'

The exclamation was wrung from me by a sudden spasm of terror, which shook me from head to foot. I fell back against Power with such violence as nearly to upset him, and then clung to him trembling. 'Quick! let us go back. Don't look. This is no place for us. Flesh and blood cannot stand any more,' I gasped.

'For heaven's sake, old man, what's the matter?' cried Power. 'Here, drink this.' He handed me his flask.

The spirit revived me, and with a violent effort I collected my wits again. 'Take some yourself, Charles,' I urged. 'You will need it.'

He did so. 'Tell me what it is,' he demanded.

Holding my torch in my left hand, I pointed straight in front of me with my right. Power's eyes followed my finger. His torch dropped from his hand and I flung my arm round him just in time to save him from falling.

'My God!' he cried. 'How awful!'

Immediately in front of us yawned an open grave. The earth flung up on either side of it had grown hard and caked in the years that had rolled by since first it was dug, and almost turned to stone by the ceaseless drip of water from the roof. At one end lay a pick and shovel, carelessly cast aside. At the other were two fleshless grinning skeletons, in such a position that they seemed to be peering into the grave beneath them. The light of the torches played on the ghastly forms, throwing flickering shadows upon them, until they looked like a pair of mocking demons, laughing into the nethermost pit.

'Let us go,' cried Power.

'No, no,' I said in an unsteady voice. 'They cannot harm us. They are dead enough. Let us examine the grave.'

'Not while *they* are keeping guard over it,' protested Power.

With one sweep of my sapling I thrust back the ghastly pair, and they fell, crumbling into dust, by the side of the grave. We then peered into the open shaft, our torches drooped forward to throw in the light. There, in the shallow grave, were two forms that had once been human. The upper, a skeleton such as we had just removed, hid the form that lay below it, a form which, though emaciated, and in the last stages of decay, preserved some lingering likeness to humanity. With a determined effort I thrust forward my sapling, when the hideous thing on the top instantly fell a crumbling ruin like the others.

Leaning forward, we held the torches far down into the grave. In one glance we recognised the face of the man we had seen in the waterfall earlier that night. I scarcely think we were surprised, and when our first feeling of dread had passed away, the same thought struck us both simultaneously: 'Can we find the key to this mystery?'

'We can try,' said Power. 'Look! There is an old coat, near the pick and shovel. Let us begin by searching it.'

The coat was fast falling to pieces, but had originally been

149

of good material and make, such as would be worn by a man in easy circumstances. Inside the collar, though almost effaced, was the name of the maker, one of the principal tailors in Sydney. We looked at each other.

'Schuylen came from London and opened that shop about seven years ago,' said Power. 'So this must have been left here within that time.'

'Evidently,' I replied, feeling in the pockets. 'But here is something which may prove more definite,' and drawing out a small tin box, about three inches square, I handed it to Power.

'There is an inscription on it,' he said; 'but the torchlight flickers so, I can't make it out. Let's have the lantern.' I turned the bullseye full on the lid of the box and Power read out the inscription. It ran:

GEORGE WOODFALL
Pott's Point, Sydney

'George Woodfall!' exclaimed Power. 'Why, he must have been murdered after all.'

With a great deal of difficulty I forced open the lid and drew out from the box a small sheet of paper, folded square. 'Shall we read it now?' I asked, 'or wait till we get outside?'

'Now,' answered Power eagerly. He had already begun to unfold the paper and after one glance at its contents uttered a cry of surprise. 'It is a confession,' he said, and read on.

'Yes,' he repeated presently, 'it is the confession of George Woodfall, who lived among us so long, beloved and respected. It is his own story of how he sinned and suffered.'

We read it together, by the flickering light of our torches. The statement was short and to the point, giving few details, but setting forth a crime and the long mental agony endured by its unhappy perpetrator in consequence. It was as follows:

'At length I confess. I am driven to make this statement of my crime, lest I go mad before it is done. Twenty years ago I did it—twenty years ago on the 20th September, now close at hand. There were three of them, and I killed them all three. It was for gold. We had been mates at the diggings and were coming down to Sydney with our gold dust and nuggets. We had a good deal; more than enough to set each of us up, and a fortune for one. That's what tempted me. I don't know who they were, as each passed under some nickname. Blackguards all of them, and a rough lot, while I was what they call a gentleman! I thought I saw a chance to rebuild my fortunes with that gold, so I took it. I killed them in a cave we had struck one day while prospecting. It was a damnable deed, and black treachery. Whatever their crimes, they had always been good enough to me, letting me join their gang when I first came to the diggings, and sharing fair and square in everything. They were sleeping, too, when I robbed them of their treasure and their lives at one and the same time. At least, two of them were sleeping; the third awoke just as my knife was raised to strike him. He never said a word, but hurled himself straight at me. I caught his throat as he came and held on. I made sure he was dying before I loosed my grip and stooped to pick up my knife which had been dropped in the struggle. I leant over him to see if he was dead, but he had recovered and struggled into a sitting posture. His face was livid, his eyes protruded from his head and his tongue from his mouth. He could not speak, but he clasped his hands in prayer for mercy. I flung myself upon him and buried the knife in his heart. As the breath left his body, he uttered a yell which seemed to echo for long minutes through the cave. It rings in my ears now, and will ring till my dying day.

'I began with much difficulty to dig, or rather to hew out a grave, but at length desisted, reflecting that no one would be likely to discover the cave in so lonely and remote a spot, and that even if it should be discovered, there would be nothing to connect me with the bodies of my victims. So I laid the corpses in the shallow pit I had excavated and threw a few loose stones upon them. Thus I left them, and came to Sydney with my ill-gotten gold. Here I was quite unknown, and for a time I kept quiet, giving out that I had recently arrived from England and was on the look-out for a good investment for my small capital. At last the opportunity came. One week I invested almost all I had in the Benamburra mine; the next I found myself rolling in riches and the talk of the town. From that day all I touched turned to gold. It seemed that I could not make a mistake. Of course, I kept my eyes open, but my luck was phenomenal. In the first flush of success, my excitement was so great that I almost forgot my crime. I went everywhere, did everything, and before the year was out had nearly persuaded myself that I *had* forgotten. And then something happened that warned me I should never forget.

'It was long past midnight, and I was sitting alone in the smoking-room of the house on Pott's Point. I had a house-ful of companions, wild reckless fellows; but one by one they had dropped off to bed, and I was sitting alone at the open window, looking out on the quiet waters of the bay, my thoughts running in no particular direction. As I sat, a wave of bitter regret suddenly rushed over me, and I felt I would have given all my wealth and even my life to free my hands from the stain of blood. Had I acted on that impulse, gone to the nearest magistrate, confessed my crime, and paid the penalty, I might have saved myself an eternity of suffering; but I resisted and the impulse passed. My emotion, though transient, had been deep, and with a shaking hand I mixed myself a stiff glass of brandy and water, which I drained at a gulp. The last vestige of my hesitation disappeared and I turned to close the window. "Dead men tell no tales," I muttered, with my hand upon the sash, when, spoken as it were from the verandah immediately below me, I heard the

153

words, very softly uttered, "It is time; let us begin." Burglars, was my first thought, as I sprang back from the window and felt for my revolver. Concealed behind the thick curtain I awaited their entrance, but no one came. At last I crept to the window and peered out, my finger on the trigger and every nerve on the alert. Bright moonlight illuminated the verandah, the lawn, and all down the shrubberies to the water's edge, yet nothing was to be seen, nor did the faintest sound break the stillness of the night. "They have heard me and made off," I said to myself; and, revolver in hand, I slipped through the window and made a tour of the gardens and outhouses, without finding anything for my pains. Returning to the house, I went in and, having closed the window, put out the lights. As I turned to take up the bedroom candle, I started back with a cry of alarm, for a heavy body fell with a thud at my feet. Then, before I had time to recover myself, or even to wonder what it could mean, sharp and sudden and terrible, arose a cry. And then, in a flash, all was clear to me. I staggered back into a chair and covered my face with my hands. But I could not shut out those awful sounds that echoed round me, just as they had echoed in the cave on that fatal night. I knew it could not be long before the household was aroused, and then I should explain everything. So I sat and waited, for how long I do not know, until at last it was borne in on me that I alone could hear this devil's concert. With that thought the sounds ceased and silence once more fell. Then, while still I could see nothing, I heard the voice of the man with whom I had had that desperate struggle. "George," said the voice, "you are growing forgetful. We are here to remind you that this day week will be the 20th of September." The tones of the voice were low and very even. I could not answer, though I strove to speak, and presently the voice went on. "Your time has not come yet, George. Before it does, we will teach you to remember. Thursday will be the twentieth. We shall expect you in the cave. You will come, will you not?" "Yes, I will come." I whispered, and then I knew no more.

'I need not go on. I kept the tryst and passed through a night of such agonising horror that I wondered afterwards how I came to retain either life or reason after it. I have kept both, however, during twenty miserable years. I am glad I have written this, for it has strengthened and comforted me. It may be had I written it, had I spoken it, earlier, I might have been forsaken by those awful things, which for these twenty years have haunted me perpetually, never leaving me, and surely as the date comes round, forcing me on that dreadful pilgrimage to the scene of my crime, there to spend one long night of terror on the spot where once I fell.

'Now something tells me the end is very near. One more pilgrimage will I make, because I must, to that spot of bloodstained memories, and when I return, I will give myself up, and place this confession in responsible hands. Then it may be that my tortured soul shall find rest and peace at last.

'GEORGE WOODFALL.'

We buried them all in the one grave, and over them Power read the burial service from his Prayer Book. Then, when we had piled a cairn of quartz over them, we turned away and left them.

Note by the Rev. Charles Power

Two ideas strike me with such force that I cannot refrain from giving expression to them. In the first place, it is evident that George Woodfall never came back from that last miserable journey on which he set out shortly after writing his statement. Why was this? Was it that, going with his confession unmade, he was delivered into the power of the spirits of darkness? And, in the second place, were not our steps guided to the cave that night, in order that his confession might be found, so that his long-tortured soul may find 'rest and peace at last?'

The Countess
of
Belvedere

¶ The story of the *Countess of Belvedere* appears in the *Ghost Book* without any indication of how or from whom *Lord Halifax* obtained it. It is not a ghost story at all, but was the kind of tale which never failed to delight him, both for its strangeness and for the fact that it dealt with the history of families with which he was acquainted. His friend, *Mr. Athelstan Riley*, married the daughter of the 8th *Viscount Molesworth*, a descendant of the father of the *Countess of Belvedere*.

MARY MOLESWORTH WAS THE ELDEST DAUGHTER, BY A first marriage, of Richard, 3rd Viscount Molesworth, an officer of distinguished bravery, who had been aide-de-camp to the Duke of Marlborough at the battle of Ramillies. After having attained the rank of major-general, he retired from active service and held many high and important situations in Ireland. For many years he was commander-in-chief in that country, residing with his family in Dublin.

It was during his tenure of the command that his eldest daughter Mary attracted the regard of a Mr. Rochfort, a gentleman of a very ancient and honourable family in County Westmeath. He is described as a man of considerable talent and ability, with expensive tastes and the most polished manners; but as being at the same time possessed of a haughty and vindictive temper, selfish, unprincipled, and dissipated in his way of living. At the date when he met Miss Molesworth, he was twenty-eight, a widower, and childless, his first wife having died a few months after the marriage. He had some interest in high places in England, a circumstance which possibly commended his suit to Lord Molesworth who, besides being charmed by his excellent manners, was sufficiently worldly to encourage the addresses of a man for whom honour and advancement might reasonably be anticipated. Indeed, at this time Mr. Rochfort was considered a most promising young man and was so much in favour with the reigning monarch, George II, that he was soon to be created Baron Bellefield, and a little later a Viscount. Eventually he became Earl of Belvedere; and as it is by this title that he is best known, he will be so termed throughout this narrative. He was a man of striking and handsome appearance. The only portrait of him extant shows him at a comparatively advanced age, when he was no longer a smiling and successful courtier, but had begun to show in his features the working of the hand of time. He is in his parliamentary robes, tall, dark and handsome, but with a stern, gloomy, and saturnine expression on his face. Probably his appearance had altered since the days when he paid his court to Miss Molesworth and a milder manner and a more amiable temper would be expected of him. She at this time was only sixteen, an attractive and accomplished girl, with a gentle and thoughtful disposition. She seems to have been not altogether unaware of her suitor's true qualities. She saw in him a man who might well adorn a court, but was less likely to make his own family happy. She had observed that, kind and attentive as he invariably was towards herself, he was haughty and inconsiderate towards others; and the prospect of marrying him gave her little pleasure. However, she was only sixteen, too young and too gentle to offer much resistance to a match which all around her were pressing on her. With many forebodings she at length gave her consent, the marriage taking place on

160

August 1st, 1736. It is said that just before its celebration, she sat for her picture, and that when it was suggested that she should be painted in some fancy costume, she chose one which, especially in the shape of the coiffure, recalled a well-known portrait of that ill-fated captive, her namesake, Queen Mary of Scotland.

In a very short time, Lady Belvedere's forebodings began to be realised in the coldness and neglect of her husband. He was surrounded by flatterers who, for reasons of their own, had opposed his marriage and were now on the watch to prejudice him against his young wife. There was a woman in particular who was her persistent and mischievous enemy and to whom she afterwards attributed most of her misfortunes. Having enjoyed for some time a strong influence over Lord Belvedere, the woman was naturally jealous of his young wife.

Although a year after the marriage Lady Belvedere disappointed her husband's hopes for an heir by giving birth to a daughter, in due course she presented him with a son, a fine and promising child; and it may be supposed that for a time at least Lord Belvedere's affection for his wife revived. The birth of the heir was magnificently celebrated, the child being christened George Augustus after the king, who stood godfather by proxy and continued, until his death more than twenty years later, to be a firm friend to the child's father.

During the first years of their married life, the Belvederes mostly resided at Gaulston, in County Westmeath, and here, in course of time, two other sons were born to them. The house was a large, gloomy building, dating from the days of Edward III. Later it belonged to Chief Baron Rochfort and is alluded to by Dean Swift. Such painful associations were to gather round it that the second and last Earl of Belvedere sold the house to Lord Kilmaine, who replaced it with a more modern and less forbidding structure.

As might be expected, a rural and domestic life had little attraction for Lord Belvedere. His absences were long and frequent, most of his time being spent either at the English Court or in Dublin, which, in the days before the Union, had its own Parliament and was the residence of the Irish aristo-cracy. Fortunately for Lady Belvedere, she preferred a quiet life in the country. She was a fond and attentive mother, and in the care and society of her children she was able to forget the estrangement from her husband. The three boys were still in their infancy, but the daughter was beginning to be of a companionable age. Afterwards Countess of Lanesborough, the girl gave early promise of that affection, gaiety, and beauty for which she was to be distinguished.

As time went on, the visits of Lord Belvedere to his wife and family became rarer and shorter, and when they occurred they added little to the happiness of the house. There was a gloom on his brow and a severity in his manner which filled his wife with fears for the future. She was convinced that his old friends and flatterers, and in particular her own enemy, had been poisoning his mind against her; nothing else could explain his suspicious looks and savage tones.

Eight years after the marriage, the storm broke. Lord Belvedere appeared at Gaulston and charged his wife with having been unfaithful to him, the partner of her guilt being alleged to be a relative of his own. The accounts which have survived state that Lady Belvedere at first received this accusation with surprise and anger, but that at last, in desperation, she astonished her friends by acknowledging her guilt. She was, in fact, entirely innocent, but, having failed to conquer her husband's suspicions, she hoped to strengthen the grounds for a divorce and so rid herself of a man whom she now found it impossible not to hate. Subsequently she repeatedly protested her innocence, and on her deathbed, some thirty years later, made a solemn oath to that effect.

The other party named was a married man, of exemplary character, an affectionate father and a most attached husband. He and his wife were both sincerely sorry for their young and neglected neighbour, whose husband's profligacies were well known to them. Living, as they did, close to Gaulston, there was a constant intercourse between the two houses. Lady Belvedere knew that she would always find a ready and sympathetic welcome in the home of her friends, and it may well be that in their company she did not always resist the temptation of dwelling upon her unhappiness.

The charge of infidelity was followed by proceedings in

163

court. The principal witness was Lady Belvedere's enemy, who had laid her plans so well that damages to the amount of £20,000 were awarded the earl; whereupon the ill-fated defendant, unable to meet so formidable a demand, fled the country. After residing abroad for many years, his Irish property being meanwhile neglected and his sole comfort being the society of his attached wife and family, he was induced to return with them to Ireland, believing that lapse of time would have softened Lord Belvedere's heart. It was a vain hope. He was arrested and sent to prison, where eventually he died, protesting to the last his innocence of the charge against him.

Meanwhile Lady Belvedere had discovered that her hopes of obtaining a divorce from her husband were illusory. Latterly he had spent little time at Gaulston; now he determined to abandon it altogether. The house was old and inconvenient, and the property, apart from the gardens, which were very fine, had little to recommend it to a man of his taste. He accordingly removed his establishment to a beautiful mansion some few miles away. It was a new house, immediately adjoining the demesne of Rochfort, the residence of a collateral branch of his family. The name of Rochfort is now almost extinct in the neighbourhood, but was at one time well known and esteemed, a member of the family representing Westmeath in Parliament for many years. Between Rochfort and Lord Belvedere's new house lies the artificial ruin of an abbey, the tradition being that this build-ing arose out of a family feud. The ruin was actually built by Lord Belvedere himself and was a further illustration of his vindictive nature. He had quarrelled with his younger brother, who lived at Rochfort, and wished to be spared the annoyance of seeing the other's house when he looked out of his windows. So, at great expense, he built the ruined abbey, fetching over for the purpose from Italy a celebrated Floren-tine architect.

But when Lord Belvedere moved from Gaulston, he had no intention of taking his wife with him. She was to remain, and her house was to be her asylum or prison, where he could keep her under close surveillance, and such was his influence throughout the countryside that he had no lack of allies to help him to carry out his detestable plan.

Lady Belvedere was accordingly closely confined to Gaul-ston, forbidden visitors and restricted in her movements. Otherwise she appears at first to have been treated reasonably well. She had sufficient servants, the use of a carriage for driving about the extensive grounds, and all the clothes she required. It is said that drawing was her favourite occupation, and for this she was given every facility. She was also allowed to write letters, and it is a mystery why she did not complain of her treatment to her family or her friends; or if she did, why they took no steps to help her. Perhaps they feared to interfere between man and wife; and probably Lord Belvedere had

165

taken the precaution of giving his father-in-law a version of his daughter's conduct, such as would persuade him that strict seclusion was the only way in which further disgrace to the family might be avoided. It may be added that very soon after the confinement took effect, Lady Belvedere's mother, who might have exercised her influence in her daughter's favour, died; whereupon Lord Molesworth took to himself a second wife, who presented him with a large and increasing family. What at least is certain is that Lady Belvedere's relatives took no steps whatever to procure her liberation.

One consolation was at first allowed her. She was permitted from time to time to see her children, who were and continued to be deeply attached to her.

The years began to slip by. At the date of her confinement Lady Belvedere was not quite twenty-five, and as she grew older, her desire for emancipation became stronger. Doubtless she repeatedly appealed by letter to her husband; if she did, her efforts were quite unavailing. He would not even see her, though he paid frequent visits to the grounds and gardens of Gaulston.

One day, however, fortune seemed to favour her. Lord Belvedere unexpectedly entered the garden without having taken his usual precautions against seeing his wife. Unhappily he was accompanied by one of those friends who were especially hostile to Lady Belvedere. The latter, however, seeing her husband approach, rushed forward and threw herself on her knees before him. She would not ask forgiveness for a crime she had not committed, but in a few hurried words she told of the hardness of her lot and begged to be released. So moving was her appeal that for a moment Lord Belvedere was shaken in his resolution, but only for a moment. His friend, without allowing him time to reply, turned reproachfully to him with the words, 'Remember your honour, my lord,' and drew him from the spot.

From that time onward Lord Belvedere hardened in his attitude. So far from modifying the treatment of his wife, he increased the restrictions on her liberty. She was allowed to walk in a certain portion of the demesne only, and at such times a person was appointed to accompany her. Her attendant was even given a bell, which he was instructed to ring when he and his charge were taking the air, so that everyone might know they were about and avoid them.

After twelve years of captivity the lady at length succeeded, with the help of some faithful servants, in making her escape from Gaulston. How she got away is not known, but the news was quickly taken to her husband who, anticipating that she would seek the shelter of her father's house in Dublin, took immediate steps to forestall her. Lord Molesworth was then living on the south side of Merrion Square, and Lord Belvedere, reaching the house before his wife could arrive, worked so powerfully upon the feelings of his father-in-law that the latter gave strict orders for his daughter to be refused admittance. Poor Lady Belvedere was completely overwhelmed by such a reception. At her wits' end, and thinking of no danger but the chance of recapture, she took the one step that would be fatal to her. She gave her coachman orders to drive to Sackville Street, where resided the wife and family of the man, now dead, with whom she was supposed to have misconducted herself. There, if anywhere, she believed herself sure of a welcome.

Whether she ever got to her friends or not, we do not know. She was, however, followed, and Lord Belvedere's rage, on discovering her destination, may be imagined. She was seized, and within less than twenty-four hours after she had left Gaulston, she was back in her prison again. In future, her treatment was to be greatly altered. She was deprived of her comforts; the servants who had been too sympathetic with her were dismissed; she was not allowed to see her children; and even her little amusements and occupations were forbidden her. In fact, she was reduced to the bare necessaries of life and surrounded by a set of attendants who treated her harshly and were constantly on the watch lest she should elude their vigilance. But indeed she had guessed what her capture would entail for her. It is stated that immediately after her unsuccessful flight her hair turned white in the course of a single night.

She endured this rigorous imprisonment for no less than eighteen years. It is hard to believe that this could have been possible in a civilised country during the eighteenth century. It is equally surprising that her reason did not give way under her treatment. There was indeed a general though erroneous idea abroad, fostered probably by her husband, that her mind had become deranged. We have no exact account of how she passed her time. A few particulars, however, have reached us. One informant was an old and valued servant, who lived and died with the Rochfort family. He was at one time a footman at Gaulston, the only one of the old staff who was allowed to remain after Lady Belvedere's attempted escape. As it was, he stayed until the day of her release. When he was a very old man and his memory, particularly of recent occurrences, was beginning to fail, he could still recall with energy and feeling every circumstance connected with his unhappy mistress. He would relate how she would ask him anxiously for news of her children or of what was happening in the country. The children, however, were her chief concern, and the footman was the only person from whom she dared to ask for information of them. Many a time, he said, when he was seeing to the fire, she would purposely delay him in his task, so as to prolong the conversation. At other times he would see her walking in the picture gallery and gazing at the portraits as though she were trying to talk to them.

When Lady Belvedere had almost abandoned hope, the hour of her release arrived. In November 1774, Lord Belvedere died, in the sixty-sixth year of his age, heavily in debt

169

and regretted by few. No sooner was the funeral over than his eldest son, accompanied by his brothers, hastened to Gaulston to set their mother at liberty. Eighteen years had wrought great changes in all parties, and especially in poor Lady Belvedere. She had, we are told, become prematurely old and haggard, had a scared, unearthly look, and spoke in a harsh, agitated whisper. When her sons arrived, they found her wearing the fashions of thirty years back, when her imprisonment began. As they entered the room, she was at first speechless; then faltered, 'Is the tyrant dead?'

Her sons, of course, were now fully grown, the eldest being in the prime of life; and so strong was the family likeness between him and his brothers that their mother was compelled to ask which was the new Lord Belvedere. They took her from Gaulston at once. The eldest son, who had just married, was about to travel to Italy with his wife, and thinking a complete change of scene might benefit his mother, proposed that she should accompany them. This well-meant plan failed in its object. The excitement of a journey was too much for one so long accustomed to solitude. Eventually it was arranged that while Lord Belvedere and his young wife went on to Italy, his mother should stay at a convent in France; and it has been erroneously stated that she died there, having first joined the Roman Catholic Church.

The truth is that, after spending the winter in Florence, Lord Belvedere returned for his mother and took her to London, where for twelve months she stayed with a friend of the family who had apartments at Kensington Palace. Her long imprisonment had so impaired her nerves that she now sought solitude and shunned the company of all but her nearest relations. Her dread of appearing in public was not irrational. Her story had begun to attract attention and was circulating round London in different versions, some less charitable than others; while the strangeness of her appearance made her an object of curiosity wherever she went. All that kindness and care could do for her was done, but her disquiet increased, and after the death of one of her younger sons she wrote to Lord Belvedere and expressed a wish that she might return to Ireland. She spent the remainder of her life in Dublin, first with her eldest son and afterwards with her son-in-law and daughter, Lord and Lady Lanesborough. So she ended her days in peace, surrounded by her grandchildren; and on her deathbed, after receiving Holy Communion, she confirmed with the most solemn oath her innocence of the offence for which she had suffered so long a captivity.